"A nice rural flavor, complete with authentic rustics, living conditions, and social customs, blends with family secrets and a slightly twisted plot to make [*Marrow-Bone Pie*] an enticing first historical for all collections."

    —*Library Journal*

"The story is wonderfully enhanced by herbal lore (decoctions, potions, and balms) and a heated forbidden romance.... There is always someone lurking behind an arras or scuttling along a secret passage."

    —*Publishers Weekly*

"A brilliant novel about food, books, and murder in Elizabethan England... Emerson's storytelling is nearly flawless."

    —*Maine Sunday Telegram*

"Emerson grows more confident in each of these stories, enriching them with details of daily life, the miseries of travel, the uses of the herbs, and the horrors of the English penal and justice systems in 1565."

    —*Booklist*

"Lively paced, evocative of its historical period, with surprising twists of plot and interesting dialogue."

    —*Tampa Tribune*

"[*Banqueting House* is] spirited and studded with wry humor....the extensive glossary stands alone as a reading pleasure."

    —*Kirkus Reviews*

FACE DOWN BESIDE
ST. ANNE'S WELL

Face Down Beside
St. Anne's Well

A MYSTERY FEATURING

Susanna, Lady Appleton

Gentlewoman, Herbalist, and Sleuth

Kathy Lynn Emerson

M M V I
PALO ALTO / McKINLEYVILLE
PERSEVERANCE PRESS / JOHN DANIEL & COMPANY

A PERSEVERANCE PRESS BOOK
Published by John Daniel & Company
A division of Daniel & Daniel, Publishers, Inc.
Post Office Box 2790
McKinleyville, California 95519
www.danielpublishing.com/perseverance

Book design: Studio E Books, Santa Barbara, www.studio-e-books.com
Set in Perpetua

Cover painting by Linda Weatherly S.

10 9 8 7 6 5 4 3 2 1

LIBRARY OF CONGRESS CATALOGING-IN-PUBLICATION DATA
Emerson, Kathy Lynn.
  Face down beside St. Anne's well : a Lady Appleton mystery / by Kathy Lynn Emerson.
    p. cm.
  ISBN 1-880284-82-0 (pbk. : alk. paper)
  1. Appleton, Susanna, Lady (Fictitious character)—Fiction. 2. Great Britain—History—Elizabeth, 1558–1603—Fiction. 3. Mary, Queen of Scots, 1542-1587—Fiction. 4. Women detectives—England—Fiction. 5. Tutors and tutoring—Fiction. 6. Herbalists—Fiction. I. Title.
  PS3555.M414F295 2006
  813'.54—dc22
                    2005012555

✶Cast of Characters✶

† indicates a real person

SUSANNA, LADY APPLETON of Leigh Abbey, Kent; widowed gentlewoman, herbalist, and sleuth; foster mother of Rosamond

ROSAMOND APPLETON illegitimate daughter of Sir Robert, Lady Appleton's late, unlamented husband

GODLINA (LINA) WALKENDEN daughter of a wealthy London merchant

DIONYSIA (DIONY) TALLBOYS heiress to land adjoining the Hawleys' Bawkenstanes Manor in Derbyshire

ELEANOR, LADY PENDENNIS Rosamond's mother

SIR WALTER PENDENNIS of Cornwall, Eleanor's husband

MADAME LOUISE POITIER waiting gentlewoman and tutor in French conversation

ANNABEL MACREYNOLDS once Sir Robert Appleton's mistress; waiting gentlewoman (aka Jacquinetta Devereux)

SIR RICHARD HAWLEY owner of Bawkenstanes Manor

LADY BRIDGET his wife; daughter of an earl

PENELOPE (NELL) HAWLEY their daughter

WILL HAWLEY their son and heir

WYMOND TALLBOYS Sir Richard's neighbor; Dionysia's father

MARGERY COTTELLING waiting gentlewoman

FAITH HOPKINS tiring maid at Bawkenstanes Manor

GILES BANNISTER Lady Bridget's music master

MELKA Lady Pendennis's Polish-born tiring maid

JENNET JAFFREY Lady Appleton's housekeeper and friend at Leigh Abbey

ROB ("MOLE") JAFFREY Jennet's son

† Thomas Greves warden of the baths at Buxton
  Henry Flower his servant

† Elizabeth, countess of Shrewsbury also called Bess of
    Hardwick
† Owen her groom
† Bessie Pierrepont the countess's granddaughter

ᦡ *Other Real People Mentioned in the Story*

Elizabeth Tudor queen of England

Mary Stewart queen of Scots until her abdication; now a
  prisoner in England

Mary Tudor now deceased; Elizabeth's older sister and queen
  of England 1553–1558; her attempts to return the country to
  Catholicism earned her the nickname "Bloody Mary"

Robert Dudley, earl of Leicester Queen Elizabeth's
  favorite courtier; reputed to be her lover

William Cecil, Lord Burghley Queen Elizabeth's most
  trusted advisor

George Talbot, earl of Shrewsbury Bess of Hardwick's
  fourth husband; in charge of keeping Mary Stewart a prisoner
  in England

Catherine de' Medici, queen mother of France the
  power behind the throne during the minority of three of her
  sons; Mary Stewart's former mother-in-law; one of those
  responsible for the St. Bartholomew's Day Massacre in 1572;
  reputed to use young women as spies

❧ Glossary ❧

(Also please see Glossary in
Face Down Below the Banqueting House)

almonry office of the almoner, one who distributes alms

ashlar squared block of building stone; masonry of such stones

banns announcement of an intended marriage

bladders any of various distensible membranous sacs from an animal, filled with water for one of the cures at Buxton Baths

bonnet generic term for a woman's French hood; low, flat men's hats were also called bonnets

branle also called bransle and brawl, this was a dance with easy steps in which many people could participate at once

bugloss herb also called oxtongue; in the sixteenth century it was believed to strengthen the heart; added "for good measure" to many remedies but has no healing properties on its own

by-blow illegitimate child

capcase small bag used to carry personal belongings; overnight case

cittern instrument similar to a lute, but easier to play

cordwainer shoemaker

crowner coroner

doxy loose woman

dump slow, mournful-sounding dance tune

dutchman slang term for a person radical in religious matters

ekename nickname

embrasure opening in a wall for a window; often a recessed area large enough to provide privacy for conversation or romance *feverfew* herb taken for chest complaints, fevers, and colds; believed to cleanse the kidneys and cheer the heart when taken in wine (for over-indulgent eaters)

French hood small bonnet made on a stiff frame and worn far back on the head; folds of material fell below the shoulders from a short, flat panel at the back; worn over a crespin or creppin (a fine linen cap)

galliard fast, spirited dance also called the cinquepace; sometimes courtiers laid aside their rapiers and cloaks and danced the galliard in doublet and hose

gavotte French peasant dance that was also a kissing game

gill one-quarter pint

gimmal ring made of two interlocking parts

heartsease herb used in the sixteenth century to treat epilepsy, asthma, and diseases of the heart

knot garden garden consisting of closed flower beds outlined with low, close-growing plants like hyssop and germander and arranged to form elaborate designs; the open spaces in the patterns might contain daffodils, primroses, or hyacinths

make a leg to bow

marchpane dessert made with blanched almonds and sugar

May Queen honorary title granted at some May Day festivities

merrybegot another term for a bastard

night rail garment in which some wealthy women slept by the mid-sixteenth century; sleeping in the nude or in a shift, shirt, or smock was more common

pantofles cork-soled scuffs worn to raise the wearer's feet out of the mud

pavane stately, processional dance

peascod peapod

puritans term used by 1565, by their critics, to refer to those who wanted a purer church than the Church of England; they called themselves the godly, or professors, or the elect

quat purulent pimple

rushdip type of candle with a rush wick in tallow; also called a rushlight or a rush candle

sarcenet fine, soft silk

snoskyn muff made of cloth or fur; smaller models hung suspended from a woman's girdle (belt)

spatterdashes boothose; worn in lieu of boots

spaw spa

troll-my-dames game played indoors with leather balls on a trolling bench

tup to fornicate with

virginals keyboard instrument similar to a harpsichord, it was placed on a table or stood on legs; "a pair of virginals" referred to only one instrument

waiting gentlewoman upper servant usually of gentle birth herself

waits professional musicians

Xeres sack wine drink imported from Xeres in Spain; sherry

FACE DOWN BESIDE
ST. ANNE'S WELL

❧ 1 ❧

March 26, 1575
Buxton, Derbyshire

THREE SHADOWS slipped silently past a small outbuilding and dashed across the open space separating it from New Hall. For an instant each was silhouetted against a moonlit sky before being absorbed by the greater darkness in the lee of the earl of Shrewsbury's fortified tower. It rose, brooding, above the marshy dale, square, solid, and forbidding.

"If anyone saw us, they will think us spirits of the night. No one will dare venture close enough to notice what we are about." Rosamond Appleton forced a note of confidence into her voice, determined to keep the others in line.

Physically, she could not compel them. Although she had her father's look about her—tall and slender, with dark brown hair, a narrow face, and a high forehead—and had inherited his ability to coax and cajole, Rosamond lacked both the muscle and the training at arms to force anyone to follow her into danger. Her only weapon was self-assurance, what her detractors criticized as an exaggerated sense of her own importance.

Although Rosamond was the instigator of all their acts of rebellion, she was the youngest of the three, only a few months past her twelfth birthday. At first her friends had been scandalized by her suggestion, but she'd overcome their objections, ignored their

common-sense warnings, and convinced them, by virtue of forceful personality alone, to come with her.

"Are you certain no one is within?" Godlina Walkenden, the
braver of Rosamond's two companions, sounded as if she were
about to bolt. She glanced nervously at the upper levels of the
stone tower. "The warden of the baths lives here all the year
round, even when there are no visitors."

"Master Greves has gone to visit his family. You heard Sir
Richard say he will not return until after Easter. No one else will
venture out to catch us, not at the full of the moon." It hung low
in the sky to the southeast, providing sufficient light to guide their
steps without need for a lantern. Superstitious folk, of whom
there were many hereabout, held it the time of the month when
wickedness stirred abroad and good Christian souls should
remain close to their hearths.

In spite of her bold words, Rosamond signaled for silence as
they inched their way along a windowless outer wall. She trailed
one gloved hand along the ashlar to orient herself, glancing up
every few feet to determine if the windows of the tower were still
overhead. The ground level contained household offices, but on the
two floors above were sufficient lodging chambers to accommo-
date as many as thirty of the earl of Shrewsbury's invited guests.

After what seemed an endless distance at their cautious pace,
Rosamond found the turning and a few moments later felt the
difference as stone became brick. A nasal whine had followed her
around the corner. "You said there was a way in." Dionysia Tallboys sniffled and swiped at her nose with a white handkerchief.

"It is here." Rosamond's searching fingers found a jagged
break where the mortar had given way, tumbling several courses
of bricks inward. The earthquake that had shaken all the Midlands
just a month earlier had left a hole in the wall large enough for the
three of them to scramble through. Thomas Greves was not so
dedicated a servant that he'd rushed to make repairs. Buxton was
the highest, coldest village in all of England. Like any sensible

person, he'd left unnecessary outdoor work until the weather warmed.

In spite of bulky skirts, two lithe young bodies and Godlina, who was inclined to plumpness, squirmed through the opening and regained their footing amid the rubble on the other side. Dionysia gasped. Godlina giggled. Rosamond grinned.

"The First Chief Bath," she whispered in triumph.

They were in a walled courtyard that measured, at a guess, ten yards long and six wide. A rectangular pool took up most of the space, the largest of the thermal baths for which Buxton was famous.

"I cannot see what's in there," Diony complained, moving close enough to stare into the depths.

"Do you expect sea monsters?" Although the bathhouse had no roof, moonlight did little to reveal what might be hidden beneath the water.

A shiver of anticipation ran through Rosamond as she produced a small tinderbox from the pocket of her cloak and struck steel against flint to make a spark. From the tinder she ignited a brimstone match and used that to light the three candles she'd brought with her. The entire process took a nerve-wracking span of time, and in the end the lights did little to add to the illumination. Shadowy corners lurked at every side.

Mysterious sounds issued from the western end of the bath itself. Although she could not see it, Rosamond knew there was a reservoir there, an ancient basin of gritstone. Water issued from the rock through a fissure more than a foot wide to be conveyed through lead pipes to other cisterns under the floors.

Curious about the area around the pool, Rosamond plucked up one of the candles to examine the small rooms opening off one side. Although they were empty now, she supposed they must be used for robing or storage. Opposite that series of doors stood a gigantic hearth. Fires were necessary, even in high summer, to offset the cold air of Buxton.

When Rosamond's circuit of the perimeter was complete, she returned to the pool and held the candle over the water. It had a faint blue cast but was passing clear. She could see what looked like paving tiles on the bottom of the bath, and benches had been built all around its sides. Submerged up to their necks, those who thought such treatment could cure them sat there in the thermal waters to let the healing power of underground springs work its magic. Rosamond had no difficulty imagining her mother sitting just so, her misshapen legs buoyed up by the warm water.

Eleanor, Lady Pendennis, had visited Buxton the previous summer. She had not been cured but she had succeeded in another area. She'd met important people. One who lived locally, Lady Bridget, wife of Sir Richard Hawley, had agreed to take Rosamond into her household.

Ignoring a faintly unpleasant mineral smell, Rosamond released the clasp that held her dark green wool cloak in place and let it fall to the stone floor. Then she undid the points holding skirt and bodice together, and removing both, tossed them carelessly away.

With less abandon, the other girls followed her example.

"A pity we could not bring Faith," Lina said as she and Diony helped each other undo ties and laces. At Bawkenstanes Manor the tiring maid they all shared assisted them with dressing and undressing.

"You know why we left her behind." Rosamond shivered as she discarded the last of her clothing but she counted the chill in the air small cost for an adventure of this magnitude. "If Faith knew our plans, she'd tattle." Her first loyalty was to Lady Bridget, who had hired her, her second to Lady Bridget's husband. The girls in her care placed a poor third.

"We should not be here," Diony whined. "It is not meet."

"Even an apprentice bound for seven years to the strictest of masters is entitled to slip away from his dull duties a time or two," Rosamond argued. "Boys in London frequent the brothels, or so

I've been told. A visit to Buxton's healing waters, fed by the same springs that bubble up into the holy well of Saint Anne, cannot be half so wicked as that!"

On the heels of this defiant statement she strode, naked, to the very edge of the bath. Ahead of her stretched an expanse more than three times her own height and almost as wide as it was long. Rosamond knew her friends depended upon her to lead the way. Taking a deep breath and using two fingers to pinch her nostrils together, she jumped into the water with a loud and gratifying splash.

Her knees bent on landing and she submerged for a moment, but as soon as she surfaced again she realized the depth was not at all alarming. Besides, unlike most girls, Rosamond had been taught how to swim.

Lina peered down at her. "Is it truly the temperature of hot honeyed milk?"

"Come in and see for yourself." Rosamond flicked wet hands in Lina's direction and missed dousing her only by inches.

Giggling and hugging herself to keep warm, Lina ventured closer. After a moment, when she gathered enough courage to insert a toe in the pool, Rosamond seized her by one plump ankle and tugged. Lina tumbled into the water, sending up a large wave.

With a squeal, Dionysia retreated, all angles and gangly limbs, but she was back at the edge an instant later, in time to see her friend's dark head pop up. Lina sputtered only a little before she began to giggle again. "There are bubbles, Diony, and it *is* lovely and warm."

Frowning, moving with the awkward lack of grace of one as yet unaccustomed to newly acquired height, Dionysia closed her eyes and ran toward the pool. She tripped just as she reached the edge and fell forward with a shriek, landing on her belly and producing a geyser. Flailing wildly, she sent spray straight into Rosamond's face.

"You did that apurpose!"

"I did not!" Finding her feet, Diony scraped a pale lock of hair out of her eyes and glared.

Rosamond scooped up a handful of the tepid water and threw it, scoring a direct hit. "Did, too!"

A lively and protracted battle ensued until, exhausted by their frolic, Rosamond flopped onto her back to stare at the rectangle of moonlit sky above. The others followed suit and stillness descended.

The lukewarm, bubbly water felt strangely soothing on Rosamond's bare skin. Far off, she heard the gentle rush of the spring that fed the pool. Closer at hand the only sounds were water lapping against the sides of the bath and quiet breathing. She floated, lost in a dreamlike trance, until the peaceful interlude was abruptly shattered by a shrill feminine voice.

"This will not do. *Allons, demoiselles! Ne restez pas dans la fontaine.*"

Startled, Rosamond tried to right herself but only succeeded in submerging. Nearby, Lina was in similar difficulty, but she sloshed about, gasping and swallowing copious amounts of tepid water until she was hauled upright by Diony. Once she regained her own footing, Rosamond spared them only a glance, enough to see that, mortified, Lina stood with head down, hiding behind the dripping mass of her hair. Wet, it was the color of ebony. Dry, it more closely resembled mud. Where she grasped Lina's arm, Diony's bony hand trembled.

Reassured that both would survive, Rosamond turned her attention to their discoverer. Madame Poitier, one of Lady Bridget's waiting gentlewomen, stood at the edge of the bath. Backlit by the candles, swathed all in black as befit a widowed refugee who'd fled the wars of religion in her homeland, Louise Poitier's face was set in an implacable expression. One foot tapped impatiently on the stone flooring and her arms were folded across her chest. In this mood she seemed a formidable figure, but Rosamond hoped it was only a trick of the light. The tallow candles she'd brought were so old that they sputtered like rushdips, casting deceptive shadows and adding a sense of menace to everything about their surroundings.

Rosamond took her time wading to the edge of the pool. The other two girls had already scrambled out of the water and gathered up their discarded garments by the time she reached it. Since none of them had thought to bring towels, Diony used her chemise to dry herself before she put on any clothing. Lina, more anxious to cover her nakedness, simply pulled her undergarment over her wet and shivering body.

The night air felt harsh as well as cold, especially after the soothing warmth of the healing waters, but Rosamond refused to be hurried. Her movements slow, she dressed herself. All the while, her mind raced. She knew why she and her friends were here, but what had drawn Madame Poitier? When she dared meet Madame's eyes, the anxiety she saw there only confused her further.

"Return at once to Bawkenstanes Manor and contemplate your transgressions," the Frenchwoman said. "Say nothing of this to anyone. On the morrow, after church, you will come to me to work on your embroidery and we will speak further of your sins and how you may be absolved of them."

Lina and Diony bolted, glad of the reprieve. Rosamond hung back. "Do you mean to tell Lady Bridget you found us here?"

"Run along home, *jeune fille*," Madame Poitier answered, her smile enigmatic. "If you obey me now, this will remain our *petit secret*."

❦2❦

"WHO IS that girl?" Annabel MacReynolds asked the question in French.

"Which one?" Louise Poitier, as she now called herself, peered into the shadows and answered her companion in the same language.

"The bold, dark-haired child." Now that all three young gentlewomen had departed, Annabel left her place of concealment in the passage that led to New Hall and ventured into the moonlight.

"Her name is Rosamond Appleton," Louise said.

"Is it, by God? No wonder she seemed familiar. I knew her father once, long ago."

Only by a diminution in their glitter could Annabel tell that Louise's eyes had narrowed. "Will that complicate our quest?" Louise asked.

"'Twill depend upon why she is here. The last I heard of Mistress Rosamond, she was living with her father's widow in Kent."

Taking the candle Louise handed her, Annabel led the way into the deserted tower house where the earl of Shrewsbury's personal guests stayed during the bathing season. As soon as she'd confirmed what Louise knew, she would be on her way, riding hard by the light of the full moon, her only escort the two silent men she'd hired in Derby.

"The widow must have remarried," Louise said. "Rosamond's mother is not called Lady Appleton. She is a Lady Pendennis of Cornwall."

They reached a large, comfortably furnished chamber, its windows shuttered against the cold and to prevent light from showing. Annabel had been tempted to start a fire in the hearth while she waited but had settled for a brazier full of coals. She burrowed deeper into her fur-lined cloak. Mistress Rosamond was reckless indeed to bathe at this time of year in such a frigid clime, even in a hot spring.

Annabel repressed a smile. On the other hand, that was just the sort of thing she'd have done herself at Rosamond's age.

She offered Louise mulled wine and waved her toward a cushioned bench, waiting until she was settled there before she sipped from her own goblet. Then, too restless to sit, she prowled the room.

"If young Rosamond has but half her father's cunning or a modicum of her mother's guile," she said after a moment, "she could endanger the most innocent scheme. Add to those traits the peculiar skills of her father's widow and the connections her stepfather once had and our plans could indeed be in jeopardy."

"Explain." The sharpness in Louise's voice betrayed her concern even as her words betrayed her true religion. "In this heathen land where divorce and remarriage have been all but impossible since the ouster of Mother Church, our Rosamond has one too many parents living."

Annabel lifted plump shoulders in a shrug meant to convey casual unconcern. She did not want to panic Louise, only warn her. "Rosamond Appleton is what the English call a merrybegot— a bastard. Her father, Sir Robert, never paid much attention to his marriage vows. Eleanor, Rosamond's mother, was but one of his mistresses."

"And you were another? You traded your favors for information?"

"But of course." She'd been ordered into Robert Appleton's bed by no less a personage than Catherine de' Medici, the queen mother of France, and she'd enjoyed the assignment. "Eleanor captured his attention a few years later. When Rosamond was born, Robert was out of the country, up to his neck in espionage and intrigue. Eleanor, destitute and desperate, threw herself on the mercy of Robert's wife, Susanna. Lady Appleton is a most...unique individual. She provided for both mother and child."

"Would Rosamond recognize you?"

"I do much doubt it. The girl was not yet three years old the only time I ever encountered her. My appearance has altered much in the interim." Since then, Annabel acknowledged with a rueful grimace, she had nearly doubled in girth. The slender, supple young woman she'd once been was now well disguised by furrows in the brow, pouches under the eyes, dewlaps, and double chins. Hidden by her headdress, silver strands outnumbered those that remained a bright but natural red. She could still ride like a centaur but feats of running, climbing, and seducing courtiers in window embrasures were no longer part of her stock in trade.

Louise was some years younger. In the concise manner of one accustomed to making reports, she detailed all she knew. "Lady Pendennis met the Hawleys last summer and struck up a friendship with Lady Bridget, after which she arranged for Rosamond to come to stay at Bawkenstanes Manor. Lady Pendennis was badly injured some years ago and can walk only with great pain. She hopes, I do think, to receive frequent invitations to visit her daughter...and the baths."

"If the waters did not bring about a cure at once, is it not foolhardy to return?"

"I am told they eased her suffering." Louise laughed softly. "Mayhap the real reason she came, the reason she means to come again, is to be cured of infertility. Lady Bridget says Sir Walter Pendennis does much desire a son and heir."

Annabel's hand clenched her goblet. "If a man would be certain of his child's paternity, he'd do well to accompany his wife here to Buxton."

Louise's eyebrows lifted so high that they almost disappeared beneath the front brim of her French hood. "Is that because of the reputation of spaws on the Continent? Or Sir Walter and Lady Pendennis?"

"Both." Annabel paused to refill her goblet. "I have met Lady Appleton, too. When Rosamond's father was murdered, suspicion fell upon his widow. She is by way of being an expert on herbal poisons and even wrote a book on the subject. In order to clear her name, she was obliged to seek out her husband's former mistresses, on the theory that one of them would have had the best reason to kill him. By the time Lady Appleton discovered the identity of the guilty party, she'd brought together a goodly number of people from Robert's past, including his daughter Rosamond, Eleanor, Sir Walter, and myself. At the time, Sir Walter Pendennis was one of Queen Elizabeth's premier intelligence gatherers. A master spy."

The words landed like cannon shot in the quiet of the little chamber. Louise swore softly, the sound underscored by an ominous rattle from the shutters. A wind had come up in the dale.

"It is as well that you do not remain in Buxton," she said. "It would never do for you to come face to face with such a man."

Silently, Annabel agreed. When last she'd seen Sir Walter, he'd been about to have her arrested for espionage. Soon after, newly married to Eleanor, he'd gone abroad, taking his new bride with him and leaving Rosamond with Susanna Appleton. Whenever she'd been on the Continent herself after that, Annabel had taken care to stay well away from her old enemy.

"Finish your report," Annabel said abruptly. "Tell me first about the others in the household." It was vital she know everything before she proceeded to the next step.

"You will have gathered already that Lady Bridget is the daughter of an earl." Annabel nodded. Her title gave that away. If she were naught but a mere knight's wife, she'd be called Lady Hawley. "She married beneath her," Louise continued, "and she never lets anyone forget she is nobly born. Her husband has no land save Bawkenstanes Manor, which he inherited from a cousin. The Hawleys have two children, a daughter named Penelope and a son." A slow smile curved Louise's lips. "Young Will Hawley fancies himself in love with me, which has been useful."

"How young?"

"Fourteen." Louise was twenty. Annabel restrained her impulse to comment. "Your little friend Rosamond may make a match with him, if their mothers have aught to say about it. I understand she is a considerable heiress."

Annabel supposed Susanna Appleton had seen to that. She might have been betrayed by her late husband, but she was not the sort of woman to take her revenge on a helpless child. Leigh Abbey and all its riches, Annabel recalled, had come to Robert at his marriage to Susanna. Upon his death, his childless widow had inherited everything. His only other kin yet living had been an unacknowledged half sister.

"What of the two girls who were with Rosamond just now?"

Louise sent her a curious look. Annabel supposed her impatience showed. In truth, she was angry at herself for wasting so much thought on what was long past.

"The plump one, Godlina Walkenden, is the youngest daughter of a wealthy London merchant." Louise hesitated, almost as if she wanted to add something else, then shook her head. "He is of no importance, but the other girl is a Derbyshire lass and her father is Wymond Tallboys. Tallboys shares certain mining interests with Sir Richard Hawley, but none of his religious sympathies. I have heard there is a new term for those as radical as Master Tallboys in their beliefs. They are called puritans because they want a purer church than now exists in England—no music, no vestments, not even any bells to mark the hours."

Annabel nodded, filing the import of that information away to consider at a later time. "Has he any weaknesses?"

Louise chuckled. "He is fond of me."

"So is every man breathing and a good many women, too."

"Tallboys believes every lie I tell him, even when my words must seem passing strange for one who professes to be an exiled Huguenot."

"You are certain he does not suspect anything?"

"He is too besotted."

Annabel believed her. "Continue, then. Tell me about the upper servants at Bawkenstanes Manor."

Louise dismissed them with a wave of her hand. "None of any use to us. Margery Cottelling and I are Lady Bridget's waiting gentlewomen." She went on to enumerate the members of the Hawley household, from steward and cook to musician and stableboy. Halfway through the recital, Annabel's mind began to wander.

The mention of Robert Appleton brought back memories, many of them most pleasant. Life had been exciting in the days when Mary Stewart ruled Scotland and Annabel was one of her ladies. That she'd been at the Scots court as a spy for France had been of no moment.

"That is the lot," Louise said, jerking Annabel out of her reverie.

Present reality was harsh. More than seven years ago, Mary had abdicated in favor of her infant son and fled her own realm. She'd sought sanctuary in England, only to become Elizabeth Tudor's prisoner instead. These days, Mary Stewart was in the keeping of the same earl of Shrewsbury who owned New Hall and Buxton's baths.

Even before Mary's imprisonment, Annabel's activities had come under scrutiny by English spies. For that reason, she'd avoided involving herself in any of the many attempts to rescue the Catholic Queen Mary and put her on England's throne in place of the Protestant Queen Elizabeth...until now. Now there was a new plot brewing.

Annabel drained her goblet and tossed it aside. She had no time to indulge in nostalgia and precious little to expend on interrogating Louise. She gave the other woman a curt nod. "There seem to be few surprises here. Now tell me all you know about the other conspirators. If there is a potential turncoat among them, I would weed him out now, before he has opportunity to betray us."

As Annabel had hoped, Louise accepted the logic of this statement. "There are three men, all as devoted to Queen Mary's cause as we are," she said, and gave Annabel the particulars she'd need to locate them.

❦3❦

March 27, 1575
Buxton, Derbyshire

THE MORNING after her clandestine visit to the First Chief Bath, as Rosamond was about to set off for St. Anne's Chapel, she looked for Madame Poitier. She was surprised to see no sign of the Frenchwoman. This was the sixth Sunday in Lent, otherwise known as Palm Sunday, a holy day of enough importance that the Hawleys forsook the comfort of the private chapel at Bawkenstanes Manor and assembled the entire household to walk into Lower Buxton for services.

For this special occasion Lady Bridget wore her most elaborate gown over a warm wool kirtle and a new French hood decorated with pearls. Her thick brows drew together in annoyance as she noticed the absence of Madame Poitier, one of her waiting gentlewomen. "We must not be late," she fretted. "We must set a good example for the villagers."

"Let us go on, then," said Sir Richard. With an impatient flip of a lace-encircled wrist, he signaled his steward to take the lead.

Of a muscular build, though beginning to show the effects of excessive consumption of food and drink, Sir Richard was taller than his wife. Almost everyone was, even Rosamond. On this day, however, the difference in height seemed less. Lady Bridget wore pantofles with three-inch cork soles strapped to her shoes. They served a dual purpose, keeping her feet out of ice or mud on the road while adding to her stature.

"Wait," she objected. No one was surprised when she countermanded her husband's order. They were often at odds. "Appearance is all. You, girl!" She pointed the fur snoskyn keeping her hands warm toward Rosamond. "Walk beside my other waiting gentlewoman."

When Rosamond had taken her place next to Mistress Cottelling, the procession set out. Dressed in their finest clothing, wearing warm and colorful cloaks against the frigid air, they followed the same route from Upper Buxton into the dale that Rosamond and her two companions had taken the previous night. The way was steep, uneven, and slick with ice, for although the sun had risen it was scarce visible through a gloomy mist. Damp ribbons of fog curled around Rosamond's ankles like living tendrils and cold eddied up beneath her skirts with every step.

When Lina shrieked and dropped the silver box full of comfits she always carried with her, everyone jumped except Will Hawley.

"Did some evil, crawling thing reach out of the murk and touch you?" he taunted her.

"An apt description," Rosamond muttered. She had no doubt it had been Will himself who'd startled her friend.

Behind her she heard a snicker turn into a cough as Lady Bridget's music master, Giles Bannister, tried to hide his amusement. She turned to grin at him but her smile faded at the sight of Will pushing rudely past Diony's father and his own sister to come level with Rosamond and Mistress Cottelling.

"Where is your sense of fun, Ros?" he asked as he trotted along beside them.

She spared him one disdainful glance, enough to observe that in a face covered with pustules, he had a new quat. Uncharitable of her as it was to wish for such a thing, she hoped it would stay red and inflamed and torment him for at least a week.

"There is a new litter in the stable," Will said. "The orange tabby's hidden them somewhere in the straw."

She pretended to ignore this blatant attempt to engage her in conversation but his overture made her uneasy. Had there been a threat behind the silken words? She'd seen Will torment dogs by tying sticks to their tails. She hated to imagine what he could do to a tiny newborn kitten.

"We could slip away once the vicar starts droning on and go for a walk instead," Will whispered. "I've somewhere I want to show you."

With anyone but Will, Rosamond might have been tempted. Palm Sunday services went on longer than most, what with reading the story of Christ's entry into Jerusalem and so on. But she'd always enjoyed the pageantry that followed. She was not certain what they'd do in Derbyshire, but in both Kent and Cornwall the entire congregation made crosses of catkin-bearing willow to carry when they processed out of the chapel. Long ago, or so her foster mother had once told her, before such things were banned in English churches, the priest would have blessed the foliage, giving it powers to protect the bearer against evil.

Mistress Cottelling, who had as much reason as Rosamond to be wary of Will Hawley, walked faster to get away from him. She had closed the distance from Sir Richard and his wife to mere inches when Lady Bridget, coming abreast of St. Anne's Well, stopped short. Mistress Cottelling narrowly avoided plowing into her. Will caught Rosamond's arm to keep her from colliding with the waiting gentlewoman.

"The gate is open," said Sir Richard.

"See to it, husband." Lady Bridget let her impatience show.

"Allow me, Mother." Will moved swiftly past his father.

A protective wall enclosed the well. Made of stone in some places and red plaster hard as brick in others, it had not been damaged by the earthquake. Furthermore, the earl of Shrewsbury, who did not want people to take free samples, had left standing orders that the only gate into the enclosure should be kept locked whenever an attendant was not on duty. Rosamond frowned. She saw no sign of the padlock. Had it been absent last night? Had they missed a golden opportunity to visit the sacred well without supervision? A pity if so, but when they'd crept past in the darkness she had not noticed whether the gate was secured or not.

Curious, she trailed after Will, hoping for a peek inside. She'd heard there was a stone basin there, one that had been used to collect medicinal spring water since Roman times. She'd just reached the gate when Will staggered back as if he'd taken a blow. Retching, he fell to his knees at her feet.

Rosamond froze where she stood. Behind her she heard Lady Bridget make a choked sound and Sir Richard curse. Mistress Cottelling screamed. With an effort, Rosamond managed to inhale but she was unable to look away from the terrible sight before her.

They had found Madame Poitier. Limbs twisted and stiff and whitened by a light coating of hoarfrost, her body lay face down beside St. Anne's Well.

༄4༄

April 18, 1575
Canterbury, Kent

JENNET JAFFREY'S twelve-year-old son, Rob, was a scholar at the King's School. The Leigh Abbey housekeeper chose the time of her visit carefully, arriving at the elaborate gate that led into the Mint Yard during the second of the two hours between morning and afternoon classes. The boys customarily ate their dinner at the common table in company with other members of the cathedral foundation, but Jennet had allowed time for Rob to finish his meal. She expected to find him among the dozen or so scholars who'd fled the chill of the ancient grey stone buildings for the sunlight out of doors, but she searched among them in vain.

A cluster of buildings interspersed with trees crowded into the Mint Yard, so-called because for ten years it had seen service as a royal mint. What had once been the cathedral's almonry chapel had become the schoolroom, although some of the scholars slept there, too, including Rob. Other boys lived in Canterbury and went home to their families at night, or were lodged in the Headmaster's House at the west end of the yard, in rooms formerly occupied by the staff of the almonry, or in the Lower Master's House.

Reasoning that Rob would not willingly have stayed indoors on such a bright, sunny day, and reluctant to believe he might have been kept in for some infraction of the rules, Jennet made her way to the Green Court Gate, one of two entrances to what had once been a monastery. Beyond its north wall she could see the magnificent buildings of the Archbishop of Canterbury's palace.

Jennet's attention, however, focused first on the Prior Selling Gate. On his last visit home, Rob had regaled them with stories about the legends surrounding it. Jennet saw nothing out of the ordinary. There were lodgings above. Below, according to Rob, were the monastic *necessarium* and a long, gloomy passage running through what remained of the former monastery. This was the infamous Dark Entry, reputed to be haunted.

Jennet was not sure if she believed in ghosts or not, but she'd listened as eagerly as her husband and two daughters to Rob's tales of a canon who'd lived in the gatehouse in old King Henry's day. This canon had employed a cook named Ellen Bean. As was the custom, she'd been known as Nelly Cook, but there'd been more to her duties than cooking. When the canon brought home a young woman, calling her his niece, Nelly Cook grew jealous and retaliated by poisoning them both. According to Rob, she'd been walled up alive in the Dark Entry for her crime. Young scholars ever since had sworn they could hear her screams, especially on moonless nights when the air was still.

Jennet shivered. Rob had too much imagination, that was his trouble. And he should not be gadding about unsupervised. She did not want to get him into trouble by asking Master Gresshop, the headmaster, where he was, but she was beginning to feel concerned. Every other time she'd visited, she'd located him without difficulty. He'd been with his friends, or sitting on a bench, reading, but always out of doors in the fresh air.

Puzzled, she returned to the Mint Yard. *Had* Rob been kept inside for punishment? He was not expecting a visit from his mother. She'd planned to surprise him, as she had once or twice before when she journeyed the five miles from Leigh Abbey on the excuse of making purchases in the buttermarket beside the cathedral.

The scholars began to drift inside as the hour to resume their lessons neared. Jennet plunked herself down on a conveniently placed stone bench to consider whether or not to abandon her effort to see her son. A short time later, her tired feet much restored, she decided to give up and return to Leigh Abbey. The absence of boys in the Mint Yard and the angle of the sun, as well as the sight of Robert Rose, the Lower Master, scurrying toward the chapel, told her that the afternoon session was about to begin.

At the precise moment Jennet stood to leave, she at last caught sight of her wayward son. Her mouth open to call out to him, she froze. Rob was headed toward the gate through which she'd entered the Mint Yard.

Jennet's lips closed with an audible snap and her eyes narrowed. Struggling with a bulging pack, Rob cast nervous glances over his shoulder, as if he feared pursuit. Furious and alarmed in equal parts, Jennet flung herself across the courtyard and swooped down upon her hapless son in a flurry of dark blue skirts and swirling grey wool.

"And just where do you think you are going?" she demanded, planting herself directly in his path.

"Mother!" His voice cracked on the first syllable but he recovered quickly. When he spoke again it was in a lower register. "Step aside."

The command was so unexpectedly forceful that Jennet almost obeyed. One hand over her bosom to still the frantic pounding within, she gaped at him. When had her child matured into a young man? He'd been home for a visit less than a week earlier. Why had she not noticed then that he was taller than she was? What had happened to the small-boned, pale-skinned boy with the shock of mole-brown hair and the sweet nature?

Jennet had never considered her son a weakling, but his sudden transformation into a young man of purpose and passion deprived her of breath. She swayed, beset by sudden dizziness. Mayhap she should not have tried to run. As an alarming blackness edged closer, Rob caught her arm to guide her back to the bench.

"Give me a moment," she wheezed.

With deft fingers, Rob loosened both her grey cloak and her best linen collar. "Your face is red. What is it? What is wrong?"

Although she still felt weak, Jennet did not need long to collect her wits. In his alarm he'd become her little lad again, concerned for his mother. "You tell me, Rob. What is the meaning of that?" She indicated the pack Rob had dropped beside the bench, but before she could question him further, he regrouped and challenged her.

"Why did you come here, Mother?"

"Cannot a fond mother visit her only son? I missed you. I have marchpane in my market basket. And a honey cake."

"I just spent Easter holiday at Leigh Abbey." He sounded exasperated.

"It is no good trying to distract me, Rob. That I am here is not the most important matter at the moment." She eyed his pack with disfavor. "'Tis plain enough you meant to run away from school, but why?"

Rob thrust out his chin. His pale blue eyes met hers with a defiance she'd have admired had it come from anyone else. "Rosamond needs me."

No answer could have made Jennet more livid. Her temper flared, bringing with it another wave of light-headedness. "Rosamond! Rosamond is in Derbyshire."

"Yes." Rob held himself stiff, shoulders squared. "That is where I mean to go."

"Rosamond..." Jennet muttered.

Rosamond Appleton had been a bad influence on Rob from the day she'd arrived at Leigh Abbey, where Jennet was housekeeper to the widowed Lady Appleton and Rob's father served as steward. Rosamond, the by-blow of Lady Appleton's late husband, had led Rob and his two sisters into all manner of trouble. The final straw had been when she'd blithely renamed Jennet's son, dubbing him Mole for the color of his hair. The demeaning ekename had stuck. Even Lady Appleton had been heard to use it.

Jennet managed to stop grinding her teeth long enough to speak. "Do you want to kill your poor mother? Will you worry me to death?"

"There is no need to be concerned about me. I've made long journeys on my own ere now."

Jennet gnawed at her lower lip, as was her habit when she was agitated. Did he think to comfort her by reminding her of the last occasion on which he'd run away? Rosamond had been the cause then, too, and it had been pure chance that Rob had come to no harm.

One look at her son's set features warned Jennet that she'd never be able to make him see the risk in what he intended. He dismissed her concerns and discounted, too, the potential for personal danger on such a long journey. With the optimism of youth, he believed he was invincible.

"Lady Appleton will not be pleased to hear you've abandoned your schooling without a by-your-leave. Nor will the school let you return if you go." When this reminder caused his brow to furrow, Jennet pursued her advantage. "You have an obligation to Lady Appleton. She is the one who provides the money for your expenses here. At twelve pounds per annum, it could take you a very long time to repay her." Jennet herself earned but twenty-six shillings a year and her husband's position as steward commanded only fifty.

"But, Mother," Rob objected, "Rosamond needs my help." His voice cracked with the intensity of his desire to convince Jennet he should go to Derbyshire.

"What? Something that girl cannot do on her own?"

"She *thinks* she can manage," Rob admitted, "but I fear for her safety." He hesitated, then blurted out the rest. "She has set herself the task of investigating a murder."

🐚5🐚

Later that afternoon
Leigh Abbey, Kent

THE DISCORDANT sound of keys clashing against one another as their wearer sped along a passage warned Susanna Appleton that something was amiss. Jennet Jaffrey, who wore the ring of keys as a symbol of her position in the household, did not willingly hurry anywhere these days. Moving too fast made her heart race and her breathing irregular, to the point where Susanna had insisted she take a little feverfew in wine each day and avoid nuts, cheese, meat, and fruit.

With a final jangle, Jennet entered the study. She placed one hand on the keys to still them as she stepped over the threshold. Pale blue eyes, just a shade lighter than Susanna's, went straight to her in the cushioned window seat. Whatever had happened, it had left Jennet's expression grim and her face flushed.

"There is too much pink in your cheeks," Susanna said, putting aside the letter she'd been reading, a missive from her neighbor and sometime lover, Nick Baldwin, who was presently on the Continent. "A pity it is too early in the year to gather fresh heartsease." She could, however, distill a drink using herbs she kept on hand—borage, bugloss, saffron, balm, basil, rosemary, and roses. Jennet was Susanna's housekeeper, but for many years she had also been her companion and friend. Susanna had no intention of letting her neglect her health.

Fists planted firmly on rounded hips, Jennet huffed out a breath. "Naught's wrong with me but that I am angry."

"Sit down and tell me why." Susanna patted the cushion beside her.

That Jennet obeyed without further protest was as alarming as her agitation. The slender girl who'd first come to Leigh Abbey as a tiring maid had passed through the pleasing plumpness of young motherhood to become a rotund matron of thirty-eight. Having safely passed her thirtieth birthday, Jennet might reasonably hope to see sixty, but she would have to contend with an increasing number of ailments along the way. Jennet *would* take that healthful infusion, Susanna decided, if she had to pour it down her stubborn throat with her own hands!

Aloud, she said only, "You went to visit Rob today. Was there trouble in Canterbury?"

Jennet did not stand on ceremony. She unburdened herself in a rush.

Although Susanna tensed at the first mention of Rosamond, she did not interrupt. The child was as dear to her as if she'd been her own flesh and blood, but that did not blind her to Rosamond's faults.

It had been to attempt to cure her of fits of temper and a tendency to sulk that Susanna had relinquished custody to Rosamond's natural mother and her husband. Susanna knew she had been too lenient with the girl. She had hoped living at Priory House in Cornwall with Eleanor and Walter would teach Rosamond to be less self-centered and channel her excess energy into productivity.

For a time the plan had seemed to work. Rosamond liked Sir Walter Pendennis and therefore had been willing to obey him. She'd enjoyed living in a place where she could ride for miles on Courtier, the roan Susanna had given her. Indoors, she'd pursued the course of studies Susanna had set up—lessons in French, Latin, and Greek, and in ciphering and cosmography. Then Eleanor had decided she needed more, proper training as a gentlewoman in someone else's household. By the time Susanna had been informed of Eleanor's decision, Rosamond was already in Derbyshire.

Since the previous autumn, Rosamond had written several letters to her foster mother at Leigh Abbey. She'd sounded content. She'd made friends with the other girls at Bawkenstanes Manor and she liked learning to dance, an activity markedly absent at both Leigh Abbey and Priory House.

"Rosamond told my Rob she's investigating a murder."

"Murder?" The word caught Susanna's attention as nothing else could have. "What murder?"

"None at all that I can see." Jennet seized a leather pillow with tassels, plumped it, and replaced it on the window seat with rather more force than necessary. "According to what Rob told me— he would not let me read Rosamond's letter for myself—one of Lady Bridget's waiting gentlewomen fell while dipping water from a well. Saint Anne's Well, he called it. She struck her head and drowned in the basin."

"An accident?"

"So any sensible person would suppose."

"But Rosamond thinks otherwise?" Susanna reminded herself that her foster daughter loved excitement and relished being the center of attention. She might well suspect foul play where none existed.

"She *says* she does." Jennet's exasperation underscored every word. "Her letter convinced Rob of it. Believing that wild tale, he was ready to run away from school."

"Did she ask him to?"

Jennet's scowl gave Susanna part of the answer. She'd have liked to blame Rosamond for everything, but in fairness could not. "She wanted him to discover all he could about poisonous mushrooms and send the information to her. She believes this Madame Poitier was poisoned."

Susanna winced, sensible of her own culpability. Rosamond's knowledge of poisons and how easily they could be ingested came from *A Cautionary Herbal*, the book Susanna herself had written some years ago. She had no doubt that Rosamond had taken her own copy of the slim, leather-bound volume with her to Derbyshire. It dealt only with herbs, not mushrooms, but in the entry for wormwood Susanna had included the astrological argument for using it as an antidote for mushroom poisoning. She had her doubts about the effectiveness of the treatment. Wormwood, after all, was also a deadly poison.

"Mushrooms," she muttered under her breath. Many varieties were poisonous and she supposed she should have devoted more attention to them. She might have, if most English people had not had a natural aversion to eating fungus.

Susanna left the window seat and crossed the room to one of several large chests filled with books and papers. The bulk of the material dealt with the properties of plants, although there were a goodly number of travel narratives as well.

"Master Corraro's book speaks of mushrooms," she told Jennet. "As I recall, he suggests the sylvester pear given in strong wine as an antidote. And Pliny the Elder's *Natural History* details the appearances of various edible and poisonous species."

"Oh, madam, never tell me you mean to credit that child's

stories." Jennet stared at her mistress in dismay. "Certes, young Rosamond does but exaggerate to make herself seem more important. Bawkenstanes Manor is a respectable house."

"I do not know enough to say if the woman's death was accidental or not, Jennet, but murder can happen anywhere, court or castle or hovel. Did Rosamond offer Rob any proof?"

"She gave none, and further said that no one in authority in Derbyshire is investigating this so-called murder."

"That means, I hope, that she has not shared her suspicions with the local justice of the peace." Susanna wished Rosamond had chosen to confide in her, while at the same time being glad she'd had sense enough to keep such serious accusations to herself. One of Rosamond's most conspicuous faults was a tendency to blurt out whatever she was thinking.

"The people of Buxton doubtless wish to hide the circumstances of this death, even if it was an accident," Susanna mused as she turned with Pliny's book in her hands. She did not open it. Instead she stared out the window at fields newly planted and orchards just coming into flower. The peaceful sight failed to calm her turbulent thoughts. "Saint Anne's Well is the source of the healing waters in the thermal baths. News that they'd found a body beside it might discourage custom."

"Well, then. That's all there is to it. Rosamond misinterpreted the reason matters were kept quiet. This has been much ado about nothing. You must write and tell Rosamond so. That will put an end to these wild claims."

"Can we be certain there is no basis for them?" Setting aside the book, still unopened, Susanna picked up the discarded letter from Nick. Simply holding it comforted her. She wished she could have his advice, but it would take weeks for any missive she sent to reach him and as long again for an answer to come back.

"Why would she think anyone would use mushrooms to kill?" Jennet argued. "What sensible person would eat one?"

"This Madame Poitier was a Frenchwoman," Susanna reminded her. "In France they consider many varieties of fungus to be delicacies."

A derisive snort told Susanna what Jennet thought of that.

"Did Rob have information to give Rosamond?"

"He had consulted a copy of Pliny," Jennet admitted, "and made notes in his copybook. I persuaded him to give them to me. I promised I would send them on with the letter I would ask you to write."

"And that was enough to dissuade him from leaving Canterbury?" Rob was devoted to Rosamond. He'd defied his mother before to please her. It would not have surprised Susanna to learn he was already on his way north.

"I reminded him that if he left school he'd owe you a very great fortune," Jennet said, "one he'd be unable to repay for many years because he'd not be able to attend university. We'd have to apprentice him in a trade, I told him, and that would mean he'd have neither income nor freedom for seven long years."

"Jennet! You know you would never do such a thing. The boy has a brilliant mind. He must go to Cambridge as my father did."

Inwardly she winced at her own words. Was it disloyal to Nick to imply that a lack of formal education hindered a man's success? Nick had as brilliant a mind as any university scholar. As a merchant he had served an apprenticeship after grammar school, but the fact that he'd never gone to Oxford or Cambridge, or to the Inns of Court, had not stopped him from amassing great wealth. He was a justice of the peace for Kent. In time he might be knighted for service to the queen, although he seemed to have no interest in such honors.

Jennet smoothed her fingertips over a bit of the decorative carving on the nearest book chest, but her thoughts were clearly still in Canterbury with her son. "I know you would speak for him, persuade the school to allow him to return, but I saw no advantage in letting *him* believe it. He wants to make something of himself, madam—a physician or lawyer, or a dean or archdeacon.

A man can rise above the most humble beginning if he has a university degree."

Susanna felt a twinge of sympathy for young Rob, torn between loyalty to a friend and his duty to fulfill the commitment he'd made when he entered the King's School. His parents' expectations made the weight of that burden even heavier. "He might have left as soon as your back was turned," she suggested.

Jennet shook her head, confident even in her exasperation. "He gave me his promise in return for mine. Besides, I spoke with Master Gresshop before I returned to Leigh Abbey. Rob will be closely watched for the next few weeks."

And likely beaten, Susanna thought. Discipline was harsh in most grammar schools, but she chose not to distress Jennet by mentioning that. She could only hope his punishment and the restrictions put upon him did not make Rob all the more determined to go his own way. A clever lad, he would not find it difficult to escape.

"He will honor his word," Jennet insisted, "no matter the provocation."

"What promise did he demand of you?" Susanna asked.

"That I share his concerns with you, madam. Rob knows how much you love Rosamond. I persuaded him to trust your judgment. I will tell him when next I visit Canterbury that you have no qualms about her safety and that he need no longer feel obliged to rush to her aid."

Uneasiness engulfed Susanna. *Was* Rosamond safe? The girl had been pampered when she lived here, indulged and made much of, the more so because Susanna had never had any children of her own to spoil. She'd encouraged Rosamond to think for herself, and been pleased when she'd developed an active imagination. If she said she'd begun an investigation into a suspicious death, then she would pursue the matter until she had all the answers she sought.

It seemed unlikely there had been anything untoward about

the way the waiting gentlewoman died, but what if Rosamond's questions threatened to reveal other secrets? Most people had something they'd prefer to keep hidden. A few, as Susanna had reason to know, could be driven to use deadly force when they felt threatened.

She smoothed her thumb over the wax seal on Nick's letter. Speculation about Rosamond's doings availed her as little as wondering when Nick Baldwin would return. There was, however, a simple way to discover the truth or falsehood of her foster daughter's claim.

"Eleanor Pendennis swears the month she spent in Buxton last summer produced a great improvement in her health. Would such waters, I wonder, ease the pain of that old injury to my leg? In cold weather, the persistent ache is most annoying."

Horrified, Jennet hopped to her feet. "Derbyshire is a very great distance to travel on a child's whim, and it is cold there all year round."

"Healthful, they say, and neither of us is as lithe or limber as once we were."

Unlike Jennet, Susanna had never been tiny. She had inherited her father's sturdy build and height, together with his square jaw and his love of learning. Her mirror told her she was in danger of being called stout. Too much sitting around at home, she concluded. Nearly three years had passed since she'd traveled farther from home than London. A change would do her good.

"We have never been to Derbyshire," she said, "and it has been a long time since I last saw Rosamond. You need not go with me," she added in response to Jennet's glower. She knew in advance what reaction that offer would provoke.

"As if I would let you go haring off on your own! You need me to look after you, madam." Shaking her head at the foolishness of the decision, she nevertheless looked nearly her old self again as she bustled out. "At least we've not yet packed the fur-lined cloaks away," she muttered as she went, "or the heavy wool stockings."

6

April 21, 1575
Priory House, Cornwall

"YOU'VE NO need to go to Buxton." Sir Walter Pendennis scowled at his wife.

Eleanor glared back. Her husband was the most stubborn, opinionated creature on God's green earth. Once he got an idea into his head, it took an explosion to dislodge it. Well, then, she'd give him one. Her temper was primed and ready to ignite. "I was much improved after my last visit," she said through clenched teeth. "You cannot deny it."

Walter smoothed one hand over his sand-colored beard, carefully trimmed in the newest fashion. He wore it longer now than when she'd first met him, no doubt to compensate for the steady loss of his hair. Only a fringe was left, sticking out from beneath his bonnet like stray silk threads. It glinted in the candlelight, as did the gold embroidery on his red velvet doublet.

They faced each other across the expanse of Eleanor's high, ornately carved and painted bed. She sat propped against the headboard, a plump bolster covered in soft, tufted velvet at her back and a coverlet of cream-colored silk tucked in around her hips. The cloth concealed the misshapen legs stretched out in front of her.

"You were in high spirits when you returned," Walter said, "because you'd managed to place Rosamond in Lady Bridget's household."

"That pleased me, yes." The ache in her lower limbs had also been lessened by the care she'd received at Buxton and he knew it. She refused to play on his sense of pity. Pressing her lips together, she waited to hear what he would say next.

Walter circled the bedstead and leaned close, bracketing her narrow hips with his strong, long-fingered hands. His shoulders were broad enough to block out the room behind him. "You do not appear to have conceived."

"Further treatments are required." Forcing a sultry smile, Eleanor reached up to toy with the laces holding his collar closed. Walter had always had the power to stir her senses, even when she was wroth with him. A playful flick of her hand knocked his bonnet clear off his head.

A dangerous glitter came into his ice blue eyes as the expensive head covering landed among the rushes on the floor. "If a second visit to Buxton results in a child, then the more fool I," he muttered. "I warrant unchaperoned mixed bathing has more to do with curing infertility than any healing properties deriving from the thermal springs."

Eleanor's hand cupped the back of his head. "Come with me, then." The idea excited her. She could imagine Walter immersed beside her in the bubbling depths of the bath, both of them naked, no one else about. Her legs did not impede her underwater. She might even succeed in conceiving the son he so ardently desired.

He pulled away. "God's teeth, woman! I have no time for such nonsense."

"Then perforce I must go alone. Never fear, Walter. I will not make you wear a cuckold's horns." What other man would *want* a crippled woman?

"So you say." Walter turned his back on her and pretended to stare at the wall hanging. She'd replaced the tapestry map of Cornwall that had once been there with a scene of Venus presenting Aeneas with armor. She wondered if he appreciated the sentiment.

"Come with me," Eleanor coaxed. Since this felt uncomfortably like begging, she let a sarcastic note come into her voice. "Mayhap the waters will prove a remedy for your suspicious nature."

He gave a short bark of laughter. "There is no cure for that."

"No, I do not suppose there is. Well, then, if not out of duty to me, why not visit Buxton in the service of crown and country?" It was no good using sweet reason with Walter Pendennis. It was

probable he loved her, although there had been a long period
of time when he had tried not to, but the very intensity of their
feelings towards one another meant they'd never have a placid
marriage.

At last, she had his full attention. "What does that mean?"
Catching hold of the back of the Spanish chair, he carried it to her
bedside and straddled it. His intense blue gaze bored into her as
he waited for her explanation.

She met his eyes with a boldness she was far from feeling.
Ever since the accident that had damaged her legs, she'd also had
to contend with a disfiguring scar on one cheek. Once she'd taken
pride in her appearance—the perfect oval shape of her face, the
turned-up nose—but now it was a daily struggle not to give in to
despair. She wondered that Walter could think she'd be able to en-
tice another man into her bed. She had all she could do to keep
him coming back, and she could never be certain what weighed
more—lust for her or the desire for a son.

"Eleanor? If you know something about this so-called spaw in
Derbyshire, you had best tell me."

"Only what you do," she said in her sweetest voice. "Such
places attract spies and traitors. You would be in your element."

"I am no longer an intelligence gatherer, only a simple country justice of the peace."

"Hah!" Temper flaring once more, she tugged at her wedding
ring. If she could have pulled it off, she would have hurled it into
the glowing coals in the fireplace.

"Did you encounter intrigues at Buxton when you were
there? Something to do with your old friend Queen Mary, mayhap?" Walter's voice was suddenly silk over steel. He would never
let her forget the consequences of her one attempt to give aid to
Mary, queen of Scots. She'd betrayed all Walter stood for and for-
giveness had come hard. "Mary is allowed to go to Buxton to take
the waters, but only under guard. No one will get close to her
there."

"Are you so certain of that?" Taunting her husband was one of Eleanor's few joys. Her maid, Melka, claimed it put a sparkle into her eyes. Eleanor doubted that, but she did believe it was a wife's sacred duty to save her husband from the sin of overweening pride. She smiled sweetly at him. "Your sudden interest in such matters seems to belie your claim that you have abandoned your old life."

"I still correspond with acquaintances. Most of the news they send, I share with you. You know already that the countess of Shrewsbury is out of favor with the queen just now."

Eleanor nodded. According to the gossips, Lady Shrewsbury had conspired with the countess of Lennox to arrange a secret marriage between her daughter Catherine and Lady Lennox's son Charles. In the ordinary way of things, no one would have objected to such a match, but the countess of Lennox was the daughter of the elder sister of King Henry VIII and as such had a claim to England's throne. So did her son, and any children he might beget. Bad enough that young Charles had married without the queen's permission, which was against the law, but his new mother-in-law had the keeping of the captive queen of Scots, another contender for the English throne. All in all, the situation looked suspicious to those on the lookout for treasonous plots.

"Lady Lennox was sent to the Tower," Eleanor said. "Lady Shrewsbury was not."

"No. She is back at Sheffield with her husband and their royal prisoner." Abruptly abandoning the chair, Walter kicked it out of his way and stalked across the chamber to the window. The rushes underfoot whispered as he passed, giving off a faint fragrance of marjoram.

For a moment, Eleanor simply admired the sight of her husband framed by the casement, his form silhouetted against the sky and clouds behind him. Walter held himself stiff and tall as a mainmast, and he'd shortly unleash a razor-sharp tongue, but nothing could spoil Eleanor's pleasure in his appearance. He was a well-built man. His doublet and hose clung to broad shoulders and tight buttocks. Even his legs were fine. He needed none of the padding some men used.

Eleanor sighed. Once she'd been his physical match. They'd made a handsome couple, richly dressed, the world at their feet. That dream was gone now, but there could still be a child, a son who combined the best of them both.

"Tell me what you know of intrigue at Buxton," Walter demanded, turning to face her once more. "What did you hear of the doings of the countess of Shrewsbury? Was she present during your visit?"

"No. Nor was the earl. But if you will let me return to Buxton, I will be your eyes and ears. In the informal atmosphere of the baths, many a confidence is exchanged."

"You could also pass on information."

"What do I know? We have been immured in Cornwall too long to be aware of any *important* secrets."

He gave her a speculative look as he strode to the pedestal table. Covered with an exquisite piece of Persian carpet, it held a pitcher of Xeres sack and another of barley water. Walter filled two goblets with the former before coming to sit beside Eleanor on her bed.

"I do not believe in the magical powers of well water and I do not want you playing at being an intelligence gatherer. Stay here and tend to your house, madam." He handed her one of the goblets.

She sipped the potent liquid. "Why should I, when you will be away?"

Startled, he spilled a little of the wine. A rueful smile followed a curse. "Mayhap I should reconsider your qualifications as an intelligence gatherer."

"I saw the queen's seal on the letter that arrived two days past and I know you've made preparations for a journey."

"The queen's commission was not one I could refuse. I may be gone for several months."

"Then let me go to Buxton to visit my daughter. If the baths themselves trouble you so, I will not go near them. I will spend all my time sewing with Lady Bridget and her waiting gentlewomen." She made a face and sipped the sack, a drink of which she'd become most fond. It eased the pain in her legs remarkable well.

"So that is what this is about. You envy me my travels." Walter's smile was that of a poacher who'd just found juicy prey in his snare.

"Perhaps. Will you take me with you?" She sipped again and leaned into him. "I'd gladly return to the Continent instead of making the journey to Derbyshire."

"I cannot." His left hand slid along her shoulder. The fingers toyed with a lock of her hair.

"Then give me leave to visit Rosamond. I do not care what you choose to believe about my reasons for wanting to return to Buxton, but it is cruel of you to keep me a prisoner here while you are away." She let her lower lip slip forward into a pout.

He kissed away the sullen expression, then removed the goblet from her hand. His drink had already vanished. "I will consent, if you are a sweet and obedient wife to me tonight, to discuss the matter further. In the morning."

With that, he rose and left both her bed and her chamber.

Alone, Eleanor permitted herself a small, self-satisfied smile before she called for Melka. She'd greet her husband freshly bathed and enticingly perfumed. She'd relish the next few hours—a time to prepare, and plan and anticipate—but she'd enjoy what came after even more.

❦ 7 ❦

"MY DEAR Lady Appleton," said Lady Bridget, "welcome to Bawkenstanes Manor." She ignored Jennet, who stood just behind her mistress, observing everything.

Sir Richard's wife wanted something, Jennet decided. For all that she was an earl's daughter, there was a fawning quality to Lady Bridget's greeting, as if she wished to ingratiate herself with Lady Appleton. Did she hope the gentlewoman from Kent could do her some service in future?

Gracious as ever, Lady Appleton smiled and said the right things, but when their hostess was not looking she exchanged a speaking glance with Jennet. *Be wary of this woman,* it said. *She is not to be trusted.*

Jennet did not think much of Sir Richard, either. He was handsome in a dissipated fashion, tall and fair-haired. He was also anxious to escape. He regarded his unexpected visitors through heavy-lidded eyes and drawled some excuse about his duties to his son. The boy had his father's look about him and the same arrogant manner. Will Hawley scowled at the delay and rudely showed his impatience by shifting his weight from foot to foot while his right hand clenched and unclenched on the fishing pole slung over his shoulder.

"The Wye is accounted a fine trout stream," Lady Bridget murmured as both explanation and apology when her menfolk departed in unseemly haste a few minutes later.

"Do not concern yourself over the matter," Lady Appleton insisted, and turned the conversation by making admiring remarks about Bawkenstanes Manor.

Jennet thought it a pity the Hawleys did not live up to the promise of their house. The exterior of Bawkenstanes Manor, solidly built of local stone, was impressive. The house consisted of two storeys with attics in three straight-coped gables roofed with green slate. In a niche above the top windows some industrious stone carver had reproduced the family coat of arms. Below it was a date large enough to be read from the ground: 1549.

They entered the Great Hall from a porch, passing through an inner oaken door to a huge room with a fine paneled ceiling. An oriel window at the dais end was filled with stained glass in a series of roundels depicting the months of the year, while the canopy over the high table had been divided into panels by molded oak ribs.

"Each panel is decorated with a different coat of arms," Lady Bridget said when Lady Appleton remarked upon the piece. Preening, she pointed out several of them—all kin of hers and representing a fair portion of the nobility of England. Then she led Lady Appleton up a timber staircase into the family wing.

Through a window at the top of the stairs, Jennet could see two wings at right angles to the one they were in. This created a three-sided courtyard closed off to the north by outbuildings— barn and dairy, bakehouse, brewhouse, and laundry. Several fishponds were visible beyond. She also caught a glimpse of a small chapel at the northeast corner and wondered if Sir Richard had been granted a license to hear services at home. Lady Appleton was allowed that privilege at Leigh Abbey, although on most Sundays she and her entire household walked into nearby Eastwold to hear the vicar preach.

The south-facing chamber to which Lady Bridget led her guest, with Jennet trailing behind, compared well to the luxury of Lady Appleton's present lodgings in the earl of Shrewsbury's New Hall. In addition, it was filled with music, feminine chatter, and sunlight that poured in through windows overlooking the gardens.

A lute player sat on a bench by one of them, strumming a soft melody to provide a pleasant background in which to work. This golden-haired young man was not much more than twenty, slen-

der and fine-boned with long fingers. As was proper, he kept his
eyes on his lute strings. He was, Jennet realized, as much a part of
the decor as the two walls paneled in oak or the one covered with
an arras depicting scenes from mythology. She did not recognize
them, but the figures were colorfully embroidered, wearing rich,
stylish garb nearly as fashionable as that worn by the cluster of
women and girls sitting in a circle on cushions near the windows.
Each of them had a piece of needlework in her lap, but they sat
and wrought with varying degrees of enthusiasm.

Jennet's gaze went first to Rosamond. The elongated oval
in her hands, a sleeve panel, bore a design of peas and peascods.
Jennet wondered if she had selected it herself or had it assigned to
her. Whatever the case, the girl exhibited little care with her
needlework. Several strands of silk thread hung loose and the
whole appeared to be a bit lopsided.

Rosamond herself had grown in the nearly four years since
Jennet had last seen her. Were those breasts? It was one thing to
know Rosamond was fast approaching marriageable age and quite
another to see proof of it. If her mother, Lady Pendennis, had the
sense of a goose, Jennet thought, she'd find Rosamond an older
man to wed, someone with a character forceful enough to control
her.

At that moment Rosamond looked up. Annoyance chased
surprise across her face. "Mama! Jennet! Whatever are you doing
in Buxton?"

"Why, we have come to see if the baths will alleviate the pain
in my leg," Lady Appleton said, ignoring the girl's less than welcoming tone. Lady Bridget sent a reproving glance Rosamond's
way but she, too, pretended not to notice that the girl was, in her
own way, every bit as ill-mannered as Sir Richard had been.

Jennet was not so forgiving. She glared at Rosamond. What a
waste of time this journey had been. She'd warrant there'd never
been any real cause for concern. Murdered gentlewoman indeed!

Lady Appleton said, by way of explanation to Lady Bridget, "I endure a persistent ache when the weather is cold and damp, the result of an injury I suffered many years ago."

"Have you been able to secure lodgings nearby?" A line of worry puckered her brow at the possibility she might be expected to offer hospitality.

"Aye, at New Hall."

Lady Bridget looked both relieved and impressed. Lady Appleton did not bother to tell her that she had known the countess of Shrewsbury when she was plain Bess Cavendish. More to the point, it was early in the season. The rush of courtiers seeking the society of fellow bathers and the healing powers of the waters would come later, after the weather warmed.

"You will no doubt find Buxton Baths most soothing," Lady Bridget said. She sounded sincere but was quick to change the subject. "Allow me to present my daughter, Penelope."

One of the embroiderers, caught in the act of fumbling for a pair of shears, looked up, flushed, and promptly dropped both the shears and her thimble. Penelope Hawley did much resemble her mother, poor thing, with the same light brown hair, small eyes, negligible chin, and lack of stature. Jennet would have taken her for Rosamond's age had Lady Bridget not announced that Penelope was eighteen and about to become betrothed to their neighbor, Wymond Tallboys.

"An attractive choice of subject," Lady Appleton said in a kind voice, indicating the young woman's handiwork. "Taken from the illustration 'Two Frogs on a Well-head' in Gabriel Faerno's *Fables*, is it not?"

"And this is Dionysia Tallboys," Lady Bridget cut in before Penelope could reply. "She will by that marriage become Penelope's stepdaughter."

Dionysia, a tall, gawky lass with hair of such a pale shade of yellow that it was almost white, managed a nervous smile and a nod before returning to her needlework. She had to squint to see the simple design of rainbows, as if she needed spectacles.

The girl seated between Rosamond and Dionysia, introduced as Godlina Walkenden, had muddy brown hair, plump fingers, and significantly greater ability with a needle than either of her companions. She stitched an intricate design containing a rose, a lily, and a thistle. Jennet wondered if she'd also done the embroidery on the clothes she was wearing, but a closer look suggested that had been professionally done. The fabric beneath shouted of wealth. Whoever her father was, he was generous with his offspring. The finest lace decorated her collar and cuffs, and the jewel winking in a ring on her thumb appeared to be an emerald.

Almost as an afterthought, Lady Bridget presented Lady Appleton to her two waiting gentlewomen, Margery Cottelling and Jacquinetta Devereux. Mistress Cottelling's hair was completely covered by a plain white coif, but the lines in her face suggested that it had by now turned white or grey. Her eyes were dark, her complexion sallow. Her most distinguishing feature was a bump on the bridge of a rather long nose, hinting that it had once been broken.

The second waiting gentlewoman, Mistress Devereux, could not have been more different. For one thing she had dyed her hair a vivid, unnatural red, as many women seemed to do these days in a vain attempt to make themselves look like Queen Elizabeth, and wore only a small, round cap to cover it. The face beneath revealed her to be a woman of middle years with pouches under her eyes and a double chin. It was difficult to say what color her eyes were—they were hidden by a pair of round, thick spectacles.

"Jacquinetta has graciously agreed to stay on with us for a time," Lady Bridget said, "to continue lessons in French with the girls."

"Continue?" Lady Appleton inquired, all innocence. "Were they begun, then, by another?"

"A sad story," Lady Bridget said. "Mistress Devereux's kinswoman, Madame Poitier, suffered a fatal accident some weeks past."

"A close relative?" Lady Appleton inquired.

Mistress Devereux's reply was delivered in heavily accented English. "My…how do you say it?…my good-sister. But I am happy to stay for the *jeunes filles*."

So, the dead woman had been her sister-in-law. Jennet took another look at Mistress Devereux. If she'd arrived at Bawkenstanes Manor after the so-called murder and had been invited to stay on to continue teaching French conversation, she would know nothing of interest to them. And yet Jennet could not help but feel their presence made the woman wary. Jennet frowned, unable to pinpoint why that might be.

Lady Appleton's interest also seemed piqued by the Frenchwoman. A short time later, using the excuse that she needed to visit the privy, she neatly extricated Jacquinetta Devereux from her companions to act as her guide.

❦8❦

"THE GARDEROBE is there," Mistress Devereux said, indicating one of two doors leading from a large bedchamber.

Susanna opened the other to reveal a small, paneled room fitted out with a bench, a table, and a chair covered in russet satin. "This will suit our purpose better."

She entered, leaving the other woman to follow. A single corner window overlooked a knot garden. Ordinarily, Susanna would have been interested in studying it. Now she ignored the view in favor of watching her escort close the door behind them and turn to face her. Susanna said nothing, just held the other woman's gaze until "Jacquinetta" sighed.

"What gave me away?" she asked. "I do not much resemble my younger self."

"None of us do. It was your speech."

"I thought I had perfected my English by now."

"You used a Scots term—good-sister."

A Scot by birth, Annabel had spoken Gaelic as a child, and Inglis, the native tongue of the lowland Scots, then spent a number of years at the French court. She had learned to speak English as an adult, and in fact spoke it passing well, without any trace of the French accent she'd assumed as Mistress Devereux.

"*That* roused your suspicions?" Annabel asked.

"It was enough to make me look closely at your face. And now that we are standing close together, I recognize your perfume." It had a distinctive, musky smell. "It has been a long time, Annabel."

"Not long enough," the other woman muttered. "You wish, I suppose, to know why I am at Bawkenstanes Manor."

She would like, Susanna thought, to know why Annabel was in England. Aloud she said only, "It would relieve my mind if I could be certain Robert's child will be safe here. She has become most precious to me."

"She has naught to fear from me."

Susanna reserved judgment. She questioned Annabel's morals and wondered about her loyalties, which made her loath to trust her when she said she meant Rosamond no harm. "What is your connection to Louise Poitier?"

"I am here to discover what happened to her."

"Your good-sister?" Susanna did not believe in that relationship for a moment. While she waited for Annabel's answer, she seated herself on the chair. Her leg was bothering her again. She had begun to consider that the baths *might* be worth trying.

Annabel stood at the window, staring into the sunlit garden. "Louise was an old friend from my days in France. We may not have been kin but we were close."

Susanna toyed with the silver braid and silk fringe that trimmed the chair. Women with whom Annabel had been "close" when she'd served Mary Stewart in France were likely to have been intelligence gatherers for the queen mother of that country. Or genuine servants of the queen of Scots. None of them would have an innocent reason for entering Lady Bridget's service, not when the captive queen was known to be angling for another visit to the healing waters at Buxton.

As if she guessed Susanna's thoughts, Annabel said, "I was pensioned off some years ago, Lady Appleton. These days I prefer to stay well away from plots and conspiracies."

"So, there is no plot afoot to free the queen of Scots?"

"You are direct, as always. I am certain there are a goodly number of them. There always are. But I have no part in them." Glancing away from the view, she managed a faint smile.

Even that small movement made the folds of skin in her face and neck ripple. The slender beauty who had once lured Sir Robert Appleton into her bed had become grotesquely over-weight in the last nine years.

"Ask me what you will. I will answer if I can." Annabel made the offer with apparent sincerity.

Before Susanna could think better of the question, she blurted, "What did you do to your hair?" Next to the alteration in weight, it was the most startling change.

Annabel laughed. "Lead and sulphur mixed with quicklime."

"But your natural shade is a lovely soft red."

"And for that very reason I chose to appear as if I had to work hard to achieve this color."

Susanna fought a smile and lost.

"It is not the worst thing I could have used," Annabel added. "Dark-haired ladies at court have been known to apply oil of vitriol in the hope of turning their locks red-gold. At least one ended up bald instead."

"And how do you explain the new name? Is there a real Jacquinetta Devereux somewhere?"

"Not to my knowledge. I chose my *nom de guerre* at random. I could scarce announce in England that I am Annabel MacReynolds. Or have you forgot I am a wanted woman?"

"You fled to France to avoid being questioned."

"Sir Walter Pendennis was about to arrest me. The charge would have been espionage. I've no doubt the warrant is still outstanding. He was ever a most thorough man, and I'd as soon not face a hangman's noose."

"So you have given up spying?" One skeptical brow lifted of its own volition as Susanna watched Annabel's face. She'd long since forgiven the other woman for seducing secrets out of Robert—her late husband's loyalties had been flexible, at best—but if Annabel was still working against England, Susanna had a duty to stop her.

"I have always believed you to be more clever than either Walter Pendennis or Robert Appleton. Do me the courtesy to think I may also be. There were over-many risks and insufficient rewards in what I was doing. When I saw an opportunity to break free, I took it. I have lived quietly on the Continent for some years now."

"How, then, did you hear of Louise's death? And *what* did you hear?"

Annabel hesitated, then gave a very Gallic shrug. "You may as well know. Louise *was* here as a spy."

Susanna drew in a sharp breath.

"I know only the little she wrote to me. I was on my way here to persuade her to leave, to get out of England and out of intelligence gathering before it was too late, when she died."

"The little she wrote you?" Susanna waited. There was more to this. She was certain of it. And Annabel had not precisely answered the question Susanna had asked.

"Louise was not involved in any specific plot to rescue Queen Mary. She was sent only to get the lay of the land. Keep an ear to the ground. Smell out the—" she waved a hand in a vague gesture "—whatever one smells out. I do love the way you English turn a phrase."

"No schemes to spirit Mary of Scotland out of England? Or place her on the English throne in Elizabeth's stead?" Susanna let her skepticism show.

"None."

"Then why are you still here? Why have you stayed on if you do not mean to take Louise's place in some treasonous venture?"

"I wish to discover how she died, for my own peace of mind. She was a friend." Fists clenched at her sides, Annabel's expression was grim. "I no longer owe allegiance to any queen."

She spoke with such conviction that Susanna believed her, about her allegiance, at least. She wondered what had happened to the Scotswoman since their last meeting. She appeared to have undergone some sort of epiphany. What life-altering event, Susanna mused, could have given her a disgust of spying? As she studied the other woman, however, she found herself strangely reluctant to pry. Palpable waves of emotion, undefined but strong, eddied around Annabel, underscoring the tense line of her shoulders and the deep furrows in her brow.

"Do you intend to turn me in to the authorities?"

"I think not. I am inclined to accept your story, at least until I find evidence to the contrary." And she *would* look. "Your arrest would serve no practical purpose. Far better to make use of your presence here."

"You propose an alliance?"

"I do. A temporary truce. Let us work together to find out what happened to your friend Louise."

"What is your interest in the matter?"

"Rosamond was troubled by the manner of Madame Poitier's death."

"Rosamond sent for you?" Annabel's voice sharpened on the question.

"Not directly. She wrote to a friend of her concerns."

"And you thought this…concern warranted further investigation?"

"I thought Rosamond's sudden interest in poisonous mushrooms a good excuse to visit my husband's child."

By her very stillness, Annabel betrayed her lack of surprise.

"Is it possible?" Susanna asked. "Could Louise have been poisoned?"

"It seems...unlikely."

Susanna felt her patience begin to slip. "Was she murdered by some other means?"

"I wish I knew." Annabel closed her eyes and heaved a deep sigh. "I find the tale of an accident difficult to accept. Why would Louise have gone to Saint Anne's Well in the middle of the night?"

Susanna's interest quickened. The timing of Louise's death did add a new complexity to the matter. "To meet another spy?" she suggested.

"That, too, seems unlikely." Annabel glanced over her shoulder at a sound from the outer room. "We must not linger here much longer lest Lady Bridget send someone to search for us."

Susanna did not get up. "Tell me quickly, then."

"All three girls know something about the night before Louise's death."

"What?"

"I have been unable to discover that. None of them are inclined to confide in me. Mayhap you will have better luck with Rosamond."

"I will speak privily with her as soon as I may."

"Have a care, Susanna. It may be that asking too many questions was what led to Louise's death."

Susanna eyed her with renewed suspicion. The girls, she reckoned, were not the only ones holding something back. Why, she wondered, would Annabel think of murder at all in connection with her friend, especially if there was, as she claimed, no treasonous plot afoot? Then again, if Louise *had* been part of some scheme to free the Scots queen, that would not, of itself, increase her chances of being the victim of a homicide. If she'd been caught, she'd have come to a violent end, but at the hands of an executioner and in a very public manner.

"We have been too long away," Annabel said, cutting short further interrogation.

Favoring her game leg, Susanna rose and followed the Scotswoman through the outer chamber. She frowned slightly at a footstool placed beside the bed. If she was not mistaken, it had been closer to the far door when she'd last seen it. Evidence someone had been in the outer chamber during her conversation with Annabel? Had the thump they'd heard been that person tripping over or knocking against the stool? And if so, had the intruder been about innocent business or bent on listening to the exchange in the inner room?

"Will you tell Jennet who I am?" Annabel asked. If she noticed the misplaced footstool, she did not mention it.

Susanna dismissed, for the present, the question of an unknown eavesdropper. "Jennet took a dislike to you the last time you met."

"So I recall. I doubt she'll look upon me any more kindly now."

"I think," Susanna said, "that we will wait a while to renew your acquaintance."

"Unless she has already recognized me, as you did."

But Susanna shook her head, and for once she did not believe Jennet had been the one with her ear to the door.

🎕9🎕

April 27, 1575
New Hall, Lower Buxton

"I HAVE brought you a gift, Mama." As Rosamond offered the basket she'd carried from Bawkenstanes Manor to New Hall, she heard Jennet Jaffrey snort. Mole's mother never had liked her.

"Why, what's this?" Mama lifted the lid, smiling in pleasure when she caught sight of two kittens nestled in fleece. "What darlings! But you cannot want to give them away."

"This is Ailse." Rosamond indicated the buff-colored female. "And the other is named Dowsabella." The second kitten sported a irregularly shaped blob of black fur atop her head. Since the rest of her coat was white-and-grey stripes, it gave her the appearance of wearing a badly centered wig. "They need a home far away from Will Hawley."

"And you needed a way to apologize for your rudeness," Jennet muttered.

Rosamond bristled at the accusation but could not deny the charge. Neither did she intend to say she was sorry. She'd had all night to think about her foster mother's unexpected arrival in Buxton. A visit to the baths? It was possible, but Rosamond was more inclined to believe that Rob had betrayed her confidences.

"What threat does young Master Hawley pose to the kittens?" Mama asked. "He seemed a proper enough gentleman at supper."

Ailse and Dowsabella, freed from their prison, began to explore the chamber, tumbling across oak boards covered with plaster of Paris and painted to imitate marble. Rush matting padded some of the surface, but not all. Ailse promptly scaled the scarlet bedcurtains while Dowsabella stopped to investigate a floor cushion and bat at its tassels.

"He tortures small creatures for the fun of it." Rosamond winced, remembering what she'd seen him do to a rabbit he'd caught in a snare. "And he likes to set fire to things and watch them burn. Everyone at the manor is wary of him except Lady Bridget. She thinks he is God's gift to the world." Rosamond lowered her voice. "She and my mother want us to marry, but I'll never consent. He's a horrid boy."

"You've no need to marry anyone you do not like, Rosamond. You know that."

"Yes, Mama." To forestall a lecture on a woman's right to refuse a bad marriage—a speech Rosamond had heard many times before—she plunged ahead, heedless of consequences, to what mattered most to her. "Did Mole show you my letter?"

"No, he did not. Jennet learned of its contents by accident."

Mama's wry smile took some of the sting out of her critical tone. She detached Ailse, claw by claw, from a petit-point flower embroidered on the hangings and sat with her on the chest at the foot of the bed. The kitten had good taste. The fabric was a high-quality woolen cloth, more expensive per yard than silk velvet.

"In truth, Rosamond, I do not know whether I am more offended that you chose to confide in young Rob Jaffrey, disrupting his schooling in a most inconsiderate way, or in your failure to turn to me for advice."

Rosamond studied her toes, shod in sturdy leather boots. "I wanted to discover the truth about what happened to Madame Poitier on my own." She heard the sulky note in her own voice and was further annoyed by it. "I only asked Mole's help because there were no useful books here."

Mama's eyebrows shot up. "I shall take steps to remedy that situation. However, it does not change the facts. You must have known I could find the information you wanted more readily than Rob. Am I not the foremost expert in England in the study of poisonous herbs?"

"A mushroom is not an herb."

"I have *some* knowledge of fungi, Rosamond. If you will tell me why you think poison mushrooms caused Madame Poitier's death, mayhap I can ease your mind in the matter."

"You think I am fanciful."

"And disrespectful," Jennet muttered. She might look busy inspecting the unpacking the maids had done, but she did not miss a word.

Ignoring Jennet, Rosamond settled herself comfortably on the cushion Dowsabella had abandoned. The rush matting crackled as she curled her legs beneath her, once more attracting the kitten's interest. Rosamond waggled a finger at her and tried to order her thoughts. She did not want to confess that she'd been in the baths on the night before they'd found the body.

"Madame Poitier had a painted wooden box in which she stored chopped, dried mushrooms," Rosamond said, as Jennet opened one satin case lined with buckram after another. The coverings protected the clothing inside both during travel and when it was stored in wardrobe chests. "She would sprinkle them onto her food, something no one else did. If someone wanted her dead, it would have been very easy to add a poisonous variety to the edible mushrooms."

"But why, when she appears to have drowned, do you think she was poisoned?"

"Too much imagination for her own good," Jennet said under her breath. She'd moved on to the leather cases used to transport delicate objects like combs and jewelry.

Rosamond cuddled the kitten, burying her face in soft fur. "The mushroom box was missing from Madame Poitier's possessions after she died."

"You're certain someone did not just throw it away?"

"It was a very pretty painted box. And besides, Mistress Cottelling had only just begun to gather up Madame Poitier's belongings when Mistress Devereux arrived." Rosamond had been able to inspect them when she'd offered to show Mistress Devereux to her kinswoman's bedchamber, the one Mistress Devereux herself now shared with Mistress Cottelling.

"Was that when you wrote to Rob?"

Rosamond nodded. "But by then, Madame Poitier's death had been ruled an accident."

Shifting restlessly on her cushion, Rosamond watched Ailse leave Mama's lap for the warmth of the hearth, where she curled herself into a ball and promptly fell asleep. At once, Dowsabella pranced across the room and pounced on her littermate.

Rosamond glanced up from the playful battle in time to catch the look exchanged by her foster mother and Jennet. Heat flooded into her cheeks. They did not take her concerns seriously. They never had. In a flash of temper she blurted out a challenge. "How could it have been an accident? Saint Anne's Well was kept locked. Why would she break in to drink the water? She was not ill. And she was not clumsy. It makes no sense that she should have fallen and struck her head and drowned as they say."

"And someone poisoning her with mushrooms and then moving her body there *does* make sense?"

Mama ignored Jennet's muttering. "Did you bring this theory of yours to the attention of the authorities?"

Rosamond wanted to growl with frustration. "They'd never have listened to me. Even you will not listen!"

"Why did I come, if not to hear you out?" Mama abandoned her perch atop the chest and dropped to the floor at Rosamond's side, placing one hand on her forearm. "I know you would not be concerned over nothing. You feel a wrongness about the death. Have you talked to anyone about what you suspect?"

"I did not think they would believe me." She'd said nothing to Diony or Lina, only to Mole, her oldest, truest friend. And he hadn't betrayed her. That was some consolation.

"Well, then, Rosamond, let us look for proof. We will try to discover what *did* happen. To do that, we must assemble and examine all the information we can gather about Louise Poitier and her final hours."

"Madam!" An appalled look on her face, Jennet's arms tightened around the wooden hat case she'd just emptied.

"Hush, Jennet. You may offer your opinions later. Right now I have questions for Rosamond." She held up one finger. "First, what was the source of the dried mushrooms Madame Poitier kept?"

"She gathered them herself."

"Did she know how to tell which ones were poisonous? There are a great many foolish superstitions about mushrooms. According to one, both onion and garlic will turn black if they come in contact with one that is poisonous. Another claims that a silver coin will turn black if it is cooked with poison fungi. To put faith in such beliefs is most dangerous."

Rosamond's spirits lifted with each word. She would convince Mama she was right about this. Then they would hunt down Madame Poitier's murderer and everyone would say how clever she had been to uncover the crime.

"When I first arrived here it was autumn and the weather was warm. One day, right after a heavy rain, Madame Poitier took us with her into the woods to cut what she called *mousserons*."

"Who else went along?"

"Lina and Diony." Rosamond twisted her face into a comic grimace. "We had to practice French conversation as we walked. Then Madame Poitier went on and on, in English, about how surpassing tasty mushrooms are to eat, but no one else wanted to try one. Who would, after she told us that mushrooms are cultivated on beds of horse manure?"

Mama's smile was encouraging. "Yes, in caves and cellars where it is dark and warm and damp."

Rosamond nodded. "Madame Poitier said that sometimes there are ventilation shafts in the caves. She also told us that the most prized mushroom of antiquity was one called the royal agaric. Another named fly agaric is similar in appearance but highly poisonous. That one is also known as Caesar's mushroom because it was used to poison a Roman emperor. I do not remember which one."

"Claudius," Mama said. "The name Caesar's mushroom came first. It was much later when Albertus Magnus dubbed it fly agaric. But I see no reason to assume you are right about someone tampering with her supply of dried mushrooms. If she drowned *and* she was murdered, then the killer likely drowned her."

"But, madam," Jennet interrupted, "how did the Frenchwoman dispose of the box of mushrooms after she was dead?"

Rosamond turned to look at her, suspicious of support from that quarter.

"That *is* strange," Mama admitted, "but the idea that Madame Poitier was poisoned does not hold up under close scrutiny. Doubtless we will presently discover some simple explanation for the missing container."

"But, Mama, she—"

A raised hand cut short Rosamond's protest. "Something about her death made you uneasy. I accept that. Very well, then. We will proceed in a logical manner. I would have you tell me, Rosamond, how each person reacted to the grisly discovery. Bring me my writing box. We will make a list."

Rosamond sprang to her feet, spurred on by Jennet's mutters of disapproval. When the box was open to provide a writing surface, with paper ready and a fresh quill sharpened and dipped in ink, Rosamond searched her memory for details. She was dismayed to discover she did not recall as much as she'd thought. She could bring to mind the body well enough, and recount the way Will had rushed to open the gate ahead of his father, but she'd been too shocked herself at the sight of Madame Poitier to heed how the others had behaved. It had not been until much later that the idea of poison had occurred to her.

The list, when complete, contained the names of every member of the household at Bawkenstanes Manor and their guests. Rosamond's mood darkened as she reread the entries. For all she'd resented being sent here, these people had become a second family to her. There were a great many things she liked about life in Buxton. For one thing, except for Mole's sisters, she'd never had female friends near her own age before. She did not like to think of Diony and Lina as "suspects."

"Lady Bridget, Sir Richard, and Will Hawley," Mama read aloud. "All more upset on their own behalf than on the victim's. Lina, Diony, Mistress Cottelling, and Faith, your tiring maid, in varying degrees appeared to be horrified and distressed. Master Tallboys?"

Rosamond struggled to recall. "He paled. Then one of the maids got a look at the body and started to scream and Master Tallboys looked after her. He had to quiet Diony, too."

"What about Penelope?"

Rosamond shook her head, unable to remember. Nell had a gift for being unremarkable. "All the maids were wailing," she offered instead, "and Lady Bridget's music master went on to the chapel to ask for a door to carry Madame Poitier home on."

"That is Giles Bannister? The lute player?"

Rosamond nodded. "Then the whole village seemed to descend on us." And to her own mortification, Rosamond had been obliged to sit on a rock by the side of the road because her legs had suddenly felt too wobbly to hold her upright.

For several interminable minutes, only the scratch of the pen broke the silence. Even Jennet kept her comments to herself. Finally Rosamond could stand the tension no longer. "What next, Mama?"

"Why, we must visit Saint Anne's Well and examine the spot where the body was found."

❧10❧

"WHAT DO you know of Madame Poitier's history?" Susanna asked as Rosamond led the way from New Hall along a well-worn path that passed a row of lodgings situated halfway between the highway and the River Wye. It would do no good to order the girl to put aside her suspicions about the Frenchwoman's death. Susanna would have to prove to Rosamond that they had no basis. She only hoped she could, for there *was* something decidedly odd about it.

Rosamond bounded ahead, delighted with herself. Her words drifted back to Susanna and Jennet on a brisk spring breeze strong enough to make the fabric at the back of Susanna's headdress flap noisily. "After she fled her homeland because of the wars of religion, she was employed to wait on Lady Bridget and to speak French with us."

"How long ago did she leave France?" Picking her way carefully over the uneven surface of the path, Susanna caught up with Rosamond only because the girl noticed her lagging behind and waited.

"I do not know," Rosamond said, "but I think she had been here for some time. Mother met her when she took the waters last summer."

"What happened to Monsieur Poitier?"

"He was killed by Catholics in France. Many Huguenots were."

"Did you like Madame Poitier?"

Rosamond pondered briefly. "Most of the time."

"She was strict?"

"There were times she was cross with us. Impatient."

Jennet mumbled something inaudible.

"Is that the village church?" Susanna pointed to a small building, stone-built like New Hall. Most structures hereabout were stone. Lady Bridget had mentioned there was a quarry nearby at Corbar.

"A chapel. It is only used for special occasions. A long time ago, when the well was a shrine, those cured by the holy waters hung their discarded crutches on the chapel walls, but they were all taken away and burnt when King Henry dissolved the monasteries."

Susanna was surprised they had not destroyed the chapel as well. Zeal for reform had undone much that was beautiful and good. Her more radical co-religionists still wanted to tear down any monument that featured a cross or the image of a saint.

Adjacent to the chapel was St. Anne's Well. "This gate was ajar," Rosamond said, opening it. "It should have been padlocked but it was not."

"Where was the padlock?" Susanna asked. It was missing from the latch.

Rosamond looked blank. "I do not know. Strange. No one thought to look, nor have they troubled to replace it."

Together, they entered the enclosure. The well-head appeared to cover the outlet of a spring. Susanna could smell the medicinal waters even before her sharp hearing picked out a faint sound of running water. In truth, the "well" could as easily have been called a fountain.

No other structure shared the walled-in space, nor were there any growing things. The bare ground was hard-packed beneath their feet.

"She was there, beside the well, half in and half out of the basin. The coroner said she must have fallen while dipping water and struck her head and drowned."

The stone catchment, what Rosamond called the basin, surrounded the well-head and looked very old. It held perhaps an inch of murky water. An awkward process, Susanna thought, to drown oneself in that. "Why should she come here after dark? Or early in the morning, before the rest of the household left for services?"

"No one knows," Rosamond said. "Is that not suspicious?"

What was even more suspicious was Rosamond's look of wide-eyed innocence. Any mention of the night Madame Poitier died had an odd effect on her, making Susanna wonder if Annabel had been right. Did the three girls know more than they were telling? Susanna was on the brink of asking Rosamond to account for her movements on the eve of Palm Sunday when Jennet burst into speech.

"She went to meet a man, I'll wager. Honeyed words have brought many a silly girl to her downfall."

"She was not a girl," Rosamond objected. "She was older than Nell Hawley. At least twenty."

Startled, Susanna forgot all about the questions she'd meant to ask. "Twenty? I had the impression she was older. Closer, say, to Mistress Devereux's age." Had Annabel deliberately deceived her, or had she simply jumped to the wrong conclusion because they'd known each other in France?

"Oh, no," Rosamond insisted. "I am certain she was not so very ancient as that! Why Mistress Devereux must be at least as old as you are."

When she realized what she'd said, Rosamond clapped both hands over her mouth, but the eyes above the fingers gleamed with suppressed laughter. Susanna let the comment pass.

"How long after Madame Poitier's death did Mistress Devereux appear?"

"Only a few days." Rosamond's farehead wrinkled as she tried to recall. "I remember. It was Palm Sunday when she died. Mistress Devereux arrived on Maundy Thursday."

"And what do you think of Mistress Devereux?"

"I cannot like her," Rosamond said. "She calls us *mes enfants* and me *jeune fille*. Not just *girl*," she clarified, lest Susanna miss the significance, "but *young* girl. Madame Poitier called me that once, but in the usual way of things she said *demoiselle*." The distinction, to one of Rosamond's years, was most important.

They left the well to stroll through Lower Buxton, what little there was of it, before returning to Susanna's lodgings. Another question or two established that Rosamond knew nothing else about either Louise Poitier or Annabel. With the self-centeredness of youth, she'd taken little interest in the Frenchwoman until after her death.

"Lina might know more," she offered. "She thought the sun rose with Madame Poitier. She was forever reciting French poetry in the hope of impressing her."

After the simple, one-room dwelling houses in the village, the tall towers of the earl of Shrewsbury's New Hall seemed even more impressive. Four levels of windows looked down on them as Susanna, Rosamond, and Jennet returned from their walk. From the top of the lodgings on this side, Susanna realized, one would have a clear view of activities at St. Anne's Well. But there had been no guests the night Louise died. Even the warden of the baths, Thomas Greves, and his servant, Henry Flower, had been absent. New Hall and the baths had been locked up tight.

Or had they? The padlock on the gate to the well enclosure had not stopped Louise Poitier from getting inside. Had someone entered New Hall, too? There were few other places a stranger could have concealed himself without attracting the attention of the villagers. Then again, Louise had most likely been murdered by someone she knew, someone who lived in the village or at the manor.

And she *had* been murdered, Susanna acknowledged at last. Not by poisoned mushrooms. No, that was too far-fetched. But it did appear that someone had struck the woman from behind and left her, unconscious, to drown in the catchment beside the well. It was not the conclusion Susanna had hoped to reach, but it was one she could no longer discount.

Pondering, Susanna completed the journey to New Hall in silence. Rosamond, too, seemed lost in thought.

Jennet was just impatient. "What is being built across the river?" she asked, stopping to shade her eyes.

Susanna looked, too. Construction appeared to be almost complete on a rambling building with three floors.

"That is the George," Rosamond told them. "Sir Richard is up in arms about its construction, most like because he wishes he owned the property. Since the earl of Shrewsbury fills New Hall with naught but courtiers and friends, there is no lodging hereabout for bathers of the common sort. The George was an alehouse. Now it is being turned into an inn."

They had stopped near the stableyard. Within, Susanna caught sight of Henry Flower, Thomas Greves's man. "Good day to you, Goodman Flower," she called.

Few men could look, or smell, less like their names. He tugged on a greasy grey forelock to acknowledge her before he resumed shoveling muck into a small cart.

"Someone must question him." Susanna glanced at Jennet. "And the villagers."

"I can scarce understand them when they speak," Jennet complained.

"They saw nothing," Rosamond said. At Susanna's sharp look, she grinned. "The servants at the manor gossip with the villagers. Most of them are kin to one another."

"And no one saw anything?" A fleeting expression of guilt crossed Rosamond's face, arresting Susanna's attention. "The smallest detail might be important."

Rosamond stared up at the nearest tower. "Someone said they saw a light in one of the windows, but there was a full moon that night. No doubt it was naught but light shining on glass."

She seemed so anxious to convince them that no one had been in New Hall that night that Susanna's suspicions were instantly renewed.

"Where are the baths?" Jennet asked. "And how many are there?"

"Two," Susanna replied, "located right next to New Hall. Where is the entrance, Rosamond?"

Rosamond jumped like a scalded pup and looked guilty. "Lady Bridget says the baths are no fit place for young, unmarried gentlewomen."

"So you've not visited them?"

Rosamond's eyes shifted to a point beyond Susanna's ear and stayed there. "No."

"All the more reason to take the opportunity now," Susanna declared. She did not believe for one moment that Rosamond was telling the truth. "Come along."

It took only a few minutes to find the way into an empty atrium with a pool at its center. Bright sunlight poured into the space but did nothing to quell the icy sensation in Susanna's stomach. In her eagerness to make Rosamond confess whatever secret she was keeping, Susanna had failed to anticipate the effect of so much water on her own equilibrium.

When she'd thought of immersing herself in a bath she'd imagined one closer in size to the leather tub she carried with her on long journeys. She enjoyed soaking in that, washing off the dirt of the road. This was alarmingly larger. Crossing rivers less wide than this body of water in a sturdy boat made her queasy, bringing back all the harrowing details of the shipwreck that had killed her father and very nearly cost Susanna her life. The First Chief Bath terrified her.

Backing away with extreme care, Susanna made a pretense of studying the rest of the chamber. Hearth. Changing room. And a section of wall that had only recently been repaired. She had heard there had been an earthquake in these parts. She assumed that had caused the damage.

"There are seats built in," Jennet observed. "Do people really lounge there?"

"They spend hours in water up to their chins," Rosamond said.

The very thought made Susanna shiver but she forced herself to move back toward the bath. The only way to overcome her fear was to face it.

"I do not see anything special about this water." Jennet peered down at the clear surface, her nose wrinkling in distaste at the smell.

"You might like it if you tried it." Rosamond's comment sounded suspiciously like a taunt. "It is warm and there are bubbles and—" She broke off suddenly, mumbling, "Or so I have been told."

Susanna had to clear her throat before she could speak. The gentle lapping of the water had caught and held her attention, making her wonder if the legendary sirens lived at the source of the spring. Amused by her own fancy, her panic abated, but not enough to persuade her to stay longer. "Let us go back to my lodgings," she suggested, "and expand our list. You must tell me, Rosamond, all you know about each member of Lady Bridget's household and where each one might have been the night before Madame Poitier's body was found."

Rosamond scurried on ahead, as anxious as Susanna was to escape the First Chief Bath. Once outside, however, she made an excuse to return to Bawkenstanes Manor. She was gone, at a run, before Susanna could object.

❈11❈

Bawkenstanes Manor

LINA WALKENDEN was hiding something. First, there was her embroidery—all symbols associated with Mary Stewart. Then, there was the way tears sprang into her eyes every time Louise's name was mentioned.

Annabel had not been entirely honest with Susanna Appleton. Oh, she'd told Susanna partial truths, but she had not admitted to being in Buxton just before Louise was murdered, and she'd not shared her real reason for coming to Derbyshire.

That brought her back to Lina. Had Louise recruited the girl to help rescue Queen Mary from captivity in England?

Lina seemed an unlikely conspirator. Annabel's casual questions about Master Walkenden of London had elicited nothing suspicious. According to Lady Bridget, he was a wealthy draper, a widower with other children, though Godlina was his youngest. He seemed to have no known affiliation with either France or Scotland. Indeed, from what Lina herself had said, her father never ventured farther from London than Hampton Court.

"You are sad, *ma petite*," Annabel murmured solicitously. They sat side by side on the widow seat in the solar, hands busy with needlework.

"I am not so very small," Lina muttered.

Annabel hid a smile. "You are pleasingly plump." No doubt she would lose weight as she grew older. Many girls did. And then, more's the pity, increased in size once more when they'd passed their prime. Not necessarily a bad thing, she decided. She had herself found it restful to have passed beyond the point where her appearance stirred lust in every man she met.

"Madame Poitier used to say I would be big as a house if I kept eating so many sweets." Lina sighed. "Now that she's gone, there does not seem much reason to avoid them." She produced a silver comfit box from a silk bag suspended from her waist and offered Annabel a sugared almond.

Annabel accepted. She contemplated Lina's words while they munched and listened to Giles Bannister play the virginals. She recognized the piece as "My Lady Carey's Dump," a morose tune in a minor key.

Was there a connection between the rose, thistle, and lily in Lina's design, and the queen of Scots? The rose stood for England, the thistle for Scotland, and the lily for France, all countries of which Mary Stewart could claim to be queen, though in the latter case only by marriage to her first husband, now long deceased. Why choose those emblems to embroider? There could, Annabel supposed, be an innocent reason, but she had been trained to mistrust coincidences. Lina's age was no argument against involvement in treason. Annabel had been only two years older than Lina was now when she'd been recruited as an intelligence gatherer by Catherine de' Medici.

If Louise had confided her plans to someone here, Annabel mused, that person could have had second thoughts. Had Louise been silenced to keep her from naming her confederate as a traitor?

A feminine laugh drew Annabel's gaze to the musician at the keyboard. Nell Hawley stood beside the instrument, leaning over his shoulder, her face much closer to his than necessary as she observed how well he played the broken-chord bass ground with his left hand and used his right for embellishments. Annabel could not help but notice the way Nell's plain, pale face flushed with pleasure when Giles Bannister whispered in her ear.

There was trouble brewing! Annabel told herself she should not be surprised. There were few things more common in a household like this one than a gentleman's daughter thinking herself in love with one of her tutors.

Annabel's hands stilled on her embroidery as her glance slid sideways. Could it be? The conclusion made sense, and if it was correct, then at least one of Annabel's questions had an answer. She had no difficulty accepting that Godlina Walkenden might have admired Louise to the point of adoration. Such intense affection was not unheard of between girls and their governesses, though it was rarely encouraged and almost never returned in kind.

She wondered if Louise had led Lina on. She'd had few scruples when it came to exploiting the emotions she'd inspired in others. As Annabel had, she'd been trained to seduce and use lovers. As Annabel had, she'd enjoyed it, and she had not restricted herself to attracting only susceptible *men* with her wiles.

Frowning, Annabel tried to think how to question Lina without alarming her. The subject was a delicate one, and fraught with pitfalls. She did not want to say too much, for it might well be that Louise had not even been aware of Lina's feelings, feelings that had doubtless confused and embarrassed the girl when Louise was alive. And yet, if Lina had formed a strong attachment to Louise, she'd have been sure to notice how others acted toward her.

"Everyone seems to have been fond of my good-sister," Annabel said. "Fond" was the word Louise herself had used when speaking of Wymond Tallboys, she recalled. And she'd implied that young Will Hawley also doted upon her.

"Oh, yes." A sad smile creased Lina's plain, round face. "She was the only one who could persuade Sir Richard to come and sing part songs with us. He has such a deep voice. Resonant, she said it was. She flattered him into spending an entire evening in song once. Lady Bridget said it was a miracle."

Sir Richard, too? Annabel realized she should have anticipated that Louise would go after the head of the household. Nor had she ever been one to neglect a well-built man.

Father and son and neighbor, all "fond" of her—had jealousy driven one of them to murder? It was a possibility, one Annabel meant to pursue, but before she could formulate another question, Lady Bridget bustled into the room, full of plans for the upcoming May Day revels in which Nell was to play a principal part.

A short time later, Rosamond returned from her visit with Susanna. Lina and Diony converged on the girl, as if it had been days rather than hours since they'd last seen her. Shut out, Annabel kept a watchful eye on the trio. For the most part they giggled together and helped each other with the pennants Lady Bridget wanted hemmed, but there was a moment that piqued Annabel's interest. Rosamond cast an assessing gaze around the room, then drew Lina and Diony close to whisper to them in an earnest manner. Diony gave a little squeak. Lina looked worried. Both appeared to Annabel to be making a promise to Rosamond.

❧12❧

April 28, 1575
The gardens at Bawkenstanes Manor

AS A HUMBLE waiting woman, Jennet was relegated to the background while Lady Bridget escorted Lady Appleton through knots and bowers, along bubbling rills, and across a little meadow surrounded by box cut into the shapes of animals. Pausing at the top of the flight of stone steps that led from the south side of the manor house down an easy slope, Jennet sent Margery Cottelling a questioning glance. "No fountains?"

"Lady Bridget said there were wells and springs enough in Buxton. She did not want to imitate what was already here." Margery, too, had been left to trail behind her mistress, a situation that suited Jennet well. What better opportunity could she ask for to talk privily with the woman?

"She seems very proud of her gardens but they do not impress me. Too much green."

"It is early in the year yet. Only cowslips, primroses, gilly-flowers, and violets." Margery pointed to each species as she named them. "Wait until late June. Almost everything is in flower then and it is a magnificent sight."

"I will take your word for it," Jennet said. "For myself, I cannot tell a rose from a lily." That was only a slight exaggeration. She had learned over the years to recognize some few flowering plants, most of them poisonous, but she had little interest in growing things.

As their mistresses walked on, enthusiastic gestures indicating they were engrossed in a discussion of the garden, Jennet caught sight of a marble bench shaded by a rose trellis. She was already short of breath and saw no point in rushing to keep up with Lady Appleton. Jennet's mistress had wanted an opportunity to question Lady Bridget. This would give it to her. And a rest in this pleasant bower would afford Jennet the chance to ferret out Margery Cottelling's secrets.

"Let us sit," she suggested, and did not wait for agreement. Why were benches always so hard and cold, she wondered as she tried to get comfortable. This one was worse than the stone seat at the King's School.

Margery hesitated, then sank down beside her. "I must admit my feet hurt," she said. "A new pair of shoes. I do not think the shoemaker took much care with them." She lifted her skirt to reveal thick ankles and a left foot afflicted with a noticeable bunion.

Sympathy, offered and accepted, led to casual discussion of other things. When they'd finished dissecting the lack of quality craftsmen in a village as small as Buxton, they passed on to the trials of a life in service. With a silent apology to Lady Appleton, Jennet launched into a highly fanciful account of that gentlewoman's shortcomings as a mistress.

"And she wears her clothes so long that by the time she's done with them they are unfit to be passed along to me!" With that, Jennet's litany of complaints came to an end. She could not think of a single thing to add.

Margery absently rubbed her bunion, having freed her foot from the offending shoe, and contemplated the now distant figure of Lady Bridget. "You are fortunate, Jennet, if that is the worst you must endure in Lady Appleton's household."

"Why? Does your mistress beat you? Or does she prefer to flay servants with a sharp tongue?"

Margery made a choking sound, then pounded on her chest with one fist. "Oh, you must not say such things!"

"Why not? Are they untrue?"

"Lady Bridget is no worse than most. She expects to have her whims catered to. *She* is not the difficulty." Margery lowered her voice. "It is Will, her son."

"What has he done?"

"Where should I begin?" Margery murmured. "Young Will takes every opportunity to hurt or frighten anyone or anything too weak to fight back. Once he crept into the bedchamber while

Louise Poitier and I slept and stood there staring at us until I awoke. When I told him to begone and swore I would tell his mother if he did not leave at once, he laughed at me and said I was the one who'd be gone if I spoke out of turn."

"What did he mean by that?" Jennet glanced at Lady Bridget, but so far she showed no sign of wandering back in their direction. It seemed safe enough to continue probing.

"I was not certain at the time, but the next morning, on my way to fetch his mother's breakfast from the kitchens, I tripped over a string stretched across the top of the staircase and very nearly tumbled all the way down."

"You think he—?"

"I am certain of it. It was a warning, and I am no fool. I said nothing to his mother, or his father."

Jennet remembered what Rosamond had said about the boy, but she'd never considered Rosamond's opinions reliable. Rosamond also claimed to be too busy with preparations for May Day to spend time with Lady Appleton today. Jennet suspected she just wanted to avoid questions she did not care to answer. Lady Appleton was too indulgent with the girl. *If I had the minding of her*, Jennet thought, *I'd make sure she told all she knows.*

"I did tell Louise," Margery said, "but she insisted I must be mistaken and would not take me seriously."

"Did he not torment her as well?"

Margery gave a little laugh. "Only if you consider amorous pursuit a torment. She may have been older than he is, but Will Hawley wanted to tup her. For all I know, he succeeded. She was not particular about who she went with."

"Never say she was wanton?"

"Oh, yes. Saw her myself, I did, making sheep's eyes at both father and son."

"That does not mean it came to anything."

"You do not know Sir Richard! Not one to refuse what he's offered. Not that one."

Picturing Sir Richard, with his heavy-lidded eyes and his muscular body, Jennet could see Margery's point. He had an air of dissipation about him. "And the son follows in his father's footsteps?"

Margery answered with a vigorous nod. "And then there was Master Tallboys, the one who's supposed to marry young Mistress Nell. He was wont to trail after Louise Poitier like a lovesick lad. And once—" Margery broke off to look all around. Even when she'd made sure no one was close enough to overhear, she lowered her voice. "Once, I saw her in a passionate embrace with another woman!"

Jennet blinked at her in confusion. "I do not understand you. A kiss, do you mean? Women kiss each other in greeting all the time."

"Not just a kiss." Margery leaned closer. "They were clasped together like lovers, one of Louise's hands on her companion's bosom and the other up under her skirts."

"You must be mistaken. Women do not do such things with other women."

"I've tried to convince myself of that, for it was very dark in the alcove where they were, but I know I saw two figures in women's garb, and one of them was Louise Poitier. Her face was turned in my direction."

Never having heard of such a thing, Jennet was certain Margery had misinterpreted whatever it was she'd seen. When the other woman busied herself putting on her shoe and would not meet Jennet's eyes, Jennet decided she was embarrassed at having shared her strange fancy. Then another thought struck Jennet. Had Margery Cottelling been jealous of the Frenchwoman's youth and beauty? Did that account for the relish with which she'd spoken ill of the dead? And if that were the case, then how much of what she'd related to Jennet could be accepted as fact?

Frenchwomen were not the most trustworthy creatures. Jennet had met one, years ago. Like Louise, Diane St. Cyr had come to a sudden and violent end. In Jennet's opinion, Diane had deserved what happened to her. She'd had Sir Robert Appleton in her bed the night before she died, even though she knew he was married. Jennet had no difficulty believing that Louise might have bedded her mistress's husband. The real question was whether or not he would have killed her to keep that information from his wife. A possibility, Jennet decided.

And what of Wymond Tallboys? Had he been her lover, too? He was a widower and not yet betrothed to Nell Hawley. As such he was free to consort with any female he chose. Even if he had played the beast with two backs with Louise Poitier, he'd have had no reason to do away with her.

The claim about an amorous encounter between Louise and another woman, Jennet discounted as too preposterous to be believed. Women did not lie with other women. No doubt Margery had seen Madame Poitier with a man wearing a long cloak.

That left Will Hawley. What kind of woman would encourage lust in a boy only a bit older than Rob? Jennet did not like to think of Rob bedding anyone before he was ready to wed, and she was suddenly very glad he was safe in grammar school, where there were no women or girls to tempt him.

But Will was another matter. He had a vicious streak, if Rosamond was to be believed. And Jennet had no reason to doubt Margery's story that she'd awakened to find him in her bedchamber. That might be discounted as mere boyish curiosity about women, but Jennet did not think so.

Could Will Hawley have killed Louise?

"Lady Appleton and Lady Bridget are returning," Margery said, putting an end to Jennet's speculation.

"Could Will Hawley have killed Louise?" Jennet asked Lady Appleton an hour later. On their way back to New Hall she'd given her mistress a summary of Margery's remarks, omitting only that foolish talk about Louise embracing another woman.

"What motive do you think he'd have?" Lady Appleton asked.

"Jealousy? If he knew she'd been with his father, and mayhap with Master Tallboys, as well, and she refused him…"

"But did she refuse him? Did she refuse anyone? And conversely, was she the mistress of any of them? Did your new friend Margery actually catch Louise in bed with someone?"

"I think she envied Louise and said most of those things because she was jealous of the Frenchwoman's ability to attract male attention."

"It is possible. As to Will Hawley, according to Rosamond, he was the one who found the body. He rushed forward so that he would be the first to enter the enclosure around the well. What he saw there caused him to cast up his accounts. Had he expected a dead body, he'd have preserved his dignity."

"What did Lady Bridget say about Madame Poitier's death?"

"Nothing useful. She preferred to talk about gardens and for the most part I obliged her. The few questions I managed to insert into our conversation revealed only that she pays little attention to her household. Lady Bridget thinks first of herself. All others are important only in relation to her. Have you noticed how she refers to people? She calls Sir Richard 'husband' and Nell 'daughter' and the three young gentlewomen she is training naught but 'girl,' to the point where I wondered if she even knew their names."

"What does she call Will, 'son and heir'?"

Lady Appleton chuckled. "She refers to him as 'my son' in speaking of him, and I noticed earlier, calls him 'my lad' in direct address. And Margery, when she refers to her at all, is 'my woman.'"

"Could Margery have killed Madame Poitier?" Jennet asked, struck by this new thought. It occurred to her with mild surprise that they now talked as if it were a given that murder had been done, and yet there was no proof that anything untoward had happened to the Frenchwoman.

"Anything is possible," Lady Appleton replied.

❧13❧

April 29, 1575
Corbar Hill, Derbyshire

JENNET clutched her chest and gasped out another protest. "The way is too steep, madam. Think of your poor leg."

"Walking is excellent exercise, Jennet." Susanna felt a bit breathless herself but she was grimly determined to reach the top of the hill. "And I am assured the entire journey is no more than two miles."

"They say there is an easy climb on the other side of the river, to a place called Poole's Cavern and the hill above it. We'd not have been obliged to hire a boat to cross to the north side of the Wye before we could even begin to hike."

"Too late now," Susanna said with forced cheerfulness. She'd chosen to face her irrational fear of bodies of water as a test of her own resolve. Before she left this place, she *would* submerge herself in one of the baths.

They followed a well-worn track around the edge of a wood, sighting a good many small birds—tree creepers, nuthatches, and one Susanna did not recognize, with a black face and throat and bright red-and-chestnut breast—but no other climbers.

At last they came out on the bare and windy gritstone summit. No, not totally bare. There were fine lichens and moss, but nothing bigger, not even the hardy plants like Herb Robert that sometimes grew on stone walls. Hanging on to her headdress with one hand and holding down her skirt with the other, Susanna gazed north and west over a grim moorland's rolling hills, then turned to look back the way they had come.

The hilltops seemed to be of a lighter color to the south, and the peaks and valleys more angular. The river ran through a narrow dale but Susanna had no difficulty picking out New Hall in Lower Buxton. High up the plunging hillside, on the outskirts of Upper Buxton, was Bawkenstanes Manor.

"You see how the buildings are arrayed," she said, pointing. "Saint Anne's Well, New Hall and the baths, and the bowling green follow the curve of the river. It twists and winds, providing a number of secluded moorings like the one where the boat that served as our ferry is tied. With the village at a distance, even though it is on higher ground, it would be passing simple for someone to meet Madame Poitier in New Hall and slip away again by boat without anyone being the wiser."

Henry Flower, servant of the warden of the baths, hired for the day to take them across the narrow river and guide them to this windswept pinnacle, made a startled sound at the mention of Madame Poitier.

"You provided the key, did you not, Goodman Flower?" Susanna said, turning on him. "You accepted a generous payment to leave it hidden near the door so that New Hall could be used in the absence of both yourself and Master Greves."

Flower sputtered an unconvincing denial.

"Spare us! I do not mean to betray you to your master. Not so long as you tell us everything you know, and without hesitation."

"I know nowt!"

"You know who asked you to leave behind a key."

Flower—though he was more weed than blossom—wilted. "That were the dead gentlewoman, madam."

Intent on Flower's confession, Jennet left off worrying a thin spot in the sole of her shoe and seemed to forget her aching feet and shortness of breath, as well. Susanna spared a moment for relief before she concentrated on her interrogation of her hapless suspect. She'd worried that Jennet might not be up to the exertion of the climb.

Flower did not look clever enough to be a conspirator, which meant he'd likely been a dupe. Had Louise Poitier seduced him into helping her? From all she'd heard of her, Susanna would not put it past her. The woman seemed to have lured a good many others into her bed.

"Paid me a crown, she did," Flower muttered.

"To hide the key where someone could find it and use it to enter New Hall?"

"Aye. There weren't no harm done. The only sign I found that anyone had been there were a goblet tossed in a corner. Dregs of wine in it, there were, but nary a dent in the pewter."

"Still, you must have wondered, when you heard of the discovery of Madame Poitier's body, if she'd come to harm because of what you'd done."

"It were an accident," Flower whined. "Sir Richard said so. The gentlewoman drowned trying to drink the water. It were nowt to do with me."

Susanna said nothing, but the patent disbelief in her expression had Flower shifting nervously from foot to foot. After a moment, he could stand the silence no longer. A man who thought he was in peril of losing his employment, and mayhap his freedom, tended to become most cooperative.

"To say summat would nae bring her back. Were not as if she were killed *in* the baths."

"And the gate to the well? What happened to the padlock that should have kept Madame Poitier out?"

"Gone, madam. It were an old lock. Likely someone struck it till it broke."

"Well, Goodman Flower, we progress." Susanna gestured toward the view. "Look down there and tell me what you see?"

"Buxton, madam."

"Aye, Buxton. And the Wye. If I wished to leave Buxton and travel swiftly to South Wingfield, would I ride or go by water?"

"Wye flows eastward through Bakewell to the Derwent at Rowsley. Derwent flows south to within a few miles of South Wingfield. By the road the way is harder, though the distance be less. 'Twould be a full day's travel to get there by river or by road."

"It would make no sense to travel any way *but* by the rivers," Jennet said, "given that this countryside is so bleak and barren and rough. Do you not agree, Goodman Flower?"

Eager to oblige, he nodded. "Lest you follow the drover's roads," he added after a moment. "Or the saltways."

"Saltways?" Susanna did not rule them out. The transportation of salt was an enterprise that cut deep tracks into the earth, tracks that might be easier to follow at night than regular roads.

"Saltway runs from Northwick to Buxton and then on to Tideswell. Branches go to Chesterfield and Sheffield."

"Sheffield," Susanna murmured. Sheffield was the current prison of the Queen of Scots.

On the return journey, when Flower drew enough ahead of them that Susanna could converse softly with Jennet without fear of being overheard, she caught her friend's arm. "I should have mentioned something to you ere now, Jennet."

"Mentioned what, madam?"

"That there may be a new plot afoot to rescue the captive queen of Scots."

"Oh, no, madam," Jennet moaned. "Not another one!"

❦14❦

May 1, 1575
Bawkenstanes Manor

MIDNIGHT marked the beginning of May Day revels. The young people of the parish left their homes and went into the woods, accompanied by the rough music of hunting horns and cooking pans used as drums. Rosamond watched, brooding, as Nell Hawley, who was to reign as May Queen on the morrow, set out in company with her maid and two other girls from the village. Carrying torches, eager young men escorted them, including Giles Bannister, the musician.

It was most unfair, Rosamond thought, that she should be deemed too young to help gather branches and make garlands. "We should go in spite of Lady Bridget," she whispered to Lina and Diony.

"It would be fun," Lina said with a sigh.

Diony looked appalled. "We were caught last time we went out on our own after dark and we could be caught again. Do you want to be sent packing?"

"No one would do more than scold us." Rosamond feigned confidence. In truth, she had no idea what would happen to them if they were caught, but she did not intend to *be* caught. "And no one knows we went out the other time...unless one of you told."

Five weeks had passed since their expedition to the First Chief Bath, and although Rosamond had avoided being alone with her foster mother for the last three days in order to escape questions about that night, she was more than ready for another adventure.

Two heads shook in vigorous denial. Then Lina's eyes filled with tears. "Oh, Rosamond, if only Madame Poitier had lived to punish us for being in the baths that night. I'd have taken a beating gladly to have spared her life."

"What nonsense!" Diony said. "It was not our fault she decided to stop at Saint Anne's Well before following us back here, or that she fell, or that she drowned."

"If we had waited for her," Rosamond murmured, more to herself than to the others, "mayhap she would not have been—" She broke off. "Mayhap she would have been safe," she said instead.

She could not mention murder without explaining and she no longer knew where to begin. Not with mushrooms! She'd learned her lesson there. But for all that she'd been wrong about the means, Rosamond was still certain Madame Poitier's death had been no accident.

"You were the last to leave," Lina said. It sounded like an accusation.

All three of them jumped at the sound of a voice close behind the window embrasure where they'd gathered to watch the departing revelers. "Mistress Rosamond," said Sir Richard Hawley, handing Lina the handkerchief he kept in his sleeve, "what did you say to make your friend cry?"

Will stood in his father's shadow, a self-satisfied expression on his face. Ignoring him, Rosamond dropped into a curtsey and forced a smile. "I meant only to tease Lina a bit," she said in a pert voice.

She wished she could tell how much they'd overheard. Enough to guess that the three girls had crept out of the house on the night of the full moon and visited the baths? Will's smirk made her think so, but Sir Richard said nothing about it, only told them to be off to their beds.

"You have a busy day ahead," he reminded them. "Games and pageants. You want to be well rested."

Lina and Diony scurried off at once. Rosamond stayed where she was and was not surprised when Will also lingered. She regarded him warily, but he did not speak until he was certain his father was out of earshot. Then a wide grin split his face.

"You want to go with them," he said, "and so do I. What are we waiting for?"

As a challenge, it was most effective. Rosamond told herself she had nothing to fear from Will Hawley. Her stepfather had taught her one or two nasty tricks to use if anyone ever tried to take liberties with her. She'd enjoy using them on Will Hawley, but for once he seemed eager to play the gentleman. He even offered her his arm.

Moments later, they were out of the house and creeping through the topiary garden toward the edge of the wood, their way lit by a lantern Will had shown the foresight to leave by the gate. "They'll bring back birch branches," he said, "and hawthorn and sweet eglantine to decorate windows and doors and make into bowers, and they'll cut down a straight young tree for a maypole."

Excitement bubbled through Rosamond at the prospect of being part of the festivities from the beginning. She was not too young, she told herself. Certes, everyone kept telling her she was almost old enough to wed. She'd use primroses to decorate the bower and gather sweet-scented herbs to scatter on the ground—lavender, mayhap, or mint, or alecost.

She thought they'd quickly catch up with the others, but Will was in no hurry. The voices and music seemed to get farther and farther away as they threaded a path through the underbrush. "Are you sure you know the way?" she demanded.

Will kept hold of her arm and tugged.

Rosamond dug in her heels. "Stop this instant, Will Hawley. Where are we going?"

"A secret place," he whispered. She could not see his face in the shadowy forest but something about his tone of voice made her uneasy.

"What secret place? And why should I go with you?"

"Scared, Ros?"

"Of you?" She gave a snort. "Never. I just want to know where we'll end up."

If her bravado annoyed him, Will did not show it. "What if it is a trysting place? I might want to steal a kiss."

"Try it and I'll kick you in your codpiece," Rosamond told him. She made fists of her hands and lifted one foot, prepared to make good on the threat.

He released her forearm with flattering speed. "Come with me or stay here, then. I do not care." Turning his back on her, he set off up Colt Moss Hill.

In a moment, Rosamond realized, he'd be swallowed up by the trees and she might not be able to find her own way back until dawn. She'd wanted to spend the wee hours of May Day in the woods, but not all by herself! She hurried to catch up with him.

A short time later, they arrived at the entrance to a cave. A chill ran through her as she realized where they must be: Poole's Cavern. She had heard of the place, but had never before visited it. "We cannot go in there," she objected.

"Afraid?"

At the insult, her temper flared. "Are you sure you know your way? If the light goes out we could be lost far underground and starve to death."

"Poole never got lost."

Rosamond had been told the stories. "Poole was a legend, like Robin Hood."

"Not like Robin Hood at all," Will objected, "except that he and Poole were both famous outlaws. Poole was not so foolish as to give away what he stole. In the reign of King Henry the Fifth he hid in these underground caves to escape capture. He was given aid by a wealthy widow of the town."

"Like Maid Marian?" Rosamond's voice dripped sarcasm. In the story she'd heard, Poole was naught but a flasher, someone who'd clipped coins. The clippings were used to make counterfeit money, or sometimes sold for the silver.

She'd also heard at least two other versions of Poole's adventures. In one he was a giant seven feet tall and big around as a tree trunk. In another the wealthy widow had not come willingly. He'd kidnapped her in Cheshire and forced her to live in the caves with him.

Will offered temptation in a whisper: "There's treasure, Ros. Poole's treasure. And I found it."

He pressed a cold, hard disk into her hand, a coin of some sort. She could not make out the markings in the dim light, but when she bit down on it she had to admit it might be real.

"Come in with me and I'll show you where I found it."

Rosamond gave Will Hawley a considering look and decided

she did not want to go wandering underground with him, not unless someone else knew where she'd gone. "You can show me the cavern tomorrow," she said, "when we both have lanterns and Lina and Diony can come, too."

"You *are* afraid. No need to be. I've been inside Poole's Cavern many times," he boasted. "You do not want Lina and Diony. They'll just whimper and carry on because it is dark in there. They lack your courage, Ros." He extended one hand in invitation.

Rosamond hesitated, tempted. Into that little silence came the clatter of a rock, dislodged by a careless step *inside* the mouth of the tunnel. As one, she and Will ducked out of sight behind the nearest tree. Will had just shuttered his lantern when two figures emerged from the entrance. They were wrapped together under one cloak and murmuring softly to each other.

Will stared after them with brooding eyes until they descended the path far enough to be out of sight. "That was Nell," he muttered. "Wanton wench. I ought to tell Father."

Too surprised to comment, Rosamond said nothing. The woman had indeed been Nell Hawley. More shocking still, the man had been Giles Bannister, Lady Bridget's music master.

"Come on." Will started after them.

"Wait." She caught his arm. "You cannot betray your own sister."

"Why not?" The stubborn set of his jaw warned her she would lose this argument if she was not surpassing clever.

"Because I warrant she'll pay you to keep silent."

A break in his stride was the only indication he'd heard her suggestion.

"If you tell your father they met in Poole's Cavern, he'll want to know what *you* were doing there."

He glanced at her over his shoulder but continued to plunge downhill. "If you want to explore it in daylight, slip away during the footrace. I'll meet you afterward at the entrance."

❦15❦

May Day, 1575
Buxton

ON THE WAY to church, guests at New Hall joined residents of Bawkenstanes Manor and villagers of Buxton on the green to admire the brightly painted maypole erected at dawn by the young people of the community. Pennants and handkerchiefs flew from the top. Garlands sprouted everywhere and were heaped in profusion around Nell Hawley. As May Queen she was carried to church, as she would be later to her bower, on a flower-decked chair.

Susanna regarded the young woman with curiosity. She looked different somehow. Her eyes bright, her cheeks flushed with pleasure, she came close to being pretty.

After church services—it was also the feast of Saints Philip and James the Apostles—dancing in the village chapel marked the beginning of a long afternoon of festivities. The congregation soon adjourned out of doors, where the sun shone brightly and the air, for a change, was so mild as to be almost balmy.

Susanna lingered after the rest had gone to examine the parish register. It had been set out in anticipation of new entries, and on the page headed DEATHS—1575 there were but a few notations. Buxton was a very small community.

Matilda, commonly called Halting Maud, had been buried in early April. No cause of death was given, nor even the exact date of her demise.

The entry above that was the one Susanna sought: "Louise Potter widow drowned in ye sacred well of St. Anne xxvij March. Crowner quest in church porch March 29th and same day buried in ye churchyard."

Not very illuminating. Susanna considered correcting the spelling of Louise's surname, then decided it did not much matter. She doubted that Poitier had been the woman's real name, any more than Jacquinetta Devereux was Annabel's.

As if Susanna had conjured her up by thinking about her, the Scotswoman appeared at her elbow. "Would you care to play at bowls?" she asked.

The bowling alley was a logical place to meet if they were to speak together without risk of being overheard. Other activities had sprung up all over the village. The archery contest and the dancing on the green—more spirited than that inside the chapel had been—would draw crowds of spectators as well as a goodly number of participants. There would be no privacy in the vicinity of either and to remain longer indoors might also attract unwelcome attention.

Susanna sent a rueful look in Annabel's direction. "You will have to teach me the rules."

"They are simple," the other woman assured her, "and the sport provides very healthful exercise. I am told that the doctor who wrote so eloquently of the benefits of Buxton's baths particularly recommended it to all who come here."

They skirted the piece of ground where a game of Barley Break was in progress. Susanna knew how it was played. The field was divided into three parts. The middle portion, known as "Hell," was occupied by the couple who'd drawn the short straw. Hands linked, they waited for a signal to break apart, whereupon they attempted to catch one of the other players, all of whom were obliged to change sides by running through the middle. The goal of the game was to avoid being the last one left in Hell. This seemed to require a great deal of shouting and shrieking to accomplish.

It was just the sort of game to appeal to Rosamond, but Susanna did not see her anywhere about. Earlier, she'd noticed Rosamond in animated discussion with Dionysia Tallboys. Since Diony looked most unhappy, Susanna had concluded that Rosamond was winning their argument. At a guess she had been urging her friend to do something that Diony did not want to. Susanna resolved to find time later to speak privily with Rosamond. The girl's evasions had gone on long enough.

"Here," Annabel said. They'd reached the bowling alley, a turfed area between hedges on the grounds of New Hall. Annabel handed Susanna two wooden balls that had been painted bright blue. She picked up two red ones for herself, together with two stakes. The balls were surprisingly heavy, given their size. Each appeared to be a little more than three inches in diameter.

"Have you placed a wager on the footrace?" Annabel asked.

"I avoid gambling. I am surprised you indulge."

Annabel chuckled. "It is expected in this case. Young Will Hawley is one of the runners. Those wishing to remain in his mother's good graces are advised to show faith in his ability to run the two-mile distance faster than any of the village boys." She planted one stake at one end of the alley and started toward the far side with the other.

"And can he?" Susanna followed her, still carrying the balls.

She shrugged. "His father insists he spend long hours learning to fence and ride and hunt, but a footrace requires stamina and determination. Will strikes me as one who looks for the easy way out. Here, this stake marks your casting spot." Annabel pushed it into the ground with her hands. "The other is your target. It is called the 'Mistress' in bowls. We take turns casting, and when all four have been cast, the one closest to the respective Mistress scores one point. If one of us has the two closest balls, that earns two points. If one ball is touching the mistress, that doubles the points. The first player to have seven points wins."

"It sounds simple enough," Susanna said, and cast her first ball. It skimmed past the Mistress and into a hedge. "Have you made any progress since last we spoke?" They'd had no opportunity to talk privily together since that first day at Bawkenstanes Manor. In the interim Susanna had learned little more about Louise Poitier's life beyond what Rosamond had told her and what Jennet had discovered from talking to Margery Cottelling. If the Frenchwoman had been acquainted with any of the villagers who worked at New Hall, aside from Goodman Flower, they were not admitting it, and if Louise had made contact with an outsider, no one seemed to have noticed.

"I've learned naught to tell me why Louise died," Annabel admitted as they walked from one casting spot to the other.

"That is not precisely what I asked." Annabel's ball had come to a stop so close to the stake that from Susanna's vantage point they appeared to be touching.

"There is the matter of the embroidery, but that may mean naught."

Susanna gave her a questioning look. Embroidery was not an area where she could claim any special insight, but now that Annabel mentioned it she did recall that the women and girls at Bawkenstanes Manor all appeared to be crafting emblems with their needles. "A coded message of some sort?"

"If it is intended as such, I cannot determine who is to receive it or how. Godlina Walkenden is the one stitching Queen Mary's symbols." Annabel scowled at her ball. Rather than touching the Mistress, it was an inch away from the stake.

"What symbols?" Susanna made her second cast and this time managed to keep the ball on the right side of the Mistress. It did not, however, end up anywhere near her target.

"The thistle, for Scotland, and the lily, for France, since Queen Mary was once queen consort there, and the rose, for England, which she has long claimed on the grounds that her cousin Elizabeth was born a bastard and cannot inherit."

Susanna contemplated this information as Annabel made her final cast. There was no question but that she would score two points for this round. Susanna suspected Annabel would have little difficulty winning the match, but playing at bowls was a pleasant enough way to pass the time on a sunny afternoon. In a small corner of her mind, Susanna considered where at Leigh Abbey she might best install a turfed alley similar to this one.

The remainder of her thoughts fixed on Godlina Walkenden. The girl seemed an unlikely conspirator. Susanna had noticed her

earlier, giggling with Diony and helping herself to the variety of
foodstuffs. There was a great deal of food available at the festival,
everything from simple bread to cracknel—a light, crisp biscuit
—to ale and cheese, meat pies, custards, flawns, and tarts.

"Young Lina was fond of your friend," Susanna said.

"More than fond. She doted upon her. Many people did."

"So I understand." The second round of bowls progressed no
better than the first. Annabel was clearly the better player.

"She took lovers," Annabel admitted, "but I cannot see that either Sir Richard Hawley or Wymond Tallboys could have assisted
her in any scheme to free the queen of Scots. Tallboys is a notori-
ous puritan. You may have noticed his immediate departure after
church services. He heartily disapproves of May Day rites."

"That Diony's father is extreme in his religious beliefs would
not prevent him from falling under a woman's spell. What of Will
Hawley?"

"A *boy*?"

"A dangerous boy, or so I am told." Annabel's astonishment
struck Susanna as overdone. She must have wondered about Will
herself. "Tell me again, Annabel—what was your connection to
Louise Poitier?"

"She was a friend."

"A friend much younger than you are. As much as fifteen or
sixteen years younger, from what I understand. That means you
could not have known her when you were with the Scots queen in
France. Your acquaintance with Louise was much more recent.
After you claim to have given up your former profession, mayhap?" Ever since Rosamond had revealed Louise Poitier's age,
Susanna had been hoping for a chance to question Annabel on this
point.

"I returned to the French court for a time after I left England." Annabel cast again, and again came within an inch of the
Mistress. "Louise was there, in the queen mother's employ. She
reminded me of myself at that age. Young. Eager. Foolish. I

attempted to take her under my wing." She hesitated. "I was fond of her, I do think, in the same way you have grown attached to Rosamond."

"You left England nearly a decade ago. Louise would have been a girl of ten at the time. Younger than Rosamond is now. Too young, surely, for even Catherine de' Medici to employ as a spy."

"I returned to the French court nine years ago. I was there, on and off, for the next seven." Annabel's last cast went wildly astray. "I knew Louise toward the end of that time."

Susanna regarded the red ball with interest as it bounced past the Mistress. Something she'd said must have affected Annabel's concentration, but what? How much of the Scotswoman's tale did she dare believe?

Annabel was an accomplished liar, an admitted spy. She'd made a practice in her younger days of seducing men in order to learn their secrets and had passed that information on to their enemies. If she were here as part of some elaborate scheme to rescue Mary of Scotland, mayhap to attempt to put her on the throne of England in Queen Elizabeth's place, then it was Susanna's duty to stop her. But first they must work together to find out what had happened to Louise Poitier. Everything else seemed to hinge on that.

In spite of her wild cast, Annabel won the game. Susanna did not suggest a rematch. She told the other woman what little she had learned about Louise. Then they walked in silence back to the green, where the footrace was about to begin.

The revels had grown increasingly rowdy in their absence. When Will Hawley won the race a short time later, a furor erupted. He was accused of cheating by taking a shortcut that had led him back to the course ahead of the others.

"Husband!" Lady Bridget cried, catching sight of Sir Richard at the edge of the green, where the poor man had doubtless been trying to keep out of her sight. "Come and speak for Will. These fools will not listen to me."

Jennet appeared at Susanna's elbow. "I am surprised anyone dared accuse the lord of the manor's son of such an underhanded trick. I'd not want Lady Bridget's anger directed at me."

"The villagers have no reason to cater to the Hawleys," Susanna said as she searched the crowd for Rosamond. "They owe their loyalty to the earl of Shrewsbury and New Hall, not to Bawkenstanes Manor."

"They must owe some portion of their livelihood to the manor. The Hall is unoccupied half of every year."

Susanna spared one glance for the lad who'd accused Will. He had a determined look on his face. Well he should. There was a handsome purse awarded to the winner, and if Will were disqualified, it would be his. An older man, by his features the lad's father, no longer looked quite so stubborn. Lady Bridget and Sir Richard in tandem presented a formidable obstacle to justice.

Susanna's gaze rested briefly on Nell Hawley, who was staring at Giles Bannister with a besotted look in her eyes. There would be trouble there, Susanna thought, if either Lady Bridget or Wymond Tallboys noticed. She shifted her attention to Diony and Lina, who were beside the pie stand, then skimmed the crowd once more, but her foster daughter was nowhere in sight.

"Where is Rosamond?" she asked Jennet.

"Am I her keeper?" Jennet's voice conveyed irritation and a trace of resentment, and when she'd surveyed their surroundings and found no trace of the girl, the tone turned sarcastic. "Mayhap she has been kidnapped. She *is* known to be a wealthy heiress."

"Lina Walkenden's value is greater, and she would be more easily lured." Susanna gave no credence to the notion that either one of them was in danger of falling into the hands of outlaws. A smile tugged at her lips as she imagined the to-do if anyone should try to abduct Rosamond. But the girl *was* missing and that made her uneasy.

"Any sort of food would do as bait for Lina," Jennet agreed, smiling in turn.

Susanna's attention focused not on Lina but on Diony as she remembered the exchange she'd witnessed earlier. With Jennet trailing after her she made her way to the pie stand. "Diony," she said without preamble, "where is Rosamond?"

Diony blanched. "I told her she should not go."

"Go where, Diony?"

"To Poole's Cavern to meet Will Hawley."

Susanna felt the color drain from her own face, until she was certain it matched Diony's in hue. The cavern was in truth a series of underground caves. Dark and uncouth, all damp and dripping, they were said to extend for miles beneath the surface. No one had ever explored the entire distance.

"But Will is here," Jennet said, "and unlikely to go anywhere for some time." The argument over the footrace had increased in volume. Everyone seemed to have an opinion and no one was shy about expressing it. Will was not well liked in Buxton.

"Certes, she will return when he does not keep their appointment." Lina's frightened eyes belied her words.

"She must already have guessed he was delayed," Jennet chimed in. "Unless she decided to explore."

The fear that Rosamond, adventurous, impulsive Rosamond, might have entered the cavern on her own, sent a chill deep into Susanna's bones. She'd been obliged to spend some time in an underground cavern once. She had no desire to repeat the experience, nor would she wish it on anyone else.

Fighting panic, she forced her way through the crowd that still surrounded young Will Hawley and seized him by his sweat-soaked shirt. "Take me to Poole's Cavern," she said. "Now."

He blinked at her in confusion. Then his eyes widened. "But she said she'd changed her mind. She wrote me a note to say so."

"Show me."

"Lady Appleton, what is the meaning of this?" Lady Bridget's glare would have daunted a less determined woman.

"Your son's carelessness, madam, has placed my daughter in danger."

"Rosamond is missing?" Distress evident in both voice and manner, Sir Richard eased his much smaller wife aside. When Will produced a page torn from a commonplace book, he seized it before Susanna could lay hands on it.

"'Will,'" he read. "'I cannot be at Poole's Cavern today but if you win the footrace I will meet you there tonight.'" Anger flashed across his face as he crumpled the paper in one large fist. "I have warned you about that place. It is dangerous. How dare you defy my orders to avoid it?"

Susanna reached for the note but Sir Richard, intent on berating his son, had stuffed it into the front of his doublet in order to free both hands to shake the boy. She abandoned the effort. "We must get to the cavern quickly. Where is it?"

"About a mile to the southwest." Diony's voice shook. "Why would Rosamond write that note? She told me she was going to meet Will. She was looking forward to exploring the cavern."

Susanna gave Will a shove. "Take me there. Now." She could think of only one reason why anyone would send a false note. He, or she, must suspect, as Susanna did, that Rosamond knew more about Louise Poitier's death than she'd revealed. Louise's murderer had wanted Rosamond to keep her appointment at the cavern, but alone. Without a companion, in a remote location, she would be vulnerable to attack.

Terrified that they would reach the cavern only to discover that Rosamond had become the murderer's second victim, Susanna pushed herself to match Will's pace. Tears streamed unchecked down her cheeks.

❧16❧

Poole's Cavern

ROSAMOND woke to screaming pain in the back of her head and total blackness. For a moment she feared she'd gone blind. Then she realized she was lying on bare rock and remembered that she'd been on her way to Poole's Cavern to meet Will Hawley.

It was the last thing she remembered—cresting a hill and catching sight of the cave's mouth. She could not recall descending into the depths.

Slowly, painfully aware of damage to elbows and knees, thigh and hand, head swimming, she eased to her feet. All around her was a vast emptiness. She could not touch walls on either side or the roof of the cavern above. Her stomach tightened as she squinted, hoping for a hint of light, and still saw nothing.

"Think," she said aloud. Her voice echoed eerily back at her, sending a chill down her spine. She was alive. That was a good thing. Wasn't it?

Rosamond took several deep breaths, eyes closed. She had not entered the cave on her own. That meant someone knew where she was. Someone who…had tried to kill her? With a delicate touch she explored the bump on her head. She'd been struck from behind. She could feel no blood, dried or fresh, just a huge, tender lump under her hair. Her coif appeared to be missing. If it had fallen outside the cavern, someone might find it.

If anyone looked here for her. Will might…unless Will had been the one who'd struck her down. She could not think why he would, but he *was* the one she'd been planning to meet here.

"Will," she called softly. "If this is a jest, it is a poor one."

She did not expect an answer and was not surprised when she did not get one. She was uncertain whether to hope that meant he was with her in the darkness, unconscious as she had been, or still out in the world somewhere.

Belatedly, Rosamond recalled that she had not entirely trusted Will Hawley and had taken a precaution lest he play just such a trick on her. She'd told Diony where she was going and with whom. Diony's response had not been reassuring. She'd reminded Rosamond that the caves extended underground farther than anyone had ever explored, and branched off in different directions. If she and Will got lost in Poole's Cavern, Diony had warned, they might never see the light of day again.

Another shudder racked her, and hugging herself against it, Rosamond's fingers brushed against the placket in her skirt. Her heart skittered. She could almost hear Mama's voice listing the useful items one should always carry in the pocket beneath. Among them were the means to make fire.

It seemed an eternity before she had her candle stub lit. It would not last long. She knew she must find other flammable material quickly. But for the present it was enough just to see again. She twisted her aching head, straining to look at everything around her at once. The tears filling her eyes and streaming down her face did not help matters.

Dashing them away with her free hand, Rosamond stared in awe at the open space surrounding her. The cavern was much larger than she'd imagined, and she had a good imagination. Another wave of panic and pain swept over her. What if she went the wrong way? What if she wandered deeper into the caves instead of finding her way out?

Tracks, she thought, and bent with the candle to study the floor of the cave. There *were* faint marks, as if something heavy had been dragged over the stone surface. Her own limp body, Rosamond realized. She choked back a sob.

Following the trail, obliged to walk bent over in order to see the faint marks, Rosamond came at last to a point where the cavern branched off in two directions. Each way seemed equally wide and neither revealed any hint of daylight at the far end. When Rosamond listened hard, she thought she heard the sound of rushing water to the right, and of a sudden she was parched with thirst. Water meant a stream, and it must lead somewhere, mayhap all the way back to Buxton. Resolute, she turned toward the sound, but she did not come to the cave's entrance. Instead, after cautiously making her way along the rock corridor for what seemed an endless period of time, Rosamond reached another underground chamber.

Heart racing, she held the candle stub higher. Walls glistened in the light, frozen waterfalls blinking back at her. Like blue curtains they shrouded the sides of the cavern, rising to heights the paltry illumination she carried could not hope to penetrate.

Rosamond's breath caught as she turned, her head tilted back in a vain attempt to see more. The sight was magnificent...and frightening beyond belief. If outlaws had buried treasure here, they had been braver than she was, for surely this was a place guarded by spirits from the underworld. Mere mortals were not meant to explore these depths.

Her strength drained, her head pounding, Rosamond sat on the cold, hard floor of the cave. If she closed her eyes she could still hear rushing water. It seemed closer. Near at hand was the sound of a steady drip. Rosamond was steeling herself to move toward it when she heard someone call her name.

Rosamond's hand shook so hard she almost dropped her candle stub. Hot wax dripped onto her thumb. Tears flowed with renewed force. She'd been going the wrong way, deeper into the caves. Rescue was behind her, back the way she'd come.

"Rosamond!" This time she recognized the voice.

"Here!" she called. The word came out as a whisper. Taking a deep breath, she tried again. "Mama! Here I am!"

※17※

New Hall

ANNABEL exerted what little authority she had at Bawkenstanes Manor to ensure that she was the one who brought
Rosamond a change of linen and what Diony called her "personal
stuff." She found the girl propped up by bolsters in her foster
mother's bed in Susanna's lodgings at New Hall. Luxurious
surroundings, Annabel thought, for a spoiled darling. The bed
was supplied with the finest blankets—made in Spain—and hung
with five inner curtains of purple baize and outer hangings of
scarlet. The coverlet was littered with empty bowls and beakers,
and sleeping kittens. Clearly Rosamond had made the most of
her perilous adventure and subsequent rescue.

With a singularly ungracious mutter of thanks, Rosamond
seized the capcase Annabel had brought, burrowing through the
contents to make sure nothing was missing. Annabel hid a smile.
She suspected Susanna's sudden fit of coughing was necessary to
cover a laugh. That the girl was right to be suspicious only added
to the humor of the situation.

Annabel had not missed the opportunity to search Rosamond's "stuff." It consisted mostly of papers, but there were two
books. One was a broadside entitled *The Woeful Lamentation of
Mistress Anne Saunders, which she wrote with her own hand, being a prisoner in Newgate, justly condemned to death*, the account of a murder
that had taken place two years earlier in London. A merchant had
been killed by his wife's lover. Wife and lover both had been executed. The second book was in Latin, a work on architecture by
Marcus Vitruvius Pollio.

"Rosamond was fortunate," Susanna said. "A few bumps,
bruises, and scratches, but nothing that will not mend."

Annabel could understand Susanna's relief even if she did not
share her affection for Rosamond. The enormity of Poole's Cavern had awed everyone in the search party. They'd been obliged to

walk a good half mile through a series of underground chambers, deep into the bowels of the earth, before they'd found Rosamond. One chamber had been at least three times as wide as most great halls were long, and as high as the nave of a cathedral.

Susanna motioned Annabel into a window embrasure overlooking the River Wye and spoke in a whisper. "I believe it best that Rosamond remain here with me for the nonce." Her eyes reflected a concern beyond worry over Rosamond's injuries.

"You cannot protect her from the knowledge that someone meant to kill her. She's an intelligent girl. She cannot fail to suspect the truth."

Wearily, Susanna made a small gesture of acquiescence. "I will discuss the danger with her. And question her. But not yet. She has been through a harrowing experience. Did you learn anything from Will Hawley?"

"The note he told us she sent him is missing." Annabel did not trouble to lower her voice. Let Rosamond and Jennet, who was listening from an inconspicuous spot in a corner, overhear. "Sir Richard insisted he returned it to the boy."

He'd also leered at Annabel, and suggested they discuss the matter later, and in private. She was not sure what to make of that, given her current age and weight.

"Do you think Will still has it?"

"Will claims it was lost in the confusion of the search for Rosamond, but he knows more than he's saying. He has a guilty look about him."

"He was most upset to realize that someone had played a trick on him."

Annabel nodded. "In his own way, I think, he is fond of Rosamond. He'd kept the note in the first place as some sort of memento."

Rosamond made a gagging sound from the bed.

"I searched his chamber. There was no sign of it there. Unless it is concealed on his person, he no longer has it."

"His father took it from him on the green. Could it have been dropped there in all the confusion?"

"On my way here, I scoured the village from maypole to kale yard. A sheet of paper that size is not a common commodity but no one would admit to picking it up, even though I offered to pay for its return. If someone did find it, I warrant that by now, at the least, the ink has been scraped off to remove the words." Scraped parchment could be reused or sold, and few residents of Buxton were wealthy enough to ignore a chance for profit.

"Or it has been burnt by whoever sent it. No matter. We know someone other than Rosamond sent Will that note, for she did not write it. Someone wanted Rosamond to go into that cavern alone. She thought Will would meet her there and that they would spend the afternoon hunting for Poole's treasure. She can remember nothing after she reached the mouth of the entrance cave."

"Yes," Annabel agreed, "someone lured her there and made sure Will stayed away. But why? What does she know that would prompt an attempt to kill her?" She shifted her attention from Susanna to Rosamond. "Do you know who killed Louise?"

"No. I should have said if I did." Rosamond folded her arms in front of her chest as her lower lip crept forward into a pout.

"I believe you. So might Louise's killer, now, since you have made no public accusation. The danger should be past." Trying not to sound too hopeful, Annabel turned to Susanna. "Will you take Rosamond back to Leigh Abbey?"

"Certes, it would make your life easier if we were out of the way." A hint of sarcasm laced the words.

"I would be delighted to have you both leave...to protect the *jeune fille*."

"*Some* might think I would no longer have had a reason to stay here if Rosamond had vanished."

"You'd have remained until you found the body. Then you'd have stayed to avenge Rosamond's death. You'd never have rested if you'd thought someone killed the girl." Annabel could not understand why Susanna was so attached to her husband's by-blow, but it was plain she was.

"It was meant to seem an accident," Susanna reminded her.

Annabel nodded, thinking over what they'd learned. "Will would, eventually, have admitted they meant to meet in Poole's Cavern and led us there to look for her." Unless he'd found her first on his own and tried to hide the body, thinking he'd be blamed. "From what I can discover, she was left for dead in the section of the caves where Will once found a gold coin."

"Just one?" Rosamond's outrage woke the kittens, who abandoned her in favor of the cushion by the hearth.

"Will is not the only one who has deceived us." Susanna fixed her attention on Rosamond. "You and Diony and Lina have been holding something back. Something that may be more important than you realize."

Rosamond responded to Susanna's gentle, coaxing tone by bursting into tears. The whole story tumbled out then, how the three girls had braved the night and the full moon to try out the waters of the First Chief Bath. And how Louise had caught them there and sent them home.

"She said she would speak with us after church services the next day. We hoped to talk her out of telling Lady Bridget what we'd done. But the next day, she was dead. She must have been killed on her way back to the manor house."

"You say she *followed* you?"

The sharpness of her question had Rosamond blowing her nose on a lace-trimmed handkerchief and nodding earnestly as she dashed away the tears.

"That makes no sense, Rosamond. If she followed you, she would have stopped you before you entered the water. From what you say, some considerable time passed before you three were discovered."

"But if she did not follow us from the manor, what was she doing there?"

"That is, indeed, the question." Susanna's gaze slid to Annabel. "And another is this: Since she did catch you, why did she not escort you home herself? A waiting gentlewoman of the household, mindful of her obligations, should have felt duty-bound to see you safely back to your bedchamber."

"She was a Frenchwoman," Jennet muttered, glaring at Annabel.

"Mistress Devereux?" Susanna prompted.

"Louise was devoted to *les jeunes filles.*"

Annabel's hopes of bluffing her way out of a confession were dashed by a gasp from Rosamond. "Madame Poitier called me that. *Jeune fille.* But only once. That night." She pointed an accusing finger at Annabel. "Were you there? Did you overhear? Is that why you say it, too?"

"Rosamond's assumption is based on little but instinct," Susanna said, "but in this case I think she is correct. Mistress Devereux?"

Annabel thought about making up a tale, then decided it was not worth the effort. "Louise came to New Hall to meet me," she admitted. "We had matters to discuss."

"Matters to do with the queen of Scots?"

"*Louise* had an interest in her fate."

As Jennet and Rosamond watched the exchange between Susanna and Annabel, their heads moved back and forth like spectators at a tennis match.

"Had Louise come to Buxton to help free the Scots queen?" Susanna asked.

"She did, yes, but her plans came to naught."

"Poole's Cavern would be an ideal place to hide an escaped prisoner." Rosamond sat up straight in the bed, eyes gleaming with barely contained excitement.

Susanna sent an appalled look in her direction.

"That was not the plan," Annabel said. But it was too close to the truth for comfort. The situation here was rapidly deteriorat-

ing, and to make matters worse, Jennet chose that moment to
peer closely at Annabel's face.

"You are no Frenchwoman!" she exclaimed.

"Excellent, Jennet," Annabel said in her most sardonic tone.
"What gave me away?"

Jennet glowered at her. Outrage at such a calm reaction to
her accusation had her spitting out the answer: "That sly look in
your eyes, Mistress MacReynolds. And a term you used when you
told us how you searched in the village: *kale yard*. That's what
Scots call a kitchen garden."

"How careless of me."

Indeed, it appeared to be words that betrayed her at every
side. *Good-sister. Jeune fille.* Now *kale yard*. Annabel glanced Susanna's way and shrugged. There seemed little point now in hiding
her real identity.

"We have met before, Mistress Rosamond, when you were in
truth a *jeune fille* of three years old. My name is Annabel MacReynolds."

"You knew my father." The words were an accusation. "Were
you always so fat?"

"Rosamond! What a thing to say!" Susanna tried to hide her
amusement but was not entirely successful.

Annabel did not take offense. Indeed, the girl's frank question
provoked a reluctant grin. "No, I was not. How is it that you
know of my…connection to Sir Robert?"

"Mother told me. She said you were besotted with him even
after he was dead."

Mother, not Mama—Rosamond meant Eleanor Pendennis.
Annabel exchanged a speaking glance with Susanna. How fortunate, she thought, that it had been Susanna rather than Eleanor
who had come to Buxton to visit Rosamond. Annabel expected
she'd have her work cut out for her to persuade Jennet and
Rosamond to keep silent about "Jacquinetta's" true identity. Convincing Eleanor Pendennis would have been impossible.

❧18❧

May 3, 1575
New Hall

TWO DAYS after Rosamond's misadventure, Susanna received a note from Annabel. She glanced at Rosamond, who had remained with her to recuperate, even though she'd been back on her feet after the first good night's sleep.

"Your mother has arrived in Buxton," Susanna announced.

Rosamond choked on the apple she'd just bitten into.

"No doubt Lady Bridget has done her best to make Eleanor welcome," Susanna continued, "but after a long, arduous journey by litter, expecting to find her daughter at Bawkenstanes Manor, she cannot be pleased to learn what happened to you, or where you are. We had best go to her at once and reassure her."

"Will she recognize Annabel?" Jennet, gathering cloaks and gloves for the walk to Bawkenstanes Manor, sounded intrigued.

"Let us hope not. Eleanor never spent much time with her. Neither has she ever been to Scotland or to France." Eleanor was unlikely, Susanna thought, to make a connection between Lady Bridget's formidable, French-speaking companion and the slender, sensuous creature who'd been her immediate predecessor as Robert Appleton's mistress. Then again, Susanna herself had recognized Annabel. So had Jennet, given time enough. It might be safest to keep the two women apart.

Once her identity had been revealed to Rosamond and Jennet, Annabel had made a show of answering questions, but she'd relayed very little real information. She'd avoided being specific about where she'd been since her flight from England nine years earlier. As for where she'd gone after meeting Louise in Buxton, she claimed they'd parted shortly after Rosamond and the other girls went back to the manor, and that she'd been on her way to Scotland when she'd heard of Louise's death.

Had she been in Annabel's position, Susanna would have considered flight, but the Scotswoman was waiting for them at the gatehouse when they arrived at Bawkenstanes Manor.

"What is this great to-do?" Susanna asked, seeing that the courtyard was crowded with men and horses. "Surely Eleanor cannot be the cause of so much fuss." Servants ran every which way, offering libations and taking charge of the animals.

"Penelope's betrothal to Wymond Tallboys is to go forward at once," said Annabel. "Sir Richard had already set everything in motion before our unlooked-for guest arrived, but professed himself delighted to have Lady Pendennis here to stand as witness. It did not, it appears, occur to him to invite the esteemed Lady Appleton to do the honors."

Susanna ignored the jibe. "Who are all these people?"

"Local magistrates. Other landowners. The vicar. Sir Richard can be certain his daughter will not wriggle out of her promise if the most prominent men in the area hear her make it." Annabel's lips twitched into a wry smile. "The wedding, I warrant, will follow in short order."

Betrothal *required* nothing more than an exchange of words between two people, a promise that they would marry. It could be done in private. Susanna had to wonder why Sir Richard was going to so much trouble over this.

Her first glimpse of Eleanor, seated in solitary splendor in her wheeled chair on the far side of the hall, drove that question from her mind. Instead she tried to fathom why Eleanor was being treated as an honored guest in this household. Walter was no nobleman. Eleanor was…kin to the earls of Westmorland. Susanna frowned. That connection had drawn Eleanor close to treason once before. Had it done so again?

Rosamond rushed off to join Lina and a tearful Diony, who was about to acquire a stepmother but a few years her senior. Susanna left them to their reunion and made her way across the crowded Great Hall to Eleanor's side, as good a place as any from which to watch the ceremony.

"Sir Richard intends to make certain the arrangement cannot be broken," Eleanor murmured.

"Mayhap he fears his daughter may otherwise devise plans of her own," Susanna said.

If the church courts were asked to enforce a contract, hearsay or common fame were not considered acceptable evidence of betrothal. They preferred two credible firsthand witnesses to the exchange of words.

It was a sensible precaution. This pre-contract would forever remove the danger that some fortune-hunting scoundrel might persuade Nell Hawley to speak words that could be taken as a promise to marry. Sir Richard wanted assurance that his daughter would marry where *he* chose, to someone who would provide for her and her future children.

Rosamond's mother had a peculiar expression on her once beautiful face. "Sir Richard has arranged for witnesses, and more."

Susanna directed her own attention to Nell Hawley and Wymond Tallboys as they began to read from the *Book of Common Prayer*. With his thinning hair and tall, loose-limbed body, Tallboys looked older than his years while Nell, so much shorter and smaller, seemed even more a child than she was. She stumbled a little over the words of the ceremony, and stood rigidly as Tallboys slid the betrothal ring onto her finger. It was a gimmal, Susanna noticed, one half of the ring he'd use for the wedding.

And then she realized that they had said the words *in verbis de praesenti*, choosing the far more binding form of the ceremony. Sir Richard did indeed want his daughter securely shackled to Tallboys. Had she said, "I, Penelope, *will* take thee, Wymond," or if one or the other had attached conditions to the promise, such as her father giving them a house, then there would have been room to escape the contract. Having sworn, "I, Penelope, *do* take thee, Wymond," the girl had already sealed her fate. Unless there was some impediment to the union, such as a pre-contract with someone else, then these two were as good as married now...for life.

Susanna's gaze homed in on Nell's face, taking note of her dazed expression. Her pupils were huge, her complexion as white as parchment, and she swayed slightly as she reached for the quill.

Eleanor caught Susanna's arm when she would have gone to the young woman's assistance. "You've no business interfering. It is a parent's right to make provision for a child, and far more sensible than letting an impressionable girl decide for herself who to wed."

Nell signed the documents.

"Will you look out for Rosamond's interests in such a manner?" asked Susanna. Unless she was much mistaken, Nell Hawley had been given poppy syrup to make her amenable. Susanna could not condone such blatant disregard for the law that said a woman had the right to refuse a marriage she found objectionable. Nell's choice had been taken away from her.

"I may," Eleanor said, her hostility a palpable force between them. "Lady Bridget's methods seem passing effective."

Across the room, the signatures having been duly recorded, Sir Richard's tame clergyman cleared his throat and launched into a lecture. "You are not to fleshly meddle together," he told Nell and her betrothed. "If you do, you sin most deadly, for 'tis not a holy and faithful conjunction until you are wed before all the congregation."

"On the next three Sundays or holidays," Eleanor said, "the banns will be read. On any of those occasions, parishioners can object to the marriage. If no one does, it can be solemnized at any time afterward, and the bride bedded." She shifted her gaze to Susanna. "Do you mean to object?"

"Someone should."

"Do not interfere," Eleanor warned. "Rosamond's future depends upon keeping the Hawleys sweet."

"Rosamond can do better than Will Hawley."

"Leave Rosamond to me. She is my daughter, not yours." And with that, Eleanor gave the wheels of her special chair a sharp spin and nearly ran over Susanna's toes as she shot forward.

Susanna tried to excuse Eleanor's behavior on the grounds she was tired after a long journey, but her sympathy...and tolerance...extended only so far. Yes, it must have been a shock to arrive and discover Susanna already here and Rosamond recovering from her adventure in Poole's Cavern, but why did Eleanor seem to condone forcing Nell into marriage? And why was she so intent on a match between Rosamond and Will? Given Eleanor's past connection to treason, it was difficult not to look for a link between Louise's death and some new plot to free the Scottish queen.

Across the room, Eleanor had cornered Rosamond. With a sigh, Susanna started toward them. It took some time to make her way through the crowd in the Great Hall, for the celebration of Nell's betrothal with food and wine and music had begun.

The clear, sweet voice of a singer filled the room: "'Love that is too hot and strong/ burneth soon to waste.'"

Nell Hawley's soft cry of anguish drew Susanna's attention to her. Tears streamed down her face as Giles Bannister continued his rendition of the popular ballad.

"'Love me little, love me long/ is the burden of my song.'"

The young woman's stricken expression tugged at Susanna's heart, but there was nothing she could do to lessen Nell's distress. In any case, her first obligation was to Rosamond. She reached the girl's side in time to hear Eleanor accuse her daughter of acting the hoyden.

"She met with an accident," Susanna said in a mild voice. That was the story they'd agreed to tell the world—Rosamond had fallen while exploring the cave and struck her head.

"She went where she should not have gone."

"This is not the place to chastise your daughter, Eleanor. Nor should she stay at Bawkenstanes Manor." Susanna had seen clashes between mother and daughter before. It was not a pretty sight.

"Are you mad? She belongs to this household. You had no business taking her away."

Rosamond's dark eyes—Robert Appleton's eyes—sent Susanna a silent plea for understanding before she pulled away from both women. "I will stay here," she said. "Mother is right. I belong here."

"I will dispatch one of the servants to New Hall for your capcase." Eleanor turned a triumphant smile on Susanna. "Mayhap you should go with him and pack it yourself."

"Mayhap I should," Susanna said.

Hurt and puzzled by Rosamond's defection, worried for the girl's safety at Bawkenstanes Manor, Susanna temporarily abandoned the field, but not before she had taken Annabel aside and extracted from her an oath to keep watch over Rosamond.

"And do not trust Eleanor," she added.

"I never did," Annabel replied.

🏵19🏵

May 4, 1575
St. Anne's Well

ELEANOR Pendennis scowled at the mineral water in her goblet. She did not much care for this part of the cure. This first full day at Buxton she was expected to imbibe three pints of the warm liquid and on the morrow, four pints, and on each of the succeeding three days, five pints and a gill. With the sugar she'd brought with her added, the drink was palatable enough, or at least no worse than whey, except that whey did not make her sneeze.

Squeezing her eyes shut, Eleanor held her breath and downed the remainder of the draught. *Faugh!* She could not care for the taste, no matter how much it was sweetened. She had come to Buxton out of a desire to bathe in the healing waters, not guzzle the stuff. If she had to consume medicinal liquids, she much preferred Xeres sack.

A pity she could not have gone to the springs at Spaw in Flanders. La Fontaine de la Sauvenieve was known to increase fertility, especially if a woman drank while one foot touched the print left by St. Remacle's shoe. That water was reputed to have a very strong taste of iron, but it could not be worse than what she'd just swallowed.

No doubt Walter could have taken her to Spaw on his way to…whatever place he had gone. The Low Countries seemed a more likely destination for him than France or Spain. They could have gone by ship to Antwerp, then overland. There'd have been no trouble about a passport, though she'd doubtless have had to take the oath of allegiance to Queen Elizabeth before she could leave England. These were troubled times.

At an impatient signal to her two burly servants, the young men lifted Eleanor's carrying chair by its poles and transported her out of the enclosure around St. Anne's Well. "Take me to the baths," she ordered when they would have returned to Bawkenstanes Manor. She wished she'd been able to use her litter for this jaunt to the well. It was far more comfortable and luxuriously lined with the silk-and-linen blend known as satin of Bruges, but the litter required the use of two horses. Chairmen were easier to direct.

At the entrance that led to both New Hall and the baths she was met by Master Greves, who kept a record of the status of all visitors, marking down their dates of arrival and departure, their illness or other reason for coming, and the fees they paid to enter the baths. He remembered that she was a gentlewoman and tried to assess her two shillings for the visit.

"I have not come to bathe," she informed him in haughty tones.

"The waters could ease your pain, madam," the impertinent fellow informed her.

"I hope that will prove to be the case, but the physician my husband consulted warned me that I must not immerse myself in the bath until at least the sixth day of my three-week stay."

Greves nodded his approval. "Aye. That is the best way. You should not be a launderer until your drunkenness is at an end. But if you do not wish to bathe, why are you here?"

"Why, to visit my dear friend, Lady Appleton," Eleanor said.

Without further delay, she was carried up two flights of stairs to the lodgings Susanna occupied. When Jennet opened the door, the height of Eleanor's chair brought them eye-to-eye. Eleanor forced a smile. Jennet had never cared for her, resenting on her mistress's behalf the fact that Eleanor had borne Sir Robert Appleton's child when his wife could not. Eleanor had no reason to suppose time had altered Jennet's opinion. She told herself she did not care.

"Put me down by the window and go away," Eleanor ordered the chairmen.

When they had gone, she surveyed the chamber, taking in Susanna's appearance—she had just finished dressing by the look of her—and the luxurious surroundings, marred only by the presence of two kittens curled together asleep in the middle of the bed. The last time Eleanor had come to the baths, she had stayed in a very plain room in the row of lodgings adjacent to New Hall. She suppressed the envy coiling inside her and continued to smile as she addressed her hostess.

"I was hasty yesterday to send you away before we'd had a chance to talk."

"An apology, Eleanor?"

"An olive branch. We are both here because we have Rosamond's best interests at heart, are we not?"

"Why, Eleanor, I thought you had come to Buxton to visit the baths."

"As you did? Tell me, Susanna, what regimen do you follow? I am obliged to rise at seven of the clock and be carried to Saint

Anne's Well even before I break my fast. After breakfast comes prayer, then mild exercise—I can walk a bit with my sticks— from eleven until one, followed by another visit to the well before dinner. Afternoons are for writing, reading, or making music, until supper at eight. At ten I make one last pilgrimage to the well, and so to bed."

"Be grateful." Susanna grimaced. "The estimable Dr. John Jones, in *The Benefit of the ancient Baths of Buckstones*, instructs patients to spend the two to three days before they enter the baths in drinking Saint Anne's water and vomiting it back up again. Drink it hastily, he advises, to the amount of two or three quarts."

"You follow those directions?" Eleanor knew her skepticism showed.

Susanna's slow smile answered her. "A visit to Buxton seemed a good excuse to see Rosamond," she admitted.

"You were pining for her company? Is that why you insisted Rosamond stay with you after her escapade in Poole's Cavern?"

A shadow crossed Susanna's face. "No, I kept her with me to prevent a murderer from making a second attempt on her life."

Eleanor felt her own smile slip. It vanished altogether when Susanna explained her theory that Louise Poitier had been murdered and Rosamond left to perish in the cavern because the killer thought she had seen or heard something incriminating the night the Frenchwoman died.

"Something?" Eleanor echoed. "What?"

"We do not know, Eleanor. That is the problem."

"Louise Poitier. I remember her."

"Ah," said Susanna. "I hoped you might. Will you join me for breakfast and help me decide what is best to do to protect your daughter?"

Once Eleanor accepted the invitation, Susanna sent Jennet for food and drink. "Now, Eleanor, tell me all you know of the Frenchwoman."

"She was introduced to me as a Huguenot refugee. We talked

once or twice of inconsequential matters. She was a friendly sort, far friendlier than the woman who has replaced her in Lady Bridget's household."

"Jacquinetta Devereux?"

"Aye."

"Did Lady Bridget tell you that Jacquinetta is kin to Louise Poitier?"

"Ah. That explains why I thought there was something familiar about Mistress Devereux's appearance. A family resemblance, no doubt. But Lady Bridget did not mention the connection. She did not even tell me that Madame Poitier was dead." Then again, Eleanor had not asked about Louise.

"Mayhap she presumed you already knew what had happened."

"Rosamond is an indifferent correspondent."

"She did not confide in me, either, Eleanor. She told Rob Jaffrey."

That revelation, followed shortly thereafter by the arrival of the food, improved Eleanor's mood. "Have you no notion who killed Madame Poitier?" she asked when she'd devoured two poached eggs, a portion of wheaten bread, and half a goblet of ale.

"Louise Poitier met someone at the First Chief Bath that night," Susanna said. "She stumbled upon Rosamond, who had gone for a clandestine swim with her friends. She sent the girls home but remained behind."

"Then the person she met must have murdered her, and having caught sight of Rosamond, thought she saw more than she did." Eleanor considered for a moment, chewing thoughtfully on a crust. "The most likely person for a woman to meet at night is a lover, but there is another possibility. Is there treason afoot? Is that why you think Louise Poitier was killed?"

"It is possible," Susanna allowed. "Do you remember anything about her that might suggest she was in Buxton as a spy?"

"She showed me a Spaw ring sent to her by a friend. Such tokens, so Walter tells me, are sometimes used as a signal that a Catholic exile is alive and well abroad."

"But she claimed to be a Huguenot."

"Protestants may have Catholic friends and relatives. Or she lied about her religion. To hear Walter tell it, everyone lies all the time."

"And for all manner of reasons," Susanna agreed. "Do you recall anything else about her?"

Uneasy now, Eleanor turned her gaze to the window. The morning sun glinted on the river where it twisted and turned as it flowed toward Bakewell. Bright beams streaked the hilly landscape beyond in shades of grey and green.

"Louise Poitier knew of my kinship to the earls of Westmorland."

The present earl, Eleanor's distant cousin, was now living in exile. He had been one of the leaders of a rebellion six years earlier, an attempt to free Mary of Scotland and put her on the throne of England. Although Eleanor had initially supported Westmorland's scheme, she had told Walter what was afoot in time to thwart the uprising. At the time, she'd believed she was dying. She'd been run down by a heavy wagon. Hooves and wheels had inflicted damage that had left her scarred and in constant pain, unable to walk more than a few steps even with the aid of crutches. As a result, for the rest of her life, she would be obliged to rely upon chairmen, a horse litter, and her special wheeled chair.

"I told Lady Bridget of my connection to the nobility when I was in Buxton last summer," Eleanor admitted. She'd hoped to enhance Rosamond's value as a bride for Will. There was no harm in that! "Louise must have overheard."

"Did she mention it to you?"

"Indirectly. I'd forgotten till now. At the time I had little interest in waiting gentlewomen." Looking back on their conversation, Eleanor wondered if Louise had subtly been testing her loyalty.

"Well?" Impatient, Susanna awaited details.

"Launderers, as those who bathe here are called, tarry two or three hours, immersed, while their clothes are hung up to air. As a gesture of our new friendship, Lady Bridget loaned me Louise's services. It was while she was helping me dress that she remarked upon the waters at Spaw. She said she had been told that they were more beneficial than those at Buxton. The earl of Westmorland, she said, had recently visited them."

"And you did not think her comment significant?" Susanna sounded incredulous.

"Servants always talk about their betters, especially those who have fallen on misfortune." She used the last of her bread to scoop up the remaining egg. Susanna was as bad as Walter—suspicious of everything.

"Did she tell you who sent her the Spaw ring?"

"No. A friend, she said." Eleanor had not cared enough to ask. "She did not give a name."

But Susanna uttered one under her breath. She spoke so softly that Eleanor almost missed what she said.

"Annabel?" she repeated.

As if a curtain of fog had abruptly lifted, Eleanor grasped the reason for that elusive sense of familiarity about Jacquinetta Devereux. "The woman is a known spy, Susanna. Send for the constable. You need search no farther than Annabel MacReynolds to find your murderer."

❧20❧

"LOUISE was alive when Annabel left her that night. She believes Louise met someone else afterward."

"What power on heaven or earth possessed you to trust

Annabel MacReynolds's word about anything?" Eleanor demanded. "The last time you dealt with her she abandoned you, fleeing
the country to avoid arrest for treason."

"She sent back what help she could once she was safe in
France. I know you never liked her, Eleanor. But I believe she
holds the key to Louise Poitier's murder, and she has expressed a
willingness to help us discover the truth. She may not have been
kin to the dead woman, but she was her friend."

"You admit she was here that night. Why are you so certain
she did not murder Louise?"

"It might be best if you may ask her that yourself. Jennet, go
to Bawkenstanes Manor and fetch Annabel. The time has come for
a council of war. And tell Rosamond that if she does not return
with you, then she must keep in company with Diony or Lina at
all times until her mother and Annabel return to the manor."

Jennet's frown expressed disapproval of this plan but she
obeyed without comment. When she'd gone, closing the heavy
door behind her with a resounding thunk, Susanna rounded on
Eleanor.

"Let us clear the air between us on another matter while we
wait. I object to your plans for Rosamond because *she* does."

"What does my daughter know? She is a child."

"As we were children when decisions were made for us. Were
they always right?"

Eleanor opened her mouth, then closed it again. As Susanna
well knew, Eleanor had been sent by her mother into servitude in
the household of an elderly relative, Lady Quarles. Her despera-
tion to escape that life had thrown her into Robert Appleton's
arms. At the time, she'd believed his promises of love and marriage. He'd not bothered to tell her he already had a wife.

Susanna's case had not been much better. Her marriage had
been arranged at the tender age of fourteen, although the wedding had not taken place until after her eighteenth birthday. Fool
that she'd been, she'd never questioned the choice of husband her

guardian had made for her. Robert Appleton had been a charming rogue, handsome and handy with compliments. Only after the wedding had she realized that his interest in her property would always be far greater than his affection for her person.

"Rosamond despises Will Hawley," Susanna said into the silence.

Eleanor sighed. "He is an annoying child, I grant you. Mayhap he will improve with age."

"He will turn out exactly like his father."

"It is a good match," Eleanor insisted. "She would want for nothing. And the family connections are excellent. Lady Bridget is the daughter of an earl."

Their discussion of Rosamond's future went round and round in this manner, resolving nothing, until Jennet returned with Annabel.

Instantly diverted, Eleanor pinned the Scotswoman with a penetrating stare. "Why should we believe you went merrily on your way, leaving Louise behind? I think you killed her."

"And left the body to be found by the well, when we had met in a chamber in this house? If I had killed her and gone to the trouble to move her after, I'd have taken her out into the wilderness where her body would have vanished without a trace."

"Can you prove she was still alive when you left Buxton?" Jennet asked.

"Produce witnesses do you mean?" A flash of amusement lit Annabel's green eyes before she sobered again. "I had two hired guides with me. They might be found and questioned. But are you certain you wish to call attention to my movements? Better to concentrate on finding out what happened after I left."

"How far did you go that night?" Susanna had not pressed Annabel for details before, but the suspicions that Eleanor and Jennet harbored sparked her own. Annabel had been holding back information. Of that she was certain.

Annabel hesitated, then shrugged. "The moon was full. I rode a goodly part of the way toward South Wingfield and arrived in time for church the next day. Word reached me there of Louise's death."

"The earl of Shrewsbury has a house in South Wingfield."

"One which has housed the queen of Scots in the past and will likely do so again," Annabel agreed.

"I told you she was up to no good," Jennet muttered. Eleanor also looked smug.

"My purpose was to prevent Louise's schemes from bearing fruit, but I have no way to prove it to you. You will have to take me at my word."

"We might have you arrested instead," Eleanor threatened. "My husband could make you answer questions."

"He would torture a woman? Has Sir Walter descended to that? I do not think so. Besides, I am reliably informed that he is not in England just at present. Let us leave him out of our calculations."

How did she know Walter was gone? Susanna bit back the question. There were others in greater need of answers. "Why meet here? I'd have thought it would be safer to use a less conspicuous place."

"The key was not difficult to obtain and I prefer what comfort I can get. We did not anticipate that the girls would be able to slip in through the cracks an earthquake left in a brick wall."

"And you saw no one else?"

"No one. If someone was lurking about, they were well hidden." Again, she shrugged. "But then, my two guides were nearby, and no one saw them, either."

"How did you know Greves, the warden, would be gone?"

"Louise discovered his plans."

"Do you think she might have told someone she intended to meet you here?"

"She could have, but I think it unlikely. She knew and trusted me and believed I was the contact she'd been told to expect."

"You...disposed of the individual she should have met?"

Annabel only smiled.

"Who sent Louise here, Annabel?"

She would not answer that question either.

"You claim you are no longer in Queen Catherine's employ. Why not?"

For a long moment, Susanna thought Annabel would not reply, but at last, on a sigh, she said simply, "St. Bartholomew's Day."

"You were there?" Susanna's stomach clenched. The French wars of religion had raged for over a decade but the worst atrocities had taken place on St. Bartholomew's Day three years past when thousands of Huguenot men, women, and children had been slain on orders from the Catholic monarchy.

"I saw the aftermath," Annabel said. "They say that six thousand died in the first purge, and a hundred thousand during the week that followed. I doubt anyone counted. Certes, no one buried most of the bodies. The wolves—"

When Annabel had to turn aside to recover herself, Susanna could not doubt the depth of her distress. It made no difference if one were Catholic or Protestant, no true Christian could countenance such wanton slaughter.

"Afterward," Annabel said, "I left France."

"To go where?" Eleanor sounded suspicious, and appeared unmoved by Annabel's reaction to the St. Bartholomew's Day Massacre.

"Here and there."

"Liege? Spaw?"

"I see you have found me out. Yes, I did go to Spaw. And yes, I encountered English refugees there."

"The earl of Westmorland?" Eleanor asked.

"And the countess of Northumberland." The look Annabel sent Susanna was one of mild amusement. "She speaks fondly of a certain lady who served briefly in her household."

"What, precisely, did you intend to do to put a stop to Louise Poitier's schemes? Indeed, what did Louise have planned?"

"That has no bearing on her death."

"Annabel, I have a certain amount of sympathy for the captive queen of Scots, but not enough to let her go free to challenge Elizabeth Tudor for the throne of England."

"Nor do I want that. Trust me, Susanna."

"Do not listen to her," Eleanor warned.

"She lied to us before," Jennet reminded her.

But Susanna was inclined to give Annabel the benefit of the doubt, at least for the present. "Whether or not Louise's murderer is part of some conspiracy, he...or she...is also someone connected to Bawkenstanes Manor. Nothing else makes sense, given the note to Will and the attack on Rosamond."

She retrieved the list she had made with Rosamond's help and settled herself on the window seat next to Eleanor, one kitten on her lap and the other between them. She unrolled the parchment.

"Let us consider what we know of each of these individuals," she suggested, "for it must be one of them who lured Rosamond to Poole's Cavern."

🕸21🕸

Bawkenstanes Manor

THE TABLE book, readable from four angles for four parts, was open to a song with which Rosamond was not familiar. She stared down at the page, nerves knotting her stomach. It was all very well to *say* solfaing was simple to master, but the truth was that she, Rosamond Appleton, capable of memorizing long passages in Latin or Greek, could not conquer vocal sight-reading.

"If I go wrong," she complained, "it will be next to impossible to sort myself out and everyone will be upset with me for ruining the evening's entertainment."

"That is why, Mistress Rosamond, you have a music master." Giles Bannister's fine-boned face was a mask of patience, but Rosamond suspected he could be got round. She'd seen him try to hide his winces when she sang.

"It is not important that I be able to sing," she informed him. "Why, I have read for myself in Sir Thomas Elyot's *Book Named the Governor* that a nobleman should use music to refresh his wit, when he has time, or else to display his knowledge of it in conversation. To my mind, that is the same as saying that a well-bred gentleman, and by extension a well-bred gentlewoman, should be able to talk about music but not necessarily perform it. Leave that to the town waits!"

"A nice logic," Mistress Cottelling said in an admiring tone, "but not sufficient reason to escape your lessons."

Rosamond scowled at her. Why should she be forced to embarrass herself in front of the others? She would retire to her bedchamber. Plead a headache.

And everyone would think her a coward.

Rosamond sighed. They knew already that she was no great addition to their singing. Her voice was loud enough, but unreliable when she tried to carry a tune. Mayhap, if they made her join them, they should suffer the consequences. She would sing even more badly. The musical notation she'd been trying to decipher was only her part. Once the song started it would be easy to lose her place. She was torn between the temptation of deliberate sabotage and the challenge of succeeding against the odds.

To one side of her stood Lina, ready to take the treble part. She had a high, sweet, clear voice, her tone light and flexible. Rosamond was to sing the mean, her range rising to meet the treble, while Will provided the tenor and his father, at Lady Bridget's insistence, the bass. There were other songs, in six parts, for which Diony and Nell would join them.

Master Bannister began to strum accompaniment on his lute. Rosamond's hands clenched, suddenly damp, on the fabric of her skirt. Why did she have to do this? It was not fair. She'd had no training in music before coming to Bawkenstanes Manor. They should not expect her to participate.

She wished now that she'd gone with Jennet and Annabel, but she'd been hoping for a chance to confront Will Hawley. That was also why she'd decided to stay here instead of returning to New Hall. Much good it had done! Not only had Will taken great care never to be alone with her, but Annabel had hovered, giving her no privacy at all. Rosamond had planned to slip out of her bedchamber after Lina and Diony fell asleep, but she'd been thwarted in that, too—tiredness had overcome her, sending her into dreamless slumber that lasted the whole night through.

A sharp poke in the ribs brought Rosamond back to the present. Lina sent her an apologetic look.

"Whenever you are ready, Mistress Rosamond." Sir Richard's attention made her feel even more self-conscious.

"Nell should sing the part in my stead."

"I prefer to hear Nell play the virginals." Sir Richard's mouth flattened into a thin line and the eyes half hidden by heavy lids were hard as diamonds.

The rectangular, box-shaped case with its small keyboard sat at a goodly distance from Giles Bannister and his lute. Rosamond had supposed Nell's betrothal to Master Tallboys had been rushed into because Will had told his father he'd seen Nell with the music master at Poole's Cavern, but he could not have named the man his sister had been with. Otherwise Master Bannister would already have been sent packing.

Rosamond glanced again at Giles Bannister. Young, golden-haired, sensitive—except for forcing her to sing—he was everything Wymond Tallboys was not. But no match for Sir Richard. He'd never dare argue about religion, or anything else, with that gentleman the way Master Tallboys did. But if Sir Richard did not know Nell fancied the younger man, why was he so intent on keeping them at opposite sides of the music room?

The song began, cutting short Rosamond's speculation. She made a valiant attempt at her part but lost her place within a stanza. Rather than plough on, she fell silent and let the others finish without her.

An elusive memory tugged at the back of her mind as she watched their faces—Sir Richard, Will, and Lina. Something about Louise Poitier, but what? And then she remembered. She'd first heard of Poole's Cavern from Madame Poitier. The Frenchwoman had suggested mushrooms might be cultivated there.

Had that been the only reason for her interest? Or had she wanted to explore it with an eye to hiding the queen of Scots there? Had she discovered it was being used as meeting place for lovers? Had she seen Nell there?

One glance at Nell had Rosamond discounting her as a potential killer. Look how meekly she'd agreed to marry Master Tallboys. But there were others who might want to keep Nell's adventures quiet. Would Sir Richard or Lady Bridget kill to prevent rumors from reaching Master Tallboys? Kill Madame Poitier because of what she'd stumbled upon in her explorations? Kill Rosamond because of what she'd seen in Will's company?

Rosamond had difficulty accepting either as a murderer. Neither of them would need to kill to achieve their purpose. Madame Poitier had been Lady Bridget's servant. She'd do as she was told. And Rosamond, unless she wished to be expelled from the household, would likewise keep Nell's secret.

Her suspicions shifted to Master Tallboys. Mayhap he'd wanted all the witnesses removed for fear one of them would object when he tried to marry Nell. If Master Tallboys had killed Madame Poitier and tried to kill her, he would also have disposed of Giles Bannister. He'd have made a point of discovering the identity of his rival.

Rosamond's eyes widened as a new thought struck her. What

if Giles Bannister murdered Louise Poitier to keep her from telling anyone she'd seen him with Nell? She could scarce breathe in
her excitement. She had solved the crime. The musician had done
it. The solution made perfect sense. Why, by his very profession,
he was but one small step above a vagabond. Best of all, there
might be a way to prove it. All she had to do was establish that he
could not be accounted for during the time she had herself been
absent from the May Day festivities. That would be enough to accuse him of following her and hitting her on the head. And once
he was arrested, the authorities would soon have a confession out
of him.

"Pay attention, Ros." The jab Will gave her was much harder
than Lina's.

She rammed her fist into the side of his thigh. He winced, but
the attack had been hidden by the table. No one reprimanded
either of them.

Giles Bannister had selected another tune and elected to sing
the solo part himself. "'I love her well with heart and mind,'" he
sang, looking straight at Nell. "'She is right true, I do it see/My
heart to have she doth me bind/Shall no man know her name for
me.'"

Rosamond joined in with the others. She hit a sour note but
soldiered on, considerably more cheerful than she had been earlier. She was certain she had identified the killer. Anyone cruel
enough to force a person with no musical talent to sing before
others would not balk at murder.

✾22✾

May 5, 1575
The gardens at Bawkenstanes Manor

"GILES Bannister is the murderer."

Rosamond's confident statement took Susanna by surprise. She sent an inquisitive look toward the girl striding along at her side, then glanced over her shoulder. They were alone among the primroses and gillyflowers and should remain so for some time. Lady Bridget had gone with Eleanor to St. Anne's Well, accompanied by Margery Cottelling. Annabel was in the schoolroom, engaging Nell, Diony, and Lina in French conversation. And Susanna could hear the clang of metal from the stable yard where Sir Richard was supervising Will's daily lesson in sword fighting. That left the musician unaccounted for, but Susanna had no reason to suppose he was hidden in the bushes about to leap out at them.

"You seem very certain."

Gravel crunched beneath their feet as they continued to stroll along paths that wound among raised beds containing herbs and a variety of flowers. A breeze had come up, eddying through the open spaces to lift skirts and chill bare skin. Rosamond had forgotten her gloves—or misplaced them again—and kept her hands tucked under her cloak to keep them warm as she explained her reasoning.

"All we need do is find someone who noticed he was missing during the footrace," she concluded.

Looking down into that hopeful, upturned face, Susanna was tempted to let her go on believing she had solved the crime. Reason prevailed. It would take very little to put Rosamond at risk again. Louise's murderer must have thought Rosamond was a threat, that she'd seen something on the night the Frenchwoman died. Her failure to accuse anyone after her rescue from Poole's Cavern would have been greeted with relief—a sign that she

knew nothing after all. But Rosamond would remain safe at
Bawkenstanes Manor only so long as she did not call attention to
herself. If she asked too many questions, if she hinted that bump
on her head was no accident, she would make herself a killer's
target all over again. Susanna refused to take chances with her foster daughter's life.

"There is a flaw in your logic, Rosamond. If Giles Bannister
saw you in the wee hours of May Day as you suppose, then Will
should have been the one he attacked near the cavern, not you.
Will was the real threat to the young lovers."

Susanna, Eleanor, Annabel, and Jennet had spent hours the
previous day considering everyone on her list, including Giles
Bannister. While it was true they had not thought of Nell's reputation as a reason to want Louise dead, Susanna still did not believe
that Giles Bannister was guilty of anything worse than loving
unwisely.

"He might have seen me at the baths. And he knows his way
about underground. Whoever left me there was familiar with the
caves."

"Anyone who lives hereabout may know as much. Will did."

"Will was running the footrace when I was hit on the head."

"But we cannot be certain where anyone else was, except
perhaps for Nell. She was in the May Queen's bower. She'd not
have been able to get away without her absence being remarked
upon. Everyone else is suspect."

"Not Diony. Not Lina."

"No, but someone at Bawkenstanes Manor did mean you
harm, and if that person realizes you know you were left to die in
the caves, then he may try again to kill you."

"I have told everyone it was an accident."

"Return to New Hall with me. You'll be safe there."

"But I want to stay here."

One look at the girl's rebellious expression told Susanna she
was fighting a losing battle. And in this skirmish, she doubted

she'd get any support from Eleanor. She remembered herself at the same age. Risks were as nothing, even when one knew full well how sudden death could come.

At twelve, Susanna had lost her father in a shipwreck she'd scarce survived herself. The grandmother who'd raised her after her mother's death had died some two years earlier. Orphaned, Susanna had been sent to the duke of Northumberland's household and there, surrounded by other young gentlefolk and nobles, had flung herself into every adventure and intrigue offered by her surroundings. She'd pursued her studies, for her father had seen to it that she'd been educated as if she were a boy, but she'd discovered new joys, among them the pleasure of leading others into mischief.

There had been a boy a bit like Will Hawley—arrogant, annoying, fascinating. He'd given her the first kiss she ever received. He'd grown up to become one of the most powerful noblemen in the land. Lord Robin Dudley was now earl of Leicester and the queen's favorite—her lover, some said.

Pushing aside nostalgic thoughts, Susanna returned her full attention to Rosamond. The wind had whipped color into her cheeks and loosened her hair, but her eyes were bright from another cause. The girl had inherited her father's stubbornness. Even if staying here placed her in danger, she was set on her reckless course and ready to challenge Susanna's right to protect her.

Resigned, Susanna tried another tack. "Tell me about your days, Rosamond. How do you pass the time?"

"In lessons."

"French conversation. What else?"

Rosamond grimaced. "They expect me to learn music, but I am not skilled at singing."

"You have my sympathy," Susanna said, "and my apologies. I should have seen to it that you were trained in music when you lived at Leigh Abbey. I had little exposure to it myself until the duke of Northumberland became my guardian." She remembered how awkward she had felt at first around the more accomplished members of that household, especially the young Dudleys. By the time Rosamond came to her, however, those days had been long past. Except for training Rosamond in the uses of stillroom and garden, the girl's lessons had come out of books.

"There is also needlework. I do not much care for that, either."

"Nor did I."

"And then there is the dancing," Rosamond burst out. "We must learn yet another one on the morrow because there will be dancing at Nell's wedding."

"Dancing is accounted excellent exercise," Susanna said. "Why, doctors recommended it to patients here at Buxton, along with walking and playing at bowls."

"Mole is not required to dance. Or to study music. I wish I could attend a grammar school."

"You would not be happy there." Susanna stooped to pluck a gillyflower growing in a wall. She twirled it between her fingers, remembering other flowers, other gardens. She herself would not have been happy with a grammar school's regimen either.

"Why not?" Rosamond demanded, contrary as usual. "I am as skilled at Latin as Mole is. And my penmanship is better."

"You write a fine italic hand. Boys customarily use the secretary style."

Rosamond looked mutinous. "That is what you had me taught."

"Because I prefer it. But more prevents you from attending grammar school than your handwriting, Rosamond, even setting aside the fact that grammar schools only admit boys." Universities had a similar restriction, as did the Inns of Court. "The scholars must speak only Latin and the hours of coming to school would not suit you. Seven in the morning, winter and summer. Four hours of study and then another four in the afternoon, and each session begins and ends with prayers. In between, the scholars are forbidden to play games and restricted in their freedoms in other ways, as well."

"I'd not go to play, but to study. And I could pass the entry requirements. Mole told me what they were. He had to read and know by heart in the vernacular the Lord's Prayer, the Angelic—"

"Rosamond—"

"Last form he translated endless sentences into Latin by writing them in parchment books. Now he is studying the familiar letters of learned men and stories from the poets. What is so difficult about any of that? It is not as if they've taught him Greek. They do not even offer the study of *modern* languages."

"All the more reason you would not like it there. You inherited your father's facility with languages."

"You read a goodly number of them."

"And find conversation in anything but English a great trial. I can never remember how to pronounce foreign words."

Rosamond's irritation faded. "That must mean I am more clever than you are, Mama. So I will be your eyes and ears at Bawkenstanes Manor. I will stay here until I can discover who killed Madame Poitier and tried to kill me."

Susanna felt her face blanch. That was not what she'd intended when she began her inquisition into Rosamond's daily schedule. She'd hoped to discover ways to keep the girl safe. "You will do no such thing," she said before she could stop herself.

"I must. We *cannot* do nothing!"

"If you must stay here, concentrate on needlework and music and dancing. Lull the murderer into a false sense of security."

"What will you be doing?"

"I will return to New Hall and write letters. I have questions about the Hawleys and Master Tallboys, and about Giles Bannister, too, and acquaintances who may be able to answer them."

"Will you tell me what you find out?"

"You have my word on it. Do I have yours that you will not make any further attempt to discover the killer's identity?"

"Unfair," Rosamond muttered.

"Promise me, Rosamond."

"Tell me who you mean to write to."

"One missive will go to the earl of Shrewsbury's house at Sheffield."

Mollified, Rosamond agreed not to do anything foolish. It was only after they'd gone their separate ways that Susanna thought to wonder if her definition of "foolish" and Rosamond's were the same.

23

May 6, 1575
Bawkenstanes Manor

"*MAIS NON. Non! Non! Non!*" Annabel's voice rose with each objection.

Had ever a woman been beset with so many difficulties? Not one of the three young gentlewomen in her charge had any aptitude for the complicated steps of the galliard.

"Let them practice the branle," Margery Cottelling urged. "The movements are simple, yet there are many variations. A candlestick branle would suit for the wedding feast—the dancers pass lighted candles between them. Others can join in and drop out as the dance progresses, so that everyone is included."

"That is not the purpose of this performance," Annabel objected. "Lady Bridget wishes to show off her young ladies, and the abilities of her son."

"The gavotte, then," Nell Hawley proposed, stealing a glance at the musician tuning his lute.

"I think not," Annabel said in her most repressive voice. The gavotte was naught but a kissing game. She considered the lute.

A cittern would be better, or a fiddle, or even Nell's virginals. They could use something, too, to mark the rhythm—a tambourine, or bells, or a small drum, or blocks. For the wedding, thank the good Lord, more musicians would be brought in.

A burst of laughter from the window seat had her head jerking round to see what Rosamond had got up to now. She and Will Hawley sat close together on the cushions, sharing a book between them. Their former dissension had been vanquished by a common delight in what they read.

"Do not keep wisdom to yourselves," Annabel admonished the pair. "What is it that provokes such mirth?"

She was not unduly surprised to discover that the volume was Thomas Elyot's *Book Named the Governor.* Lady Bridget swore by Elyot's advice. Annabel was less taken with the author's pedantic views. Elyot tried too hard, she'd always thought, to justify pleasurable activities by insisting they were healthful. He claimed the harmonious movements of the dance echoed the movements of the stars and that men and women dancing together symbolized perfect harmony.

Rosamond stifled another laugh and began to read aloud, squinting a little at the fine print: "'A reverent inclination or courtesy with a long deliberation or pause is but one motion comprehending the time of three other motions, or setting forth of the foot. By that may be signified that at the beginning of all our acts, we should do due honor to God, which is the root of prudence, which honor is compact of these three things, fear, love, and reverence. And that in the beginning of all things we should advisedly, with some tract of time, behold and foresee the success of our enterprise.'"

"That is how he describes the way every dance begins with an honor or *révérence*," Will said, "but he makes it sound more like a prelude to battle than to dance."

"Are they not the same, young Master Hawley? The tract of time is provided that you may pause, collect your thoughts, and

concentrate on worldly matters of success and enterprise. As I
recall, Master Elyot also defines the dancing couple as an emblem
for man and woman. That they dance together signifies matrimony."

Rosamond abruptly pushed the book away.

"No! No! Let us pursue this." Annabel continued to speak in
French, although Rosamond had read aloud in English. All the
young people understood both languages, but Margery Cottelling, having had a less extensive education, had difficulty following
the dialogue. Giles Bannister, or so Annabel must suppose, knowing nothing of his background, might be fluent in both tongues.

"Dance is a necessary accomplishment." Will sounded as if he
were quoting one or the other of his parents, perhaps both.

"It is," Annabel agreed. "Therefore let us resume. Stand, if you
please, Master Will, and you to partner him, Mistress Rosamond.
Mistress Diony and Mistress Lina, you must dance together, as
we have no other gentlemen. Take you the man's part, Mistress
Diony, being the taller."

Reluctantly, the girls obeyed, Diony grumbling all the while
about the disadvantages of being the tallest girl. Will leapt up with
alacrity, for dancing not only allowed him to show off his athleti-
cism and good health, but also gave him an opportunity to touch
his partner in ways not otherwise permitted.

He acknowledged Rosamond by making a leg. As he inclined
his body forward, he took up a great deal of space. In contrast,
Rosamond's bow, her body upright as she lowered it, was only a
slight dip, confined to a limited area.

"Eyes downcast, if you please, Mistress Rosamond."

"Why?"

"To show you are demure and biddable."

"But I am not."

Nell had picked up the book and now read from it: "'In every
dance of a most ancient custom there dances together a man and
woman holding each other by the hand or arm, which betokeneth

concord. Now it behoove the dancers and also the beholders of them to know all the qualities incident to a man, and also to a woman likewise appertaining. A man in his natural perfection is fierce, hardy, strong in opinion, covetous of glory, desirous of knowledge, appetiting by generation to bring forth his semblance. The good nature of a woman is to be mild, timorous, tractable, benign, of sure remembrance, and shamefast. Diverse other qualities of each of them might be found out, but these be the most apparent.'"

Will preened.

Rosamond caught Annabel's eye and struggled not to laugh.

"Let us continue." Annabel had to clear her throat. "Master Will, let me remind you of another book, Castiglione's *Book of the Courtier*. He writes that it is ill-bred to draw attention to your skills. When you dance, you must make clear that you neither seek nor expect applause. Even if your performance is sublime, you must let it be thought that you have taken no time or trouble to perfect your skills."

"But I have," Will objected.

"Many long hours," Rosamond agreed.

Too many, Annabel thought. She'd already spent an inordinate amount of time instructing these young people in the correct way to behave before, during, and after a dance. She wished Lady Bridget had brought in a real dancing master, mayhap one who also taught music, or gave lessons in riding and fencing, or taught etiquette and general deportment. *Patience*, she reminded herself.

"Dance is an essential skill for a courtier, but you must make it look as if this skill is a natural talent, not the result of practice. Begin again," she commanded, "and this time, Master Will, we will start from the point where you ask Mistress Rosamond to dance."

At least he saw the sense of putting the best foot forward in social situations. If he hoped to go to court, he had to learn how to behave. Annabel watched with critical eyes while he removed his

gloves, then held both gloves and hat in his left hand as he offered
Rosamond his right. Annabel nodded her approval. To offer the left
hand was disrespectful, as was taking your partner's hand while
wearing gloves, which suggested you did not want to touch her.

"I do not see why I cannot make long strides and leaps as Will
does," Rosamond complained.

"Your skirts would fly up." Will looked at Annabel. "Will you
teach us La Volta? In that one the gentlemen pick up their partners, putting one arm around their waists and taking hold of their
bodices with the other hand. Then they whirl around together
with such abandon that most ladies have to hold down their
skirts."

"And in all the excitement, some *gentlemen*," Nell said, "have
been known to grab more than the stiffened fabric of a bodice."
She left her chair and crossed to the bench upon which Giles
Bannister sat. "I am the one to be married and I must dance at my
own wedding. I must practice. Partner me, musician."

"But who will play for us?" Thin shoulders hunched, Diony
squinted at the room at large, unable to see much beyond the end
of her nose with any clarity.

"Mistress Devereux can." Rosamond had a devilish gleam in
her eyes as she danced Will across the room to Giles Bannister's
side and plucked the lute from his hands.

"One dance," Annabel agreed, fixing the music master with a
stern look before addressing her charges. "Begin with the pavane
for a grand entrance, and then perform the steps of the galliard as
I have taught you."

At first all went well. The three couples danced twice around
the room and then separated, the girls going to one end and their
partners to the other. The idea was to perform variations until the
music stopped, and Will at once launched into a series of high
leaps, indulging an inclination to show off.

"Enough, Master Will." Annabel stopped playing. "None can
compete with you."

"Wait. I have been practicing another step." He suspended a tassel from a wall sconce at a height level with his head, then danced toward it, jumping and twisting with the clear intent of kicking the tassel, but he both leapt and landed awkwardly, crashing into a stool and stumbling against the table beside it. Crockery fell to the floor with a great clatter.

Will picked himself up, red in the face but unhurt, and left the mess for Margery to set right. "Another dance?" he said to Rosamond.

She made a show of reluctance, but in the end gave him her hand.

"A last pavane," Annabel said, hoping the dance's stately measures would restore order to the dancing lesson. It contained no leaping or bouncing, just gliding steps executed hand in hand.

She strummed a tune on the lute and the dance began. It had not progressed very far when the back of her neck prickled. A moment later, Sir Richard Hawley's infuriated voice cut through the music, halting the young people in mid-step.

"Unhand my daughter, you blackguard!" he bellowed.

Giles Bannister stepped away from Nell with unflattering speed.

"They were only dancing," Rosamond protested.

Sir Richard silenced her with a glare and made a visible effort to regain control of his temper. He sounded calm when he spoke again, but Annabel suspected the even voice was deceptive.

"Go to your mother, Nell," Sir Richard ordered. "And you, musician, pack your bags. I want you gone by nightfall."

"Sir Richard," Annabel said in a quiet voice. "A word?"

He turned aside with her, leaving a room full of stricken faces behind him. "I could have him horsewhipped. Remember that. And remember, too, that you are only here on sufferance."

"Lady Bridget—"

"This time, Lady Bridget will do as I say."

Were she given to hyperbole, Annabel would have said there

was murder in his eyes. She, too, decided that obedience was the better part of valor.

Annabel wondered what Susanna Appleton would make of this development.

❧24❧

THE DOOR to the chamber that Rosamond, Diony, and Lina shared was opened and closed again so quietly that Rosamond, half-asleep, scarce heard the sounds. She came fully awake only when Nell spoke close to her ear. "You must help me," she whispered. "I need all of you."

"Nell?" Lina murmured in a sleepy voice. "Go back to bed. 'Tis too late."

"Not yet."

Rosamond got up and lit a candle. The grim determination on Nell Hawley's pale face matched her tone of voice. "Is someone ill?" she asked.

"I am sick at heart," Nell said. "I cannot marry Wymond Tallboys."

Deep furrows appeared in Diony's brow, as if she suspected some insult to her father. Fixing Nell with a challenging look, she demanded, "Why not?"

"Because he is old enough to be *my* father, and I do not wish to be bedded by him, not when I've known the pleasure of a young man's embraces."

Diony's mouth opened in an "O" but no sound came out. Her eyes widened to matching roundness, but Rosamond could not tell if she was offended by Nell's comments about Master Tallboys or simply shocked by the older girl's bluntness.

"Giles Bannister," Lina said.

Nell blushed. "I love him."

"But he left hours ago." Rosamond had been relieved when he'd been sent away. In spite of Mama's contention that he was unlikely to have been the one who'd left her to die in Poole's Cavern, she still harbored dire suspicions about him. "Besides, you are betrothed to Master Tallboys. There is no getting out of a pre-contract."

Diony, recovering, nodded so vigorously that her nightcap slipped sideways. "You spoke the vows."

"I must find some way to escape, and soon." Nell sounded close to tears. "Father told me tonight that the banns will be called this Sunday and on Thursday, which is Ascension Day, and next Sunday. That means we can be wed the Sunday after."

Rosamond wrapped herself in her night robe against the chill of the unheated room and reached out to tug Nell onto the bed with them. The four girls arranged themselves in a circle atop the coverlet and pulled the hangings closed, concealing them from the curious gaze of anyone who might pass through the chamber. This gave an illusion of privacy, but they were careful to keep their voices low. Servants slept in a connecting room.

When Rosamond had positioned her legs tailor-fashion and balanced the candlestick on her knee, she looked at Nell. "What do you mean to do?"

"There is only one way out for me. I must run away."

Diony gasped. Lina gave a startled squeak. Rosamond just stared at her, but she felt a rush of excitement at the thought of such a romantic and daring solution to the problem. Then she frowned. "Do you mean to go to Master Bannister?"

"Who else should I elope with?"

"But he is gone," Lina protested. "How will you find him?"

"He went no farther than New Hall."

"He can find employment there, entertaining the earl of Shrewsbury's guests," said Diony. "Oh, I am glad. That means he will be able to provide for you."

"He cannot stay *and* run away with Nell." Rosamond liked Diony, but her reasoning was ofttimes faulty. "How can we help, Nell?"

"I need you to take a message to Giles. You can go there on the pretext of a visit to Lady Appleton. You must tell him when and where to meet me and that he must find horses for us. I will bring jewels and coin to pay our way."

"But Nell," Lina objected. "Where will you find a preacher to marry you? Your father's chaplain will not do it, for fear of losing his post, and outside your own parish, any respectable vicar will ask questions, and if you lie about your pre-contract, the marriage will not be legal."

"Worse, you could be charged with bigamy for being married to two men at once." Rosamond only put into words what Nell must know—by the form of her betrothal, she was already as good as married to Wymond Tallboys.

The tears that had been threatening spilled over. Nell sniffed loudly and stuck her chin out. "I do not care. We will never return to Buxton. We will go someplace far away where no one will recognize us."

"But how will you live?" Diony asked. "A musician without an employer is a vagabond, and that is a crime. And an employer would demand to know who he worked for in the past. You will be found out."

"We will find a way." Nell dashed the moisture from her cheeks and glowered at them. "If you will not help me, then at least swear you'll say nothing of my plans."

"Mayhap my father would help," Diony said. "He cannot want a reluctant bride."

"How can he help? He is as trapped by our vows as I am."

Lina looked sly. "There is one way. I heard talk of it in my father's house, when no one knew I was listening." Intrigued, every eye turned in her direction. Preening a little, Lina lowered her voice still further. "Marry Master Tallboys and then give out that he cannot perform his husbandly duties. Then the marriage can be annulled and you can marry Master Bannister."

"You would have her lie about my father?"

"Better than to lie *with* him! And mayhap it would not be a lie." Lina's expression was all innocence, except for her eyes. They contained a glint of malevolence.

"He pleased Madame Poitier well enough," Diony indignantly shot back.

"You make Madame Poitier sound wanton," Lina protested.

"It scarce matters now whether she was or not," Rosamond interrupted. "Nothing can alter the pre-contract between Nell and Master Tallboys."

She knew a few things about annulments herself. Like Lina, she'd done her share of listening when others did not know she was there. And as the base-born daughter of Sir Robert Appleton and one of his mistresses, she'd taken an interest in legal rulings that ended up bastardizing children.

"Master Tallboys could obtain an annulment *ab causa frigiditutis naturalis* if you could not conceive," Rosamond told Nell, "but if you married again and had a child by that husband, it would be proof of your ability to conceive and would undo the annulment. You'd bear a bastard and lose its father. And if you were divorced on the grounds that Master Tallboys was impotent and you both remarried and he had a child by his new wife, then you'd be forced back together by the church courts. They'd say you deceived the Holy Church and annul both new marriages. A pity you did not use the other words for the betrothal. If you'd sworn only to marry him in the future, then the pre-contract could be undone…as long as you stay out of his bed."

"I said the words they gave me to read. 'Twas passing difficult to make sense of them. They blurred on the page."

Lina patted her arm in a consoling manner. "You were nervous. Before the ceremony you shook like a leaf in a storm. Your father had to give you a posset to calm you."

Rosamond's interest quickened. "Was there something in the drink? Were you drugged?"

"Why would her own father do such a thing?" Diony asked.

"Because he feared she would balk at the last moment," Rosamond said, then was momentarily distracted by how much Diony Tallboys resembled Wymond.

Both were tall, thin—bony, in truth—and loose-limbed. Diony had not inherited her father's hawklike nose, and her perpetual squint obscured the mild grey eyes they shared, but like him she was often ill at ease around strangers—unless she felt so passionately about something that she could not be still. Religion made Master Tallboys bold. Diony stood up for her friends.

A small sound from Nell as she hugged a pillow to her chest and rocked back and forth, drew Rosamond's attention to her once more. "Did your father know about Giles Bannister before the betrothal?"

"He could not have realized. We were careful."

"Nell," Lina said. "*Everyone* knew. You two have been making sheep's eyes at each other for weeks."

"But when did Sir Richard notice?" Rosamond looked from Lina, who'd retrieved her comfit box and was munching sugared nuts, to Diony, toying nervously with the end of one pale yellow braid. "When we watched the revelers go off into the woods to bring in the May, what were we saying, thinking ourselves alone? Sir Richard could have overheard part of our conversation."

"We made no mention of Nell." Lina chewed and swallowed. "We talked about Madame Poitier. And if Sir Richard had overheard *that*, surely he'd have said something."

They'd been remembering that night in the baths. Lina was right. They'd all have been in trouble if Sir Richard had heard them say they'd crept out of the house in the middle of the night.

"He could not have known about Nell and Master Bannister then, but he could have heard about them from Will the next day."

"No," Nell protested. "I paid Will for his silence."

"He told you we'd seen you with Master Bannister at Poole's Cavern?"

Nell nodded. "But he swore he'd not cause trouble for Giles. I gave him two gold angels to keep him sweet."

"He had no need to name your lover, Nell," Rosamond said, "to tell your father you'd been with a man. He must have claimed he recognized you but not your companion. That explains why, by the day following, Sir Richard had pushed forward the betrothal, and why he drugged you to assure your cooperation." Suddenly Rosamond's eyes lit with excitement. "Nell! If you can swear you were given a potion to make you biddable, that might be enough to nullify the betrothal. There has been at least one case in the courts where a marriage was set aside because the bride was kidnapped and forced to wed. If you did not know what you were saying, how can you be held to it?"

"What good will it do her to claim she was drugged?" Diony demanded. "Sir Richard will just insist she take the vows all over again."

"I will refuse."

"He'll beat you. No man stole you away and forced you to marry him. A father has the right to command obedience."

"That won't matter, Diony." Rosamond was certain she had the right of it. "That she was drugged is enough to set aside Nell's betrothal. All she has to do is pledge her troth to the musician in private. Once consummation makes the bond permanent, there is nothing Sir Richard can do to invalidate their union."

"But how can I prove I was drugged?" The hope in Nell's eyes was at odds with the doubt in her voice.

"I can ask Mama to help us. She knows everything there is to know about narcotic herbs."

❀25❀

May 7, 1575
New Hall

"'IN LOVING, each one hath free choice/ or ever they begin/ but in their power it lieth not/ to end when they are in.'" Rosamond heaved an exaggerated sigh as she hugged the slim volume to her chest. She was reading from a book of poetry titled *A Sweet Nosegay*, about which she professed to want her foster mother's opinion. Rosamond peered at Susanna through lowered lashes, as if this made her scrutiny less noticeable.

Curious to hear what would come next, Susanna did not let on that she could see right though the girl's thinly disguised desire to broach some subject without giving it undue importance. They were alone in Susanna's lodgings, save for the kittens. Jennet had left shortly after Rosamond's early morning arrival, bound on a shopping expedition to Bakewell, the nearest market town.

"Foolish thoughts," Rosamond declared, "but some silly girls believe them."

"A woman wrote those lines, I believe," Susanna said.

Rosamond nodded. "Isabella Whitney, or so the title page says. Her posies are not all so cloying." She leafed through the pages to find the one she wanted and read aloud: "'Such poor folk as to law do go/ are driven oft to curse/ but in meanwhile, the lawyer thrives/ the money in his purse.'"

Fighting a smile, Susanna played with the kittens and waited to see what Rosamond would say next.

"The first poem is the only one anyone at Bawkenstanes Manor quotes," she lamented after a brief silence. "All the talk there is of love and marriage and weddings and babies." She wrinkled her nose in distaste. "I do not see what all the fuss is about."

"It is a solemn contract," Susanna told her. "Matrimony. A lifetime commitment."

"And not to be entered lightly into."

"No." Where was this leading? Susanna honestly had no clue.

"Is it true that if a bride is kidnapped and forced to wed, the vows are not binding?"

"If the church courts find that is the case." Uneasy now, Susanna sat up and detached the kittens from her skirts.

"What if the bride were drugged? If she had no notion what it was she'd sworn to?"

So that was it. Nell Hawley. But how did Rosamond come to be involved? Waiting to be told became increasingly difficult, but Susanna prided herself on patience when it mattered. This conversation, she sensed, could not be rushed. "It seems reasonable to me," she said carefully, "that such a marriage would not stand, but how could it be proven?"

"By the bride's testimony?"

"Would she be believed if her family stood against her? I presume that, in this *hypothetical* case, they arranged the nuptials?"

With another sigh, this one genuine, Rosamond flung herself face down on the bed beside Susanna. "You've guessed." The words were muffled by the coverlet.

"You are precious to me, Rosamond, and have many admirable qualities, but subtlety is not one of them. Does Nell claim she was unaware of the meaning of the words she spoke at her betrothal?"

Turning her head just far enough to see out of one eye, Rosamond made a grunting sound that Susanna took for assent.

"I sympathize with the young woman, but there is little you can do to help her. She must come forward herself. Go to the bishop mayhap, to complain of her mistreatment."

"Would that free her from the betrothal?"

"I do not know. Men can justify a great deal on the grounds it is good for their womenfolk, who are, as everyone knows, too feeble-minded to think for themselves." Bitterness leaked through in spite of her efforts to maintain a casual tone. She'd spent all the years of her marriage living with the knowledge that Robert had not only made light of her intellectual accomplishments, he'd claimed some of them as his own.

"Nell loves Giles Bannister."

"So I gather." Annabel had sent word of the musician's expulsion yestere'en, followed by Bannister's abrupt arrival at New Hall.

While Rosamond gave a highly colored account of what had happened at the manor, Susanna pondered what to say to the inevitable request for aid. She did not want to involve herself in the Hawleys' affairs, other than to extricate Rosamond from danger. On the other hand, interfering in this matter might provide a way to discover more about Louise Poitier. These people were tied together, as members of the same household always come to be over time.

"And she asked me to bring a message to Giles Bannister," Rosamond said, reaching the end of her recitation.

"Let me guess. He's to meet her somewhere and they will run away together?"

Rosamond, who was sitting tailor-fashion with the kittens between her knees, looked up with eyes wide and jaw slack. "How did you know?"

"It is a frequent mistake made by young women, to think they can escape their troubles by making a clandestine marriage. Such elopements rarely end well. And in this case, until a court declares otherwise, Nell is legally bound to Wymond Tallboys. Any union with young Bannister will be bigamous."

"I still want to talk to him." Chin thrust out at a pugnacious angle, Rosamond met Susanna's skeptical gaze with a challenge in her eyes. "Why not? It is safe to do so here. You will be with me. And besides, this is our chance to ask him where he was when Madame Poitier died. And when I was struck on the head."

"Very well," Susanna said. "Let us go talk to him."

They found him in the Great Hall, scratching his name on a glass window. This seemed to be a popular thing to do. Other names and bits of wisdom were scattered over the panes. "*Hoc tantum scio quod nihil scio*, Doctor Bayley" was inscribed on one. "All I know is that I know nothing." Doctor Bayley, Susanna presumed, was Walter Bayley, Oxford's Regius Professor of Physic. She knew he had been in Buxton the previous year.

"A way to leave messages?" Rosamond whispered.

"Too obvious," Susanna hissed back. Then again, sometimes the obvious was best. Hiding things in plain sight often succeeded where too much subterfuge resulted in no one being able to decipher important information.

"Musician," she said, addressing Giles Bannister, "a word with you."

"At your service, madam. And I mean that in the most literal sense. If you would consider employing a musician in your household, you would find me most reliable."

"And talented, one would hope?"

"Modesty forbids that I say so, madam, but I am told I have a passing fine voice and some skill on an assortment of instruments."

"And he can dance," Rosamond said, *sotto voce*.

Color crept up from the fellow's collar at the reminder.

"It is information we wish at present," Susanna told him. She surveyed the hall. At the far end two women were engaged in a game of troll-my-dames, which involved rolling leather balls toward purpose-made holes in a trolling bench. They were too engrossed in their competition to pay attention to anyone else. "Tell me first, what are your feelings for Nell Hawley?"

The blush deepened, but he answered in a steady voice. "I love her, Lady Appleton. Were I a rich man, I'd have married her. But, alas, she is lost to me now. She will soon wed another."

"She wants to marry you," Rosamond blurted. "She wants to make a clandestine marriage."

"But that is impossible. The pre-contract—"

"May be invalid," Susanna interrupted. "*May*. It is not certain, nor is it certain I will help you and the young woman even if I believe that to be so. There are good reasons for parents to arrange marriages. Those based on naught but passion are apt to end in tragedy."

"I want what is best for Nell," Giles Bannister bleated.

"Do you? Or are you just out for the main chance?"

"No, madam. If I'd been willing to run off with any young lady of wealth and position, I had my chances. I have been pursued in other positions by the unmarried women of the household. Nell is different."

Rosamond looked inclined to believe him, but Susanna had more experience of the world. "Master Bannister, I will take you into my confidence. Assist me well, and I will do all I can to help you and Nell. Lie to me and I will see you never find employment again."

He bridled at the threat. "I have no intention of lying, madam. Why should I?"

"That depends, I do think, on whether or not you know anything about Louise Poitier's death."

She could tell she'd surprised him. The last thing on his mind had been a woman he'd last seen more than a month ago. Encouraged, for he'd have had another sort of reaction if he'd killed her, Susanna bade Giles Bannister sit beside her on the window seat, while Rosamond settled on a cushion at their feet, and asked him to tell her all he could recall of the last time he'd seen the Frenchwoman alive.

"It was the night before we found her body." Giles answered willingly enough, though his expression was still one of puzzlement. "I did not speak to her. She was with Lady Bridget."

"How late at night?"

"Everyone else had gone to bed. I ate something that did not agree with me and had been in the garderobe. I was on my way back to my chamber when I caught sight of the two of them at the door of Lady Bridget's bedchamber. Madame Poitier was just leaving."

"She had helped her mistress prepare for bed, mayhap?"

Giles looked uncomfortable. "Mayhap. Lady Bridget wore only a night rail and her hair was down."

Frowning, Susanna tried to imagine the scene. Why had the lady of the manor gone to the door to bid her waiting gentlewoman good night? It would have been more normal for the waiting gentlewoman to tuck Lady Bridget in, mayhap even play the lute until she slept, then slip out unremarked to seek her own bed.

A glance at Rosamond, staring at Giles with an avid gaze, had Susanna hesitating over her next question. She had no doubt the girl already knew husbands and wives had sexual congress but she was reluctant to inquire if Sir Richard might have been on his way to visit Lady Bridget. She was even more hesitant to suggest that he might have intended to while away a few hours in Louise Poitier's bed.

"Did you notice where Madame Poitier went after she left Lady Bridget?" she asked instead.

He shook his head. "It is better not to know some things," he muttered.

"Ah."

His head snapped up, eyes narrowing, but he did not volunteer anything.

"Someone may have…helped Louise Poitier to her death that night," Susanna told him. "Can you think of anyone who would have wanted her dead?"

"No one." The reply was too prompt.

"No one? What about Sir Richard? Or Wymond Tallboys? I have heard both took an…interest in her."

"Not enough interest to murder her to keep the other from having her."

"They were not jealous of each other?"

"I doubt either knew she'd taken both into her bed."

"But you did. How?"

"All the servants knew, and what is a musician but an upper

servant? I heard the talk. I saw the looks. But it was all sport, not love. Not even affection. I am not certain Madame Poitier even liked men very much."

"Did she know how you felt about Nell?"

"She may have." Again he glanced at Rosamond. "It seems neither of us was very good at hiding our emotions."

"Now tell me about May Day," Susanna said, accepting that she'd learned all he knew about the night Louise died. "Where were you when the footrace began?"

"With Nell. She slipped away from her bower as soon as everyone's attention shifted to the runners. We only had a short time together, on the bowling green where we were hidden by the hedges, before the alarm was raised."

They must have entered the bowling green immediately following her own departure with Annabel, Susanna thought.

"Had you ever been in Poole's Cavern before you went there to help us search for Rosamond?"

He hesitated, but only for a moment before giving her an honest answer. "Nell and I went there several times to be alone together."

"And you were seen," Rosamond told him, "just after midnight on May Day morning."

Groaning, Giles buried his head in his hands. "I knew we should have been more careful. The pity of it is, we never stayed long. And we never gave in to our passions." He met Susanna's eyes as he said this. "I would not dishonor so sweet a lady. She will go pure to her husband."

Somewhat to her own surprise, Susanna decided she believed him. She did not point out that if he had deflowered his lady love, he might have had a better chance of winning her. He might then have argued that the two of them had a pre-contract dating from before the betrothal to Wymond Tallboys.

"Remain at New Hall," she instructed him. "Do not run off with Nell under any circumstances. I will write to the bishop. If

Nell *was* coerced into this betrothal, it can be set aside. That does not mean you two will be permitted to marry, but at least you can be sure she'll not be forced into a union she cannot abide."

Thanking her with guarded enthusiasm, Giles gave her the promises she'd asked for and Susanna and Rosamond left him strumming a doleful lament on his lute.

"Now what?" Rosamond demanded. "I was looking forward to helping Nell get away. She will not be pleased that she has to stay at the manor."

"You must convince her this is the wisest course. But before you return to Bawkenstanes Manor, I would like to go over my understanding of everyone's movements on the night of the murder—those of you and your friends, of Louise as much as we know, of Annabel, and anyone else we can account for."

The chronology they completed a short time later still had far too many gaps.

"Item one," Susanna read aloud. "Late afternoon. Thomas Greves departs with his servant, Henry Flower. Flower leaves behind a key, hidden, after being bribed by Louise to do so. Item two: Annabel MacReynolds arrives with an escort hired in Derby and uses the key to get into New Hall."

She frowned. How had Annabel known where the key would be? She made a note to ask next time she spoke to the Scotswoman.

"Item three: Rosamond, Dionysia, and Godlina enter the First Chief Bath through a fallen section of the brick wall surrounding it. At what hour of the clock?"

"I think it must have been ten," Rosamond said. "The household went to bed at nine and the watch candle in the hearth had burned down only a little before we left."

"You heard no one else stirring?"

Rosamond shook her head. Ailse butted her shoe and she scooped up the kitten, cuddling it against her cheek.

"In a more populous place, the hourly ringing of bells would have given you the time," Susanna murmured, "or the cry of the watch."

In the country, first cockcrow was accounted to be midnight and second cockcrow halfway to dawn, but a rooster was not the most reliable of clocks. Third cockcrow, like the sound of the lark singing, heralded the dawn, a signal that the day was about to begin.

"Item four," she continued. "Louise Poitier enters through the door Annabel left unlocked for her, hears you girls in the bath, and goes there first to confront you. When you've been sent on your way, she realizes Annabel has also heard you and come to investigate. They go to the chamber Annabel has appropriated."

Susanna made another note. She must ask Annabel to recount what they said to each other, in detail. There might be some clue there.

"Item five: Louise leaves first. Annabel stays in the chamber to remove all signs of occupancy but overlooks the fallen goblet, then exits through the same door, locking it behind her and returning the key to its hiding place. She walks away from Saint Anne's Well, toward the riverbank, where men and horses are concealed. She rides away without realizing that Louise never returned to Bawkenstanes Manor."

"The murderer must have been waiting for her when she came out of New Hall," Rosamond said.

"But how did he know Madame Poitier was there?" Or *she*, Susanna silently added. Another woman could have killed Louise.

"He followed her?" Rosamond suggested.

"Then why not go inside? And if he was lurking outside, he must have seen you girls leave. Why, then, did he think you were a threat to him and not the other two?"

Rosamond toyed with the lace on her sleeve. "Because I left alone, after the others. Only a few minutes later," she hastened to add, "but it is possible he saw me and not them."

A cold fist clenched around Susanna's heart at the thought that Rosamond might easily have become the killer's second victim on the same night Louise Poitier died.

ᢟ26ᢟ

Bakewell, Derbyshire

THE WYE turned roughly east at Buxton and flowed along a twisted route to emerge from a narrow valley with sheer bluffs just to the northwest of Bakewell. A buxom matron and her reed-thin daughter, both in Derbyshire to take the waters, shared with Jennet a wherry rowed by a burly boatman. He depended for his trade upon the many sick people forced by a shortage of comfortable accommodations in Buxton to lodge elsewhere. A daily trip of a dozen miles each way was accounted as nothing in these parts.

"Is your mistress acquainted with the family at Haddon Hall?" the matron asked as they neared their destination. "They are prominent landholders in the Bakewell area."

"Lady Appleton is great friends with the countess of Shrewsbury," Jennet replied, stretching the truth a bit. It did no harm, and doubtless improved her own credit by association with someone who knew the wealthiest and most powerful noblewoman in the shire.

Bakewell straddled the Wye and possessed a fine, many-arched bridge for those who wished to cross. Off to her right at a little distance, Jennet took note of an imposing church with an unusual octagonal tower. Had travel been easier on Palm Sunday, she supposed, the household at Bawkenstanes Manor would have made a pilgrimage there for services. Madame Poitier's body might have gone undiscovered for some considerable time, especially if the murderer had troubled to lock the gate behind him.

"Can you direct me to a cordwainer's shop?" Jennet asked the boatman when he'd set them ashore.

He obligingly described the premises of Plover the shoe-wright—a building with limestone walls dressed with gritstone and a roof of Derbyshire slate pegged with oak within hailing distance of the market cross—and Jennet had no difficulty finding the shop. She heard the sound of cheerful voices while still some distance away. Plover's apprentices were singing as they stitched.

"I wish to have comfortable boots made," Jennet told their master.

Since arriving in Buxton, Lady Appleton had insisted upon a healthful regimen that included daily hikes into the hills and frequent playing at bowls. "Nothing better," she'd informed Jennet, "than a good long walk to put the humours that control the body to rights."

Lady Appleton had got it into her head that they were both in need of exercise. "Do you recall Euphemia Denholm?" she'd asked.

"I am not likely to forget her," Jennet had replied.

"She was a formidable woman," Lady Appleton had agreed, "and very large. Seeing her that first time, I vowed never to let myself get so stout as that. But I have, Jennet. We all have. Annabel is fat. You are so round that you can no longer cross a room without having to stop and catch your breath. As for myself—well, the length of the points left over to knot when I cinch the waist of my kirtle or lace up an underbodice is far shorter than once it was!"

"Boots for yourself, goodwife?" the shoemaker asked, interrupting Jennet's thoughts. "Or a pair for another?"

"For myself and my mistress. I have brought a pair of her shoes for you to copy." The shoemaker in Buxton did inferior work, according to Margery Cottelling, or Jennet would have seen to this sooner. An excess of walking required both sturdy soles and a good fit. There was nothing more painful than sore feet.

Plover took the soft leather slippers Jennet offered him in one big hand, and rubbed his thumb over one blunt, rounded toe. "Spatterdashes might do ye better."

"Not for long treks over rough terrain. Spatterdashes are naught but thick hose worn instead of a boot. But the leather *should* be soft and fit well to the foot. I've no mind to suffer blisters on my heels or toes."

"Well, then, you'll want buff leather, which is soft and pliable even at very heavy thicknesses." He gave her an assessing glance, as if weighing what her purse would bear. "I've a bit of fine Cordovan if you've a mind to have the boots in red leather."

"Imported from Spain? I think not." She gave a sniff. Bad enough that blankets and swords that came from that place were accounted better than good English versions.

"We have goats at home," Plover said with a smile. "Goatskin produces red shoes."

"And black? Black seems more sensible for heavy wear."

"Aye, it is. Waxed calf. But not so flexible as you want. Tawed leather is the softest, made snow-white by soaking the raw skin in alum salts. But cream-colored leather will do. Buff, as I said."

"And how does that achieve its color?" Jennet asked.

"It is tanned with fish oils. You'll want hobnails if you're climbing. And a buckle, to keep the fit snug."

Jennet agreed his proposals were sound. "How quickly can they be made?"

"A pity you do not want Cordovan leather." A sly look came into the bootmaker's rheumy eyes. "What you describe will take a week at the least to complete."

Jennet shot him a suspicious glance. "Do you work more quickly with red than buff?"

He chuckled. "No, goodwife. But I have here a pair of boots ready-made that may fit you. They were ordered by a gentlewoman who has since died. I do not think she will be needing them."

"A gentlewoman who died?" Jennet's mind raced. Could it be? "What gentlewoman? When was she here?"

"French by her speech, and here just before the earthquake. A terrible thing that, shaking and rattling and knocking things from shelves. As you have, she brought a pair of shoes for me to measure. Well worn, they were, but fine workmanship. I'd never seen the like. The gentlewoman demanded decoration just as detailed on the boots she ordered. That is why they took so long to make."

He produced them with a flourish and seemed gratified by Jennet's reaction to his handiwork.

"When they were ready, they sat a month or more, waiting for her to return. It was only when I sent to Bawkenstanes Manor to remind her of her purchase that I learned she was dead."

"I want them." Jennet reached for her money pouch.

"But, goodwife, will you not try them on first? I have a good eye, but if they pinch your feet you will not be happy with them."

"I still want you to make boots for me and my mistress, in *buff* leather, but I will have these, too."

She could scarce wait to show them to Lady Appleton. The design on the boots Louise Poitier had ordered was an intricate intermingling of rose and thistle and lily—the emblems of Mary, queen of Scots.

May 8, 1575
Bawkenstanes Manor

SHIFTING uncomfortably in her wheeled chair in a solitary corner of the parlor, Eleanor Pendennis grimaced. The pain was bad today, and her temper was not improved by the regimen she'd been obliged to observe. She was heartily sick of drinking so much water and looked forward to her initial immersion in the First Chief Bath on the morrow.

"Fetch Lady Appleton to me, Melka," Eleanor ordered, and watched with growing irritation as the maidservant approached Susanna and was put off.

"She say later," Melka reported when she returned to Eleanor's side.

The Polishwoman had been with Eleanor for many years, since before the accident that crippled her. She spoke little English but understood what went on around her very well. She doubtless knew that, save for Lady Bridget, everyone seemed to wish to avoid her mistress.

Even Lady Bridget was preoccupied today. Throughout church services and dinner she'd hovered over Nell like a hen with one chick—almost as if she expected Nell to bolt the moment her back was turned.

Jugglers had been brought in to entertain and Eleanor allowed them to distract her, but she was aware of the absence of the soft background music to which everyone at Bawkenstanes Manor was accustomed. A pity there were no town waits to be hired, but there was nothing big enough to be called a town in this part of Derbyshire.

Eleanor's attention shifted to Will Hawley, who stood by his father's side at a nearby window, staring out at the rain. The downpour had put paid to Sir Richard's plans to take his son hunting.

Sir Richard alternated between scowling at the weather and shooting annoyed glances at various clusters of chattering women. The brooding sort, Eleanor decided. Difficult to know.

Her brow furrowed as she compared father and son. Susanna had the right of it. In twenty years, the lad would be much like his sire. Rosamond could do far worse, but might she not also do much better?

"This rain is a judgment from God," Wymond Tallboys said in a carrying voice as he accosted Sir Richard. Will saw his chance to escape and took it. Even before his betrothal to Nell, Diony's father, a near neighbor, had often shared Sunday dinner with his daughter and the Hawleys. They knew what to expect from him.

"An *act* of God, mayhap," Sir Richard replied in a testy voice. "Scarce a judgment."

"Hunting is no proper occupation for the Sabbath. Thus does the Lord make his displeasure at your intentions known."

Sir Richard grunted. "We do not see eye-to-eye on this matter and never will."

They were, however, nose-to-nose. Tallboys's height came close to matching Sir Richard's. Otherwise, they were a study in contrasts, the one all angles and bones, the other broad and muscular, but if Tallboys was daunted by his neighbor's greater strength, he did not show it. Once he began to expound on his religious beliefs, nothing short of a knock-down blow could stop him.

With every word he spoke, Tallboys betrayed his extreme views and became, in Eleanor's eyes, more of a hypocrite. Susanna had told her just how far from saintly he'd apparently been in his dealings with Louise Poitier. Doubtless everyone in this household knew she'd been his mistress.

To amuse herself, Eleanor tried to picture the two of them in bed together. With that hawk nose, long chin, and bony limbs, she imagined he'd be a bumbling lover and wondered if Louise had mocked his prowess. Would that have given him reason to kill her? Or mayhap she had threatened to expose him as a sinner. Had he killed her in a futile attempt to keep the fact he'd bedded her a secret? Or mayhap he had discovered she'd taken up with someone else and flown into a jealous rage.

Eleanor listened for a moment more to Tallboys's diatribe and reconsidered. Murder was an even greater sin than fornication. If Tallboys had wanted Louise punished for wantonness, he'd have condemned her in public, even if complaining to the churchwardens had meant that they'd both be hauled before the church courts.

Eleanor's gaze shifted to Sir Richard. If rumor was to be

believed, he'd also been Louise's lover. It seemed unlikely that the upright Master Tallboys would agree to marry the man's daughter if he knew that. Or leave his own daughter in the keeping of the master of Bawkenstanes Manor.

What of Sir Richard, then? Had he known Louise had been in Tallboys's bed and still betrothed his only daughter to the man? Men did stranger things, Eleanor supposed. Had he also killed their shared mistress? Or mayhap they had killed her together! Eleanor shook her head to clear it. She grew fanciful. She had no reason to think either man had wanted Louise dead.

Annabel still seemed a more likely suspect to Eleanor, the more so because she was nowhere in sight. Nor could Eleanor smell her. That musky perfume the Scotswoman wore tended to precede her into a room. In hindsight, Eleanor realized that the scent alone should have made her suspicious of "Jacquinetta Devereux," for it was as distinctive to Annabel as marjoram was to Eleanor herself.

Susanna, with whom Annabel had been talking earlier, had at last begun to make her way across the parlor to Eleanor, but she was waylaid by Margery Cottelling. No doubt she wanted to ask advice on herbal remedies. She'd ramble on for hours if Susanna let her.

A muffled cry drew Eleanor's attention to Lina Walkenden. The girl's face was crimson and she'd apparently pricked her finger with her needle. Sucking on the wound, she aimed a hostile glare at Susanna's Jennet. Eleanor was surprised at the display of emotion. Lina had always seemed a lump of a girl, keeping her thoughts to herself and following wherever others led. As for Jennet, she seemed extraordinarily interested in Lina's embroidery.

Eleanor was contemplating sending Melka to eavesdrop on their conversation when a messenger in the distinctive blue livery of the earl of Shrewsbury entered the room. His appearance captured everyone's attention. Of them all, only Susanna did not seem unduly surprised.

"Lady Appleton?" he inquired. At her acknowledgment, he presented her with a letter. "From the countess of Shrewsbury," he announced.

With apologies to the company, she broke the seal and read the contents. Puzzlement, resignation, and then an emotion Eleanor could not decipher flickered across her face in quick succession. Then she turned to have a quiet word with Lady Bridget.

Eleanor wondered if she knew how little Lady Bridget liked the countess, who had been born an impoverished Derbyshire gentlewoman but married her way into the nobility. Lady Bridget's choice of a husband had taken her in the opposite direction and she did most bitterly resent it.

"It took you long enough to respond to my summons," Eleanor complained when Susanna finally approached her chair.

"I am not responding now. The message I just received concerns Rosamond. The countess of Shrewsbury wants to meet her. She wants me to bring her to Chatsworth for a short visit."

"What is her interest in my daughter?"

"She knew Robert years ago. She is curious about *his* daughter."

"And *you* are to bring her?" She should be the one taking Rosamond to Chatsworth, not Susanna Appleton.

Susanna's expression was rueful and faintly apologetic, which did nothing to lessen Eleanor's resentment. "She has sent an escort. We leave at first light."

Eleanor wanted to object, to insist on going with them, but travel was never easy for her and she feared to alienate the countess by coming along uninvited. Neither could she refuse to let Rosamond go. This was a great opportunity for her daughter. The countess was one of the wealthiest women in England...and she had unmarried sons.

❦28❦

May 9, 1575
en route to Chatsworth

ROSAMOND was delighted to be on horseback again. One of the disadvantages to life at Bawkenstanes Manor was that she could not ride out on her own over the moors, as she'd been allowed to in Cornwall. She'd brought her own horse with her to Derbyshire, a roan gelding she'd named Courtier, but for the most part the stableboys took care of exercising and grooming him.

The kittens rode in a wicker basket strapped behind Rosamond's saddle. Mama had tried to discourage her from bringing them, but Rosamond had pointed out that they were likely to be less trouble than Giles Bannister, and Mama had insisted *he* come with them to Chatsworth.

Giles Bannister was moping. There was no other word for it. He cast soulful looks over his shoulder as Buxton vanished from sight behind them and sighed a great deal. Rosamond's eyes narrowed as she studied him. He fit a little too well the role of lovelorn hero and Rosamond did not believe it was possible for someone to pine away for lost love. Who was he trying to impress with his performance? Mama? She shook her head, a smug smile on her lips. If that was his plan, it was wasted effort. Mama was even harder to fool than Rosamond. She watched with interest, however, when Jennet dropped back to speak with the musician.

"Lady Appleton wishes you to ride beside her for a time," Jennet said. "She has something to say to you."

He spurred his horse forward and Rosamond expected Jennet to follow, rejoining her mistress at the head of the cavalcade. Instead Jennet reined in until Rosamond reached her side. She rode astride, as did Rosamond. Mama preferred her sidesaddle, the one Rosamond's father had brought her, years ago, from France.

"A word with you, Mistress Rosamond."

"As you wish."

Jennet gave her a baleful stare. "Leave off that haughty manner with me, mistress. I'd not speak to you at all if it were not necessary."

"You are blunt."

"I am honest. More so than you've been, my girl."

"I keep no secrets from Mama."

Jennet's derisive sniff reminded her that they both knew she'd attempted to hide quite a few things. "Your secrets concern me less at present than those of one of your friends: Godlina Walkenden. She stitches a design that is most distinctive—an emblem of a rose, a lily, and a thistle entwined."

Puzzled, Rosamond nodded. "What troubles you about that? It is a pretty pattern, nothing more."

"No? I am told those symbols signify England, France, and Scotland, the three kingdoms in which Mary of Scotland claims she can call herself queen."

Courtier shied at the sudden tightening of Rosamond's fingers on his reins. She stroked his neck with an absent gesture, trailing her fingers over his warm, firm hide, but she kept her eyes on Jennet. "I do not believe Lina is involved in treason. 'Tis certain she had naught to do with Madame Poitier's death. Not only was she in my company that night, but I can swear to you that her feelings for the woman were never less than adulation. She admired Madame Poitier excessively."

For a moment something Rosamond had difficulty recognizing flickered across Jennet's face. Alarm? No—stronger. Not quite horror, but she'd clearly been affected by some disturbing thought.

Jennet cleared her throat. "Madame Poitier was familiar with the symbols. She ordered similar decorations put on a pair of boots she commissioned from a Bakewell cordwainer."

"He came to Bawkenstanes Manor," Rosamond murmured.

She'd been in the Great Hall when he arrived, else she'd never have known of it. "Annabel turned him away. She never asked if anyone else knew aught of the matter, just told him her good-sister was dead and would not require the boots after all. I thought at the time that she wished to avoid having to pay him for them."

"He had already been paid," Jennet said. "I asked."

"Do you think the emblems mean the boots were intended for the queen of Scots?" That went well with Rosamond's theory—rescue of the queen, hiding her in Poole's Cavern—but Rosamond did not want to be right if it meant condemning her friend.

"I do and so does Lady Appleton."

"But how would Madame Poitier get the queen's boot size?"

"She brought an old pair of boots to measure."

"How did she get them?"

"Someone must have brought them to her. Another conspirator. What difference does that make?" asked Jennet.

"The boots may have been meant as a gift for someone else, someone at Bawkenstanes Manor."

"Who?"

"Lady Bridget? No—Lina. I told you how Lina felt about Madame Poitier and Madame indulged her. Indeed, she gave her several little gifts. Why not the boots, especially if she knew Lina favored those designs?" Even to Rosamond herself, this rationale sounded weak. She urged Courtier to a faster pace, hoping Jennet would fall behind. She lacked Rosamond's experience as a horse-woman.

"The emblems meant something specific," Jennet insisted. "A signal of some sort. A message. Spies use such things. And traitors."

"They mean the person who uses them likes to embroider flowers. The rose is just a rose, the lily just a lily, and the thistle just a thistle. And Lina is no traitor!"

"Then she was Madame Poitier's pawn, tricked into displaying the emblems for some hidden purpose when Madame Poitier herself dared not."

"Lina was no one's pawn, either!" Rosamond deliberately rode away from Jennet this time. If she remained longer by her side, she would lose her temper, and Mama would be disappointed in her.

But as they journeyed onward, Rosamond could not help but wonder why Lina had been so fascinated with Madame Poitier. The only reason she'd ever heard her friend express seemed passing foolish—Lina had said that Madame Poitier's unusual violet-colored eyes were the exact same shade as her mother's.

✹29✹

THE JOURNEY from Buxton to Chatsworth with a party that included women and pack animals took the best part of a day to accomplish. They followed the course of the River Wye for a dozen or so miles to reach the market town of Bakewell and from there rode another five miles over hilly, mostly wooded land that included two moderately steep ascents and some spots that were muddy with the previous day's rain.

Approaching from the southwest in order to cross the most convenient bridge over the Derwent, Susanna had a spectacular view of the countess of Shrewsbury's house. It had been constructed entirely of brick—most unusual for these parts, where stone was so plentiful. Four towers rose above the roof level on the west front. Against the backdrop of green hillside and high moorland plateau, Chatsworth glowed like a jewel in the late afternoon sun.

"You are looking at the back of the house," said Lady Shrewsbury's messenger, a groom named Owen. "We must circle round to enter."

That, too, was unusual, but only to be expected, Susanna supposed, of a house built to suit such a unique individual as the woman who was known throughout Derbyshire and beyond as Bess of Hardwick. As they rode closer, Susanna saw that the estate's gardens and park lay wholly east of the house, and that the entrance resembled the gatehouse of a castle. They rode through into a courtyard containing an elaborate fountain.

The countess of Shrewsbury came out to greet them. It had been many years since Susanna had last seen her, but Bess had changed very little in appearance. Although she was nearly fifty years old, her hair was still as unabashedly and naturally red as the queen's, and although she was only of medium height and average build, her confident air and determined demeanor had always made her appear a little larger than life.

Susanna had been similarly impressed with Bess's energy and sense of purpose the first time they'd met. Susanna had been a new bride and Bess, then Lady Cavendish, a settled London matron with a little girl and two small sons. When Sir William Cavendish died a few years later, he had left his widow with six children and several older stepchildren. Deeply in debt, Bess had found a well-to-do knight to marry. After his death she'd been wealthy in her own right, but she'd chosen to wed again, nearly eight years ago now, this time choosing George Talbot, earl of Shrewsbury, one of the richest men in England.

Bess no longer wanted for anything and dressed the part, resplendent in a gown fit for a queen. A strand of perfectly matched pearls hung to her waist and precious gems glinted on her fingers. At her side was a girl of no more than seven or eight, dressed in similar fashion save for the color of her garments. While Bess preferred black, the child's bodice and kirtle were bright yellow, her sleeves and forepart striped orange-tawny and green.

In their travel-stained clothes, Susanna and Rosamond looked like vagabonds in comparison. Susanna was unsure whether Bess had meant to honor them with all her finery or use it to make clear the difference in rank between them.

"This is my granddaughter, Bessie Pierrepont," she said when Susanna and Rosamond had dismounted. "Frances's girl."

Susanna remembered Bess's eldest daughter from a time when she was younger than this little lass was now. "And this is Rosamond, Robert's child and my heir."

Bessie made a creditable curtsey to Susanna and smiled shyly at Rosamond. In short order, Bess had sent the two girls off together, the younger chattering cheerfully while Rosamond, carrying the basket that contained her two kittens, struggled to be polite. She could not quite conceal her dismay at being paired with someone so much her junior.

Bess's welcoming smile faded the moment the girls were out of sight. "The earl, my husband, has troubles enough without having to deal with petty complaints from Buxton. He received your letter and instructed me to handle the matter. Walk with me while we discuss what is best to do."

Murder, petty? Susanna swallowed a rude retort. She needed Bess's good will.

"My lord is short-tempered and testy of late," Bess complained as they entered the east wing of the house. "He frets about the cost of keeping the queen of Scots in custody even though her household is now reduced from thirty to sixteen."

"So small a number?"

"There are more, certes, unofficially. Even the servants have servants, and some of them have spouses as well. My lord has been most generous in letting them stay. But when his gout troubles him, he becomes irascible. This week, his right wrist aches, making it difficult for him to write. As a result, he shows exceeding choler on slight occasion—upon hearing the cost of new bed linen, for example."

Susanna tried to look sympathetic.

"I ease his burden where I may, but at present I am forbidden to stay in the same house as the queen of Scots, a consequence of my role in uniting my daughter Elizabeth and the young earl of Lennox."

Susanna refrained from comment. Bess had come perilous close to treason. Not only did Lennox have the royal blood of both England and Scotland in his veins, but his older brother, Lord Darnley, had been married to Mary, queen of Scots and had fathered the boy who now sat on Scotland's throne. The Lennox marriage should never have gone forward without first securing Queen Elizabeth's permission.

"This is the suite of rooms Queen Mary used during her last stay at Chatsworth," Bess announced. "Withdrawing chamber, bedchamber, and servant's chamber."

What Susanna presumed was the queen's bed boasted a canopy of velvet and cloth-of-gold with sarcenet curtains. The bedchamber's floors were polished wood protected by mats, and the walls had been wainscoted with colored woods and decorated with marquetry work. Two wide, high-backed chairs flanked a fireplace. Bess waved Susanna into one of them and seated herself in the other.

"The earl cannot leave Sheffield at present and since I am here at Chatsworth, hard by Buxton, he delegated me to calm your fears."

Susanna arched a brow at her. "I do not need my hand held, Bess. I wrote to the earl because I believe there has been murder done."

"The woman died by accident. The crowner's report said so."

"Did she? When she appears to have been plotting to free your royal prisoner?"

Bess waved a dismissive hand. "We have dealt with plots and schemes ere now. They came to nothing and will continue to do so."

"How can you be certain? Does Queen Elizabeth keep you informed of everything her intelligence gatherers unearth?"

"Neither the queen nor her most trusted advisor, Lord Burghley, have been forthcoming, but I pay a man in London to send me news of the city and my lord's son, Gilbert, writes from court, as do other friends."

"You cannot deny there have been plots."

"Let me tell you how little hope of success there is for any scheme to spirit away the Scots queen. In May five years ago, she came here to Chatsworth and was lodged in these very rooms until December of that year. Sir Thomas Gerard, a local Catholic squire, and two brothers, Francis and George Rolleston, together with John Hall and others, conceived a plot to rescue Queen Mary. Hall, one of the Rollestons, and John Beaton, who was then her master of the household, met at dawn on the high moor above Chatsworth. Beaton, who was a sensible man, told the conspirators that he would have to consult his queen, but that in general she discouraged all such proposals."

"Had they a specific plan to get Mary away from here?"

"They had an abundance of them," Bess said with a soft chuckle. "One proposal was to take her out a window at night, but both Mary and her servants are locked in their rooms to sleep. A second scheme called for carrying her off as she took the air on the moors and whisking her away by boat to the Isle of Man." She shook her head at the foolishness of that notion. "For more than a year the conspirators exchanged messages in cipher, but eventually one of their own betrayed them. George Rolleston saw the error of his ways."

"A better organized group might have succeeded," Susanna said. "You cannot predict the future."

"No, but I can assure you that the queen of Scots has no true desire to escape. If the matter miscarried, 'twould do her little good and much harm. She wanted no part in the rising of the northern earls, nor in Gerard's scheme, and she is not likely to countenance any other."

"Yet she corresponds in coded messages with potential conspirators."

"She gives them no encouragement. She believes that the Queen's Majesty, Elizabeth, at the request of the kings of Spain and France, will in time restore her to her former dignity. She will await that day rather than work her own delivery by uncertain means."

Susanna refrained from reminding Bess that by merely existing, the queen of Scots encouraged rebellion among English Catholics. "Will the queen of Scots come here again?"

"No doubt of it, and the queen of England, too, though not, I think, at the same time. We finished the first stage of building state apartments two years ago."

Rising, she led Susanna into another wing of the house. "Nothing is complete, nor will be for some time. There must be many more improvements before these rooms are suitable to entertain that most noble of guests, the Queen's Majesty. I have in mind blackstone for overmantels and hope to employ Thomas Accres, the master marble mason, to direct the work. I have already secured the services of Thomas Lane, the embroiderer, to provide hangings."

"This seems a remote place to build such a grand house."

"I have many visitors nonetheless. They stop en route to Buxton, and come because of the queen of Scots. Why, I expect to entertain our mutual friend the earl of Leicester ere long. It is my hope that he will find Chatsworth pleasing and persuade Queen Elizabeth to stop here on one of her progresses."

Former friend, Susanna silently corrected her. The last time she had come face to face with Lord Robin, he'd accused her of murdering her husband. Aloud she said, "I have kept to myself since Robert's death, and although the queen once threatened a visit to Leigh Abbey on progress, in the end she chose to go elsewhere." Susanna did not move in exalted circles, and unlike Bess, was content to remain a simple gentlewoman.

"Leicester has quite lost his looks," Bess informed her. "His features are much distorted with the puffiness of middle age. One might even be unkind enough to say he has grown fat, and like my own lord, he suffers much with gout and sometimes requires to be carried in a litter from place to place rather than ride."

Susanna suppressed a sigh. "We all seem to thicken with age, Bess. Save yourself. You appear remarkable fit."

"I keep too busy to gain weight." She permitted herself a smug smile and gestured toward yet another section of the house, this one in the midst of renovation.

"Carpentry? Masonry?"

Susanna's suggestions provoked a chuckle from her hostess. "I vow I am as active as any workman. I must supervise the construction, else accidents occur. And thefts. And mistakes." She led Susanna along passages and through rooms, circling the inner courtyard. "One careless workman fell from a scaffolding and broke his neck. This is the Great Low Chamber."

It was an enormous room. Instead of paneling, the walls were decorated with a set of tapestries, two on each side and one straight ahead. Bessie and Rosamond stood in front of the latter, staring up at the nearly life-sized figure in applied-work embroidery. Susanna blinked and bit back a gasp. Bess hissed and would have shouted had Susanna not caught her arm and squeezed hard.

"Do not raise your voice. You will frighten the kitten."

"I will kill the little beast if it harms that wall hanging!"

Unaware that she risked summary execution if she damaged the tapestry, Dowsabella continued to climb, needle-sharp claws digging into the exquisite, expensive cloth-of-gold.

Rosamond lifted a stricken face to Susanna, eyes pleading. She gripped the other kitten tightly to her bosom, as if afraid Ailse would follow her sister. Likely she would, Susanna thought. Moving slowly, she approached the tapestry. The name CLEOPATRA had been stitched in large letters between the figure's head and the arcade above it. If she represented that ancient queen, Susanna thought, the Egyptians had been remarkable modern in their dress. The kirtle and gown were not the latest in fashion, but clearly belonged to the present century.

"Dowsabella," Susanna called in a soft voice.

The kitten turned her head.

"Come to me, little one."

Dowsabella climbed higher, but she was young yet, and clumsy. A few more inches, and she failed to catch proper hold of the fabric. As she felt herself begin to slip, she executed a midair turn and launched herself straight into Susanna's outstretched arms.

"Open the basket," Susanna said, and wrinkled her nose when Rosamond complied. The poor creatures had been confined in there all day long, but for the present it was the safest place for them to be.

Features contorted, face purple, Bess struggled to contain her temper. Uneasily, Susanna watched and waited, for she remembered hearing that Bess could "scold like one from the Bank"—a Southwark doxy—when her anger was aroused.

Bessie Pierrepont's clear, childish voice cut through the charged atmosphere. "It was my fault, Grandmother. I made Rosamond free the kittens."

"That was very wicked of you, Bessie." There was less anger in her voice when Bess spoke to her granddaughter.

"I know." Bessie hung her head, but she watched Bess through her eyelashes.

"They are magnificent tapestries," Susanna said. "Five famous women of the ancient world, are they not?"

Bess inspected the one Dowsabella had been climbing. As there was no damage, she apparently decided to ignore the entire unfortunate incident. She nodded in answer to Susanna's question. "Lane's work, at my direction. All these women were powerful individuals notable for their constancy and devotion to those they loved. Each is flanked by two personifications of her particular virtues. Do you know their stories, Mistress Rosamond?" Bess pointed to Cleopatra. "She was a great queen in her own right."

She indicated the next panel. "This is Artemisia, attended by constancy and charity. She was the wife of a king in Asia Minor, and on his death dissolved his ashes in liquid, which she then drank to provide him with a living tomb."

Susanna looked more closely at the hanging. Artemisia held a goblet aloft.

"Here is Zenobia," Bess continued, her relief at stopping the kitten before it did any harm leading her to be unusually voluble. "The clothes and architectural setting were cut from fabrics salvaged from ecclesiastical vestments."

The tapesty pictured Zenobia wearing a crown, a ruff, and a breastplate, with one hand on a helmet and the other holding a lance—a warrior queen.

On the facing wall were two more tapestries, each one nine feet or more in height and a good twelve paces long. The first featured Penelope, wife of Ulysses, who had refused to give him up for dead and remarry. She shared the wall with Lucretia, the wife of a Roman nobleman who, after being raped by Tarquinius Superbus, killed herself rather than bring shame to her family. Foolish woman, Susanna thought. Lucretia was shown holding a sprig of myrtle and walking beside a unicorn.

Talking of her treasures had improved Bess's mood. It was further enhanced by Susanna's announcement that the musician she'd brought with her wished to join the household at Chatsworth.

"Has he talent?" Bess asked.

"Considerable. And as you will see for yourself, a pleasant demeanor."

"He can also teach you to dance," Rosamond whispered to Bessie.

From the Great Low Chamber they passed into another section under construction. Bess indicated a section of scaffolding. "In the accident I mentioned, the workman fell from there. If he had been in church as he should have been, he'd still be alive, but he preferred to pay his shilling fine for every absence and no one made a fuss."

Suddenly uneasy, Susanna peered up at the site of the accident in the fading light. If he'd refused to go to church, that meant he'd probably been a recusant—an English Catholic forbidden by his church to attend "heretic" services. "Which Sunday was that?"

"Palm Sunday."

"The same morning Louise Poitier was found dead in Buxton."

Bess scoffed at the implication that there could be any connection. "He was naught but a day laborer. I do not even recall his name."

Someone would know, Susanna thought. There must be a record of his death and burial. She would ask Bess's chaplain at her first opportunity.

She would also find a way to visit another of the earl of Shrewsbury's houses before she returned to Buxton, one that, like Chatsworth and New Hall, had served as a prison for the queen of Scots. Of a sudden, she felt a pressing need to discover why Annabel had gone from Buxton to South Wingfield.

❧30❧

May 10, 1575
Buxton

ELEANOR'S lower limbs floated, pale and emaciated, in harebell blue water. She had little hope they'd ever be restored to their former strength, but the First Chief Bath did have soothing properties, and the doctor Walter had consulted insisted the regimen would benefit Eleanor's overall health as well as her ability to conceive.

Beside her on the stone bench sat Lady Bridget, whose only

excuse for making use of the mineral springs was her desire to retain a youthful appearance, though she did also seem to enjoy watching other bathers.

There were only a few, for the season did not begin in earnest until late June. Fires had been lit in the hearths to ward off the chill in the air.

Walter had been right about one thing, Eleanor thought as she ran lazy fingers through the effervescent water. There were temptations here. She could not be lured again into treason, but when a young man of perhaps twenty entered the open-air chamber and unselfconsciously stripped off all his clothing, she had no objection to enjoying the view. Neither, she noted, did Melka. Her Polish-born servant even volunteered to take his garments and hang them up to air while he bathed.

There was no segregation of the sexes in the baths at Buxton, in spite of vicars with puritan leanings railing against the practice of mixed nude bathing in their sermons. The beautiful young man nodded at those already in the water as he passed and entered the pool only a few yards from where Eleanor and Lady Bridget sat.

"Elegant limbs," Lady Bridget commented, "but methinks he has too high an opinion of his own...prowess."

Eleanor had to fight the urge to cover herself when the young man, overhearing, responded not with chagrin or embarrassment but with a bold stare. Lady Bridget returned his presumptuous visual assessment with an insolent survey of her own. He blinked first and moved farther away from them.

Two women seated on the opposite side of the pool drew Lady Bridget's attention next. Mother and daughter from Gloucestershire, or so Eleanor had heard. Unaware of how well their voices carried, they were engaged in a quarrel over the best way to achieve full benefit from the healing waters.

"Tarry two or three hours, then go to bed with two bladders of water applied hot. That is what Doctor Jones recommends," the mother insisted.

"He says to use the bladders each morning and evening after exercise and purging but before meat," the daughter countered. "That means we must get up again to sup."

"But what of Doctor Turner's advice? He says, 'Beware of surfeiting in any wise.'"

"He also warns against anger, and against too much study," Eleanor murmured. "Save for studying his writings, I suppose." Doctor William Turner had written a book of guidelines for using the baths.

Lady Bridget chuckled. "I prefer to study other bathers."

Her admiring gaze rested on a young woman who had entered the chamber while they were talking. She stood some twenty feet away from them at the western end of the pool, contemplating the reservoir from which all the baths received their principal supply of water. She seemed fascinated by the stream flowing from the rock through a fissure more than a foot wide. What was not caught in the large gritstone basin there was conveyed through lead pipes to cisterns under the floors.

"Come in," Lady Bridget called to her. "The water is fine."

"It is not too hot?"

"Imagine that a quart of boiling water has had five quarts of running water added to it. And there is no need to be shy. Drop your towel." It was as much command as invitation.

After a moment the woman obeyed, to the delight of the young man. She was beautifully formed and in no need of healing waters that Eleanor could see. Neither had he appeared to be, now that she thought of it. For the first time it occurred to her to wonder if some bathers came to display wares for sale. Certes, the sort of bathhouses that had once flourished in London had been naught but brothels, but Buxton was supposed to be a respectable place. She had found it so last summer.

"Come and tell us all about yourself," Lady Bridget invited, apparently beset by no such suspicions, and in short order the young woman did.

She had walked from Brassington, she told them, some fifteen miles distant, to see if the waters could cure her of her barrenness. "I have a new husband most anxious for sons," she explained.

"You are young and whole," Eleanor said with some bitterness. "You will have them in due course."

"Not everyone can conceive," Lady Bridget pointed out. "The gentlewoman from Kent never had children of her own. That is, I warrant, why she is so attached to your daughter."

She does not like Susanna. The conviction was so strong that for a moment Eleanor felt chilled. A second realization followed almost at once: *Lady Bridget is not a woman I'd want for an enemy.*

"My son and my guest's daughter may make a match of it one day," Lady Bridget explained to the newcomer. "My daughter is already betrothed to a neighbor."

"Have you other children?" The countrywoman's shyness dissipated quickly, though Eleanor imagined that once she realized she was sitting next to the lady of the manor she would be abashed at her own boldness.

Lady Bridget made a face. "Would you have me spend *all* my time in my husband's bed?"

"Is congress with a man always so distasteful, then?"

Eleanor started to correct the young woman's mistaken assumption—she enjoyed that part of a wife's duties a good deal—but Lady Bridget spoke first. Aghast, Eleanor listened as the two of them traded unpleasant marital experiences. To hear Lady Bridget tell it, conceiving her children had been a great burden to her and she'd just as soon never repeat the process.

"Encourage your husband to use other women to slake his lust," she advised, "and he will not trouble you so often, but not, certes, until after you've borne him one or two sons."

Whether the countrywoman was more flustered by Lady Bridget's frankness or by the brilliant smile which accompanied it, Eleanor could not tell. Now that the subject had been opened, however, she fell obliged to pursue it. Mayhap one of the mysteries about Louise Poitier might yet be solved.

"Did you encourage him to take the Frenchwoman into his bed?" she asked.

"What Frenchwoman?" Lady Bridget gave a bark of laughter. "Not Jacquinetta Devereux? She's much too old and fat to suit his tastes."

"The other one," Eleanor clarified. "Louise."

For a moment Lady Bridget's features hardened. Then she forced another smile. "Ah. The French mistress. She led him a merry chase, I warrant."

Puzzled, Eleanor struggled to frame a question that would elicit more specific information. How did intelligence gatherers manage it without giving themselves away? It seemed intrusive to keep asking bold questions, even in the relaxed atmosphere of the bath.

The countrywoman had no such difficulty. Having recovered from her brief bout of shyness, she now plied her new acquaintances with questions about the people who came to Buxton and the grand lodgings that adjoined the baths.

"Have they music there, and dancing?" she asked in all innocence. "I have heard that is how great households pass the evenings."

"I hear New Hall has acquired a handsome young musician," Eleanor murmured.

Lady Bridget rose abruptly from the underwater bench. "A fellow with little talent and less restraint. I have had enough of the baths."

She signalled for her tiring maid, Faith, who had been waiting with the airing clothes, to bring a towel. Until the maidservant reached her side, Lady Bridget stood beside the bath, dripping and naked, and used the opportunity to bestow a long, assessing look on her new acquaintance.

"You waste your time here, countrywoman," she said, when

Faith arrived and began to pat her dry. "Dress and come back to Bawkenstanes Manor with me. We will discuss how you may best serve your husband and yourself."

Eleanor made no attempt to join them. The opinions they'd shared with such candor had left her feeling uncomfortable in their company. Moreover, she liked the sensation of warm water lapping against her skin. It would be no hardship to remain in the pool the full three hours her physican had recommended. The treatment might not make her fertile or mend her mangled limbs, but it would give her time to think.

✄31✄

May 11, 1575
en route to SouthWingfield Manor

IN SPITE of the difference in their ages, Rosamond and Bess of Hardwick's Bessie had found a number of interests in common by the time Lady Appleton's party left Chatsworth for South Wing-field. They bade each other fond farewells, embracing and even, on Bessie's part, shedding a few tears. Jennet, watching, shook her head at the display. That Rosamond should inspire such devotion from other children, even on short acquaintance, baffled her.

It was to Rosamond that they owed their splendid escort. The girl's knowledge of architecture and building, acquired from Sir Walter Pendennis as he completed construction of Priory House in Cornwall, had impressed the countess of Shrewsbury. When Lady Appleton suggested that Rosamond might like to see the older manor, for comparison's sake, the countess had obliged by making all the arrangements. She'd also insisted upon sending her man Owen with them.

"What is it you hope to find here?" Jennet asked Lady Appleton several hours later. Their destination was just ahead, perched on a wooded hill. It was a large house, built of stone with some timber work and a slate roof.

"Confirmation of Annabel's story," Lady Appleton replied.

"You think she went elsewhere that night? North, toward Scotland?"

"Oh, I believe she went to South Wingfield. But I need to know what she did there. I do not care for coincidences. Two deaths at two places having connections to the queen of Scots within two days seem suspicious, even if they *were* both ruled accidental."

All manner of possibilities streamed through Jennet's mind. She had never trusted that Annabel. No doubt she *was* part of some treasonous plot.

They entered the manor house by an arched gate at the south end of the east range of buildings. "That gatehouse does not look particularly well adapted to defense," Jennet observed.

"That is doubtless why the queen of Scots was hastily removed to a more defensible stronghold at the time of the Rising in the North," Lady Appleton said, and guided her horse through into an outer courtyard a good half acre in size. To the left of the entrance was an enormous barn that formed a third of its south side. On the others were quarters for guards and servants, stables, and other outbuildings.

As soon as she got her mistress and Rosamond settled, Jennet set out for the kitchens, using as her excuse a need for finely chopped meat to feed Rosamond's kittens. It did not take her long to become friendly with a few of the countess's servants and within the hour she had something to report to Lady Appleton.

"Wingfield belonged to the earl of Shrewsbury but his wife has a life interest through their marriage settlement. She did very well for herself," Jennet added, "since there are ironworks, smithies, and glassworks attached to the property."

"Bess always did have a keen eye for profit, but you've uncovered information more important than that. There's a glint in your eyes, Jennet. What else have you learned?"

"That a groom died, kicked in the head by a horse, between Palm Sunday, when the Frenchwoman's body was discovered, and Maundy Thursday, when Annabel took up residence at Bawken-stanes Manor. I have been thinking, madam, that Annabel might have been responsible for all three deaths. She could have killed Madame Poitier, then gone to Chatsworth and pushed that workman to his death, and then come here to dispatch the groom."

"Why kill all three?"

"They knew something about her. Mayhap they threatened to disrupt her plans to free the queen of Scots." It made perfect sense to Jennet. Annabel had lied about her good-sister. She had been an intelligence gatherer in the past. Likely Annabel had been the real conspirator all along.

But Lady Appleton did not look convinced. "*Was* Annabel here?"

"Oh, yes, madam. I am certain of that. The cook remarked upon the fact that the groom had his accident when there were extra horses to care for because there were guests at the inn. A woman with no maid, only two burly henchmen for escort. That caused a stir in the village. So did her appearance. She was a large woman, they say, with hair more red than Bess of Hardwick's."

🕸32🕸

May 12, 1575
Buxton

THE ASCENSION of our Lord Jesus Christ, although a Thursday, was an approved holy day and as such the banns could be called in church after services. A pity, Annabel thought, observing

Nell's bleak expression. If it had not been, the wedding might be delayed another week, and that would mean a further delay, since Trinity Sunday was one of the days on which marriages were prohibited without a special license.

Annabel glanced at Sir Richard. Why was he in such a rush to marry off his only daughter? Giles Bannister had been removed. Nell was not with child. And Wymond Tallboys did not appear to be in any hurry to claim his bride. Indeed, he displayed a singular lack of interest in her.

Mayhap *he* was having second thoughts about the alliance.

Annabel watched him as he conversed with Diony in the churchyard. Had he been talked into the betrothal? To hear Louise tell it, he'd been besotted with her. Had he still been recovering from the shock of her death at the time Sir Richard broached the subject of marriage to Nell? Had he been pressured into agreeing in a weak moment?

A little later in the day she sought out Diony and asked her.

"He meant to wait a few more years," the girl admitted. "Instead they will be wed in ten days' time."

"It seems odd he'd make an alliance with Nell. More often a second marriage is a love match."

Diony's thin shoulders went stiff. "He loved my mother."

"I am sure he did, *ma petite.*"

Annoyed, Diony stalked off in a huff. Shortly thereafter, Tallboys appeared at Annabel's elbow. For a moment she thought he might take her to task for her blunt comments to his daughter, but he seemed to know nothing of that conversation.

"Mistress Devereux," he said in his mild, uninflected voice, "if you have a moment I would like to talk to you about Madame Poitier."

"It will sadden me to speak of her, sir, but I strive to please."

"Good. Good. A walk in the gardens?"

A few minutes later they were private among the knots and bowers. He led her to a bench concealed from the house by topiary and sat with his hands clasped between his bony knees, his head bowed.

"We strolled here often, she and I. I fear she did not like me much at first. Said I was pompous and stuffy. Or, rather abused me with the French words to that effect." He gave a rueful chuckle. "Mayhap she was correct in her assessment."

Annabel wisely held her tongue.

"We'd never have suited, certes, but that did not seem to matter."

"Louise was...unique," Annabel allowed.

"If I were as much a dutchman as she implied, I'd have had her brought before the courts on charges of witchcraft, for indeed she did cast a spell over me." The words were ominious but there was no heat behind them. Tallboys seemed more defeated than angry. "She came close to enticing me into giving her everything she wanted. Had she but lived a little longer..." He looked toward heaven, as if asking for strength. "God help me, but in one way it is as well she is dead."

Blood turned to ice in Annabel's veins as she struggled to maintain a surface calm. *Could* Wymond Tallboys have killed Louise, murdered her because he discovered she'd been using him to advance her plan to free the queen of Scots? Of a sudden she remembered what Susanna had told her of Sir Walter Pendennis's reaction when he learned Eleanor had involved herself with conspirators. Had Tallboys been similarly enraged to learn of Louise's treasonous activities?

Annabel gathered her thoughts. To admit she knew anything about a plot would be fatal. Tallboys was a justice of the peace. His tender feelings for Louise might have protected her, but he had no reason to shield the woman calling herself Jacquinetta Devereux.

And yet she must know more. She was pleased when her words came out without a tremor. "What did Louise want of you, *monsieur*? Did she ask for jewels? Marriage? Love?"

He lifted his head, letting her see the deep sadness in his mild grey eyes. "She wanted the use of my house, for an unspecified period of time. To shelter certain friends of hers, she said. Unnamed friends, but I knew from things she said how she felt about a certain...great lady. Tell me, Mistress Devereux, did her reason for being here die with her?"

Annabel's first instinct was to claim she did not know what he was talking about. Her second was to shade the truth and ease his suffering. "I devoutly hope so, *monsieur*. She was...misguided. I believe I could have convinced Louise to abandon her scheme, had she yet lived when I arrived here."

That she'd confided in him earned her a faint smile. "I like to think I could have done the same."

Annabel stooped to pluck two springs of rosemary. She kept one for herself and gave the other to him. "For remembrance."

His eyes filled with unshed tears as he accepted the tribute. Annabel had no doubt that he missed her friend, or that he'd loved Louise.

She only wished she could be certain he had not also killed her.

🏵33🏵

South Wingfield Manor

HAD ANNABEL managed to invade the state apartments? Had she studied the arrangement of rooms at South Wingfield Manor, looking for escape routes? Susanna stood in the chamber the queen of Scots had used for sleeping when she'd lodged here and considered what she knew of Mary Stewart.

The former queen of Scotland was a woman of thirty-three, some years younger than Susanna herself. She was said to be in considerable pain from numerous ailments and therefore made frequent requests to visit the baths at Buxton. A ruse? It was difficult to tell. Any conspirators wishing to arrange her escape would hope it was.

Mary Stewart had claimed at the time of the Rising in the North that she wanted no rebellion launched in her name, but Susanna doubted she would refuse a chance at freedom were it offered. And if she could be rescued from her prison, then those who wanted to restore Catholicism in both England and Scotland would rally to the cause. Mary herself would become little more than a pawn in a religious war that would tear both countries apart.

New Hall at Buxton had been built on the model of a tower-house fortress. South Wingfield had not, but it could be kept secure. Susanna ran a hand along the side of a window casement, feeling the solid stone beneath her fingertips. Only a fool would attempt to breech these walls to rescue the queen of Scots.

Susanna felt a wry smile lift the corners of her mouth. England had no shortage of fools. Some thought they acted in a holy cause. Others were eager for land or fortune or glory. All made stupid mistakes.

Annabel was not a fool. She'd admitted there was a plot but claimed it was no longer viable. Two men had died. Two conspirators? And Louise. And another? Susanna pressed her fingers to her temples. Annabel had said that Louise *thought* Annabel was her contact. The implication had been that Annabel had replaced the real contact. Had she committed murder to get that person out of the way?

Susanna's own suspicions about Annabel had led to this visit to South Wingfield Manor, but she'd not really expected to discover a third "accident." Further questioning had elicited the fact that Annabel had not arrived until the Monday, a day later than she'd told Susanna. If she'd lied about that, then it was entirely possible she'd lied about getting word of Louise's death while she was here. That Annabel had first said she'd been on her way to Scotland after leaving Buxton did nothing to lessen Susanna's suspicions. Even before she sent to Chatsworth to inquire if a large, red-haired woman had been seen in the vicinity on Palm Sunday, she did not doubt the answer would be yes.

Annabel was up to something, but was she conspiring to free the queen of Scots or *prevent* her rescue? Whose side was she on? It almost seemed as if she were working *for* England, but Susanna could think of no reason why she should be. Although her thoughts raced round and round, considering all manner of possibilities, she could come to only one conclusion—she must not fall into the trap of trusting Annabel MacReynolds.

Muttering under her breath, Susanna turned away from the window only to discover that Rosamond was standing a few feet behind her, discontent writ large on her face.

"Is there some difficulty?"

"I do not want to stay here any longer. I do not understand why you wanted to come here in the first place. If you do not intend to arrange a marriage for me to one of the countess's sons, I want to go back to Buxton."

"Marriage! Is that what your mother thinks the visit to Chatsworth was about?"

Rosamond made a circle on the rush matting with the toe of one shoe as color swept into her cheeks. "Anyone's better than Will Hawley, and it would be nice to be wealthy."

"Rosamond, you *are* wealthy."

"Not as wealthy as Bess of Hardwick. They say she's as rich as the queen."

Shaking her head, Susanna closed the distance to her foster daughter and gathered her into an embrace. "Silly goose. Wealth is better than poverty, I grant you, but it is more important to like the man you marry than to amass worldly goods."

"Mother says it is as easy to fall in love with a rich man as a poor one. She says—"

"Enough!" Susanna held up one hand, palm out, to stop the flow of Eleanor's opinions. "You will not be old enough to wed for some time yet. Let us leave the matter until then. Now, tell me why you are so anxious to return to Bawkenstanes Manor."

"It is only ten days until Nell's wedding and I promised to help her. And now it will be even harder to arrange her escape because we left the musician behind at Chatsworth."

Stricken, Susanna stepped away from Rosamond and felt the full weight of her accusing glare. She had forgotten all about Nell Hawley.

If that young woman was drugged and duped into taking her betrothal vows *de praesenti*, then something must, indeed, be done to stop the wedding. But running away with a penniless minstrel was not the solution.

"It should not be hard for her to get away from Bawkenstanes Manor," Rosamond said. "It is not as if the Hawleys have a castle like Lochleven."

"What do you know of Lockleven?"

"Only what Bessie told me. The queen of Scots was imprisoned there when she first abdicated in favor of her infant son. A young man who fancied himself in love with her helped her escape."

"Yes, into permanent imprisonment in England. What does Bessie Pierrepont know of it other than what is sung in popular ballads?"

"More than you might suppose. Since the age of four she has been a part of the queen of Scots' household. She has only been at Chatsworth with her grandmother for a few weeks."

"Four? Passing young."

"Bessie is clever. And she is not so young now."

"Yes. All of seven or eight."

"What does age matter? She knows all sorts of things about the queen of Scots."

"Mayhap Sir Walter should recruit young Bessie," Susanna suggested, amused by the idea. "A pity no one knows how to reach him."

"You can send word to him at any time through Jacob. Sir Walter's manservant always knows how to reach him."

"I did but jest, Rosamond. Besides, I do not know where *Jacob* is."

"Melka says he is in London, at Sir Walter's lodgings in Blackfriars."

Startled, Susanna was momentarily at a loss for words. Seeing her confusion, Rosamond grinned.

"Her English is much improved, and even when she does not understand everything she hears, she can still parrot whole speeches back without an error. It is a most useful skill."

Useful, indeed, Susanna thought, and wondered just how much else Melka knew.

🍂34🍂

May 15, 1575
Bawkenstanes Manor

"BUT YOU *like* living here," Eleanor objected. She watched her daughter circle the bedchamber like a caged beast, stopping now and again to pluck up a pillow or some other soft object and throw it at the nearest wall. "If you marry Will, it will be yours."

"It will be *his*, and only after his father dies. And even if it *were* to be mine, do you think I could tolerate being Will Hawley's to command?"

Exasperated, Eleanor gripped the poles attached to her carrying chair and pushed herself upward. She no longer, while sitting, had the advantage of height over her daughter. It galled her to be obliged to look up all the time and she knew Rosamond's temper well enough to be certain she could not persuade the girl to sit beside her. "What *do* you want, Rosamond? To remain unmarried is impractical. Better to make the best bargain you may and live with it."

"Is that what you did? Does Sir Walter mean nothing to you but a source of clothes and food and shelter? Do you not resent that he can confine you to the house if he wishes, or send you away?"

Eleanor opened her mouth to give the easy reply, then closed it again. Why not be truthful with the girl? "Sit down, Rosamond, if you wish to hear hard facts. If you prefer to delude yourself into thinking you have choices in your life, then get you gone. I've no more time to waste with you."

Startled, Rosamond blinked twice, then came closer, dragging a three-legged stool after her. Only when she was settled did Eleanor relax her arms and lower herself back into a sitting position in the chair.

"You know my early history," Eleanor began. "My mother did not care enough for me to arrange a marriage. Instead she sent me to an elderly relative, Lady Quarles, to be trained as a gentlewoman in her household. I was her slave and given no hope of freedom. It was not a cheerful house like this one, with other young people my own age, but a great prison of a place. Only the necessity of going to London, to court, to plead in person for a reversion of some lands, gave me respite."

"And there you met my father," Rosamond broke in. "And he seduced you and got you with child and you were thrown out of Lady Quarles's house."

"I left of my own volition, though I admit she would have sent me away had I stayed long enough for my condition to become apparent. You know this part of the story, Rosamond. I found a place to live near London while I waited for your father to return from a mission to Spain. I was robbed of the money he had given me and all I had besides, and finally, destitute, when you were still at my breast, I went to your father's wife to beg for crumbs."

Susanna had surprised her. Instead of slamming the door in her face, she had sent Eleanor and the infant Rosamond—who already bore a striking resemblance to her father—to Appleton Manor in Lancashire. There they had lived in considerable comfort until Rosamond was three.

"While we lived in Lancashire I won the affections of a wealthy Manchester lawyer. I might have married him. But when I met Walter, I knew he was the only man for me."

"You knew he could go far as a diplomat if you pushed him." Rosamond's eyes flashed in challenge and her jaw had a stubborn set with which Eleanor was all too familiar.

"I *hoped* for many things, not all of which came to pass," Eleanor admitted.

"Why did you marry him?"

"Because he could give me a secure future. I would not be dependent upon the whim of my mother or Lady Quarles or Lady Appleton."

"No, you'd be subject to one man."

"A man fond enough of me to want me to be happy. That is all a woman can ask."

"All?" A snide note came into Rosamond's voice.

With a jolt, Eleanor realized that her daughter might only be twelve years old, but she was not entirely innocent. She had observed enough of the effects of passion to understand what a powerful weapon the desire of a man for a woman…and of a woman for a man…could be.

"No, not quite all," Eleanor admitted. "If it is possible, a woman should choose for her husband a man who knows how to please his wife in bed, but men are trainable, Rosamond. There are ways, once you are wed, to mold and shape a husband into a form that suits you."

"As you did Sir Walter?" The taunting tone was still there. Rosamond knew full well that Eleanor had not succeeded in pushing her husband into the course she wanted. After her great miscalculation, it had taken her years to win back his affection and his trust, and she was not entirely sure she had the latter, even now.

"Marriage is for life," she said, "and Walter wants a son."

That longing gave her power over him and had prompted her to put off any possibility of conception for some time after their reconciliation. This last year, however, she had hoped to find herself with child. One hand drifted to her flat stomach at the thought. She would know in a few more days if she'd failed yet again to conceive but she had hopes of that last coupling in Cornwall before she'd set out for Buxton. The passion between them then had been...explosive. As if he knew they would not be together again for a long time.

Rosamond was staring at her with a peculiar look on her young face when Eleanor came back to herself. She wondered how long she had been daydreaming, and what her own facial expression had been.

"You resent having decisions made for you," Eleanor said, "even though you often like the result. You have enjoyed life at Bawkenstanes Manor. You are devoted to your two friends. Will you not trust me to arrange other matters as I see fit?"

"Not if you require me to marry Will Hawley."

"Go your ways, then. But if you are not to marry Will, then another household may prove better for your training. Remember that, Rosamond. You'd escape Will, but you'd lose your friends."

The threat earned her a glare before Rosamond turned on her heel and stalked out of the room.

Eleanor glanced at Melka, who had been the silent witness to their debate. "She knows I cannot force her into marriage. Susanna Appleton has done a good job of teaching her to stand up for what few rights a female does have. And, I suppose, there are things about the match that no longer shine as brightly since the murder of Louise Poitier."

Eleanor's admiration for Lady Bridget had undergone a

gradual change since she had been living in the other woman's house. She was not at all sure how she felt about Sir Richard, either.

"Mayhap," she mused aloud, "I should pay more attention to Will Hawley's father. The boy is likely to grow to resemble his sire more and more with each passing year. Careful study of the elder Hawley's flaws should reveal whether or not Rosamond's dislike of the younger has any merit."

"I hear them talk," Melka said.

"Sir Richard and his son?" Eleanor straightened in her chair. Melka did not bother to mention unimportant conversations she'd overheard. "What did they say?"

The maidservant was an excellent mimic. Eleanor had no difficulty differentiating between young Will's words and those of his father. Out of context, the exchanges Melka parroted back were often tantalizing mixtures of the vague and the specific, but in this case Eleanor had no doubt that the "she" both Sir Richard and Will referred to was Louise Poitier.

"*She was a trollop.*'"

Melka imitated Sir Richard's voice, then switched to Will's when she repeated the boy's words.

"*Useful to have in the house, though. Convenient. Where would I have had to go otherwise to be initiated, Father? Derby? London?*'

"*You might have waited a few years yet. Or found a willing maidservant. There is no shortage of women when you have coin to offer them.*'

"*Did you have to pay her, Father?*'

"*She liked what she did, and did not care who she did it with.*'

"*Who else? Tallboys, certes. Not the musician?*'

"*Musicians. Horses. Goats. Why not? I'd put nothing past her. We are well rid of her sort, boy. Next time you want a woman, I'll take you to a good clean whore I know in Bakewell.*'"

Eleanor contemplated the content of Melka's recitation in silence for a few minutes after it was complete. "Well," she said at last. "Like father, like son indeed."

"Not for Mistress Rosamond," Melka said.

It was so rare for the maidservant to express an opinion that Eleanor found herself responding. "Would you have her marry for love? That is the worst thing she could do. And to wed because of insatiable passion is even worse."

Either motive for marriage was dangerous to a woman. Eleanor had gone to Sir Robert Appleton out of love, or so she'd told herself at the time, and she'd married Walter because she could not stay out of his bed.

That she had a somewhat settled marriage now, that they'd reached an understanding of sorts, and that they could still please each other mightily, in spite of her injuries, did not mean that she would wish the upheaval and suffering she'd endured on Rosamond. And yet, these last few years, Eleanor had begun to realize that what she felt for her strong-willed husband was a very special kind of love. If it had not been for the fact that he gave every evidence of being, at the least, obsessed with her, she'd have found little reason to go on living.

"I wish Walter would reply to my letter," she muttered. She'd sent it days ago, during Rosamond's absence.

"If he get it."

"I sent it to his man. Jacob always knows how to find him."

Melka said nothing more, but they both knew that was no guarantee. For all Eleanor knew, Walter might be somewhere letters could not reach. For all she knew, he could be on his way across the Western Sea, sent on the queen's behalf to revive her claim on the New World!

🕸35🕸

Bawkenstanes Manor

"I KNOW who killed Louise," Annabel announced.

Susanna stared at her, discomfitted by the unexpected declaration. Her discoveries at Derby, where she and Rosamond had gone before returning to Buxton, had left her more confused about Annabel than ever.

She'd located one of the two local men Annabel had hired as guides. He'd confirmed what Susanna had already heard from Bess, that Annabel had been in Chatsworth when the workman fell to his death. The fellow had also said that Annabel had not gone to church that day. She had been at large when that workman had fallen from the scaffolding.

Now Annabel drew Susanna deeper into the corner of the Great Hall at Bawkenstanes Manor, where they could converse undisturbed. "Wymond Tallboys had reason to want Louise dead."

"Did he also cause the deaths of a workman at Chatsworth and a groom at South Wingfield?"

"They are of no importance." She dismissed two lives with a careless wave of one hand.

Not precisely a confession, Susanna thought, but scarce a denial of guilt. She set aside the "accidents" to consider again later and listened without comment as Annabel repeated the gist of her encounter with Wymond Tallboys on Ascension Day.

"He admitted he knew why Louise wanted the use of his house?"

Annabel nodded. "He implied it. It would have been an excellent hiding place for the queen. No one would think to look for her with a known puritan. He's one of the local justices, as well."

Susanna was not convinced of either Tallboys's guilt or Annabel's innocence, but that a justice of the peace had failed to report his suspicions to the authorities did seem curious.

"Why kill her?" she asked. "Anger at discovering she was using him? Why not just order her arrest? He could claim he knew her game all along and only encouraged her to draw her out."

"Passion can drive a man to kill." Annabel shrugged. "Mayhap Louise threatened to implicate him if he betrayed her. He'd not want his spotless reputation blemished."

"And yet you say he loved her and was devastated by her death." Rosamond, Susanna recalled, had said Tallboys had gone pale when the body was discovered. A mild reaction, surely, if he'd had no notion it was there.

"Is that so difficult to accept? Such emotions are not simple to define, nor to deal with." As they spoke, Annabel had been keeping an eye on the rest of the company. Now she frowned. "He is coming this way."

"Tallboys?"

"Aye. Doubtless he will accuse me if you challenge him. Do not believe him, Susanna. If you accept nothing else, know that I would never have harmed my friend. I hoped to extract her from danger. My failure weighs heavily on me."

She darted away just as Wymond Tallboys reached their corner.

"Master Tallboys," Susanna greeted him. "Did you kill Louise Poitier to avoid committing treason?"

His eyes widened in shock and his face blanched at the accusation. Susanna had often found the element of surprise a successful tactic. She watched with interest his struggle to find words of denial and hoped revelations would follow.

"She died by accident."

"I think not."

"I cared for her deeply," he insisted. "I'd never have harmed her. And I cannot believe—"

"You'd never have harmed her? Even after you suspected she was plotting to free Mary of Scotland? Did she threaten to set the churchwardens on you if you did not allow her to use your home as a hiding place? Or implicate you in treason? Or did you willingly agree to her scheme?"

To her dismay, he rapidly recovered his composure. "The most Louise did was express the opinion that it would be best for England to get the Scots queen out of the country. Living in France, she said, would be punishment enough for anyone. She was a Huguenot refugee, Lady Appleton. Her faith was the same as mine, and as strong, for all that she had her secrets. I had no reason to want her dead."

Susanna's brows lifted, amazed at the fellow's power to deceive himself about a woman. He put the best possible interpretation on her actions and words, one Susanna found difficult to accept. It was obvious to her that Louise had lied about her religious beliefs, just as she had lied about her feelings for Tallboys.

"Did those secrets include other lovers, Master Tallboys?"

"Why do you malign her name? What is it to you, Lady Appleton?"

"Rosamond's life was threatened because someone thought she could recognize Louise's murderer."

Tallboys started to protest, then fell silent, his brow creased in thought. "Why are you so certain she was murdered?"

"Because there was no reason for her to enter the enclosure by the well that night. She had followed Rosamond, Lina, and your own Diony to the First Chief Bath, lectured them about their recklessness in slipping out of the house for a swim, and sent them home. She should have returned to Bawkenstanes Manor soon after they did. Someone stopped her."

His grey eyes grew vacant as he looked into the past. Susanna waited, all but holding her breath. "Her clothing had dried, but it must have been soaking wet at some point during the night," he murmured. "When I lifted her body, she was not just ice cold. She was coated with ice, as if she'd been immersed in water."

"But she drowned in the well basin."

Tallboys had again lost all color in his face. He scraped one hand over his eyes. "That would not account for all her garments being frozen. I did not think of it then. I was too shaken by the fact that she was lost to me. She must have done more than fall so that her face landed in the water. She must have been submerged."

After considering that suggestion for a moment, Susanna came to the only logical conclusion. "She drowned in the bath, not the well."

Their eyes locked. If that was the explanation, then there was no question but that she'd been murdered. Afterward, whoever had pushed her in—for she'd not have gone for a swim still dressed—had fished her out and carried her to the well yard.

"Why go to the trouble of moving her?" Susanna asked. "Surely an accident in the First Chief Bath would have been as readily accepted, especially after Rosamond and her friends confessed that they'd left Louise there alone."

"Someone killed her." The bleak voice told Susanna he had at last accepted the truth of that. "I meant to marry her."

"Did you tell anyone that?"

He looked uncomfortable. "Sir Richard may have guessed. I put him off when he first tried to discuss a marriage with his daughter."

Sir Richard, if common belief was to be trusted, had also been in Louise Poitier's bed. And he'd wanted Nell to marry Tallboys in order to consolidate their land holdings. He had, then, assuming he was the jealous, vengeful sort, two reasons to be wroth with Louise. But he'd had no need to kill her. He might more easily have paid her to go away. Simpler still would have been to disillusion Tallboys about his mistress's nature by arranging to have him catch Louise with another lover.

Other lovers. Were they the key? Susanna did not look forward to questioning Sir Richard. He was the sort of man she least liked to deal with—certain of his own superiority simply because he'd been born a male.

"Mama!"

Rosamond's insistent voice interrupted Susanna and caused Tallboys to start. The girl raced toward them, face suffused with fury. "I will not marry him," she said, breathless. "And I do not want to leave my friends. Tell her, Mama. Tell Mother she cannot command it."

"Will Hawley, I presume? Lower your voice, Rosamond."

"I will not marry him." Rosamond's whisper was the sort that carried to every corner. Susanna closed her eyes and prayed for patience.

"Will is not for you." The certainty in Tallboys's voice had them both staring at him. "For some years now, Sir Richard and I have intended to make a match between his boy and my Diony. I do not believe it falls within the forbidden degrees of affinity, even now that I am to wed his sister."

Delight overspread Rosamond's features. "Just to be certain," she blurted, "you could release Nell from the pre-contract."

"I fear that is impossible. The betrothal is binding and we will be wed a week from today." He excused himself then, to go to his bride.

As soon as he left them, Rosamond turned on Susanna, hands on her hips and chin upthrust. "You promised to help Nell."

With a sigh, Susanna capitulated. "I cannot talk to her now. We will have to wait until Master Tallboys returns home."

"The gardens," Rosamond said. "I will bring Nell to you there in an hour."

Amused to find herself obeying her foster daughter's command, Susanna went out at once and spent the time in quiet contemplation until Nell and Rosamond arrived.

"Why do you think you were drugged before the betrothal?" Susanna asked the young woman. She had no doubt Nell had been given something. She'd noticed the effects herself, but if she was to prove it, she needed to hear Nell's version of the story.

"Father gave me a posset. Mother said it was chamomile, to calm my nerves, but as soon as I'd drunk of it, I felt dizzy."

"Poppy syrup, mayhap," Susanna mused. "There is likely to be more of it here in anticipation of further objections at the wedding ceremony. It would be wise to locate it and replace it with a harmless substance."

"I can find it," Rosamond said. "If I steal it, will that not be proof Nell was coerced and thus nullify her betrothal?"

"I do not think it is that easy to break a contract, but having the drug in our possession may help convince Master Tallboys that there is an impediment to the marriage. He does not appear any more anxious to wed Nell than she is to marry him. But *I* will look for the drug," she added. She did not want Rosamond to risk being caught, not when someone in this household was a murderer and had already tried to silence her once.

"Time is short," Rosamond protested.

"I will start today. Are you satisfied now?"

Nell's eyes widened. "That is what *she* said. When they were about to lead me out to make my vows."

"Your mother?"

"Yes. After I had drunk the posset, Mother asked Father if he was satisfied now and he said no, but that it was a beginning."

The snippet of conversation intrigued Susanna. It almost sounded as if Sir Richard had coerced his wife into helping him drug their daughter. Had he had something to threaten her with? That surprised Susanna. Lady Bridget had always seemed to her to be the dominant partner in the marriage.

Was it possible Lady Bridget had killed Louise Poitier?

At the thought, the pieces of the puzzle Susanna had been trying to solve shifted subtly, giving her yet another aspect of the intricate relationships at Bawkenstanes Manor to consider. She no longer had any doubt that, for someone, jealousy had led to murder.

❦36❦

May 16, 1575
New Hall

MONDAY morning, after Eleanor and Lady Bridget were safely settled and out of the way in the baths, Annabel slipped up the stairs to the lodgings Susanna and Jennet shared with Rosamond's two kittens.

"There is something you should know," she said without preamble. "Louise had a secret that may have provoked someone at Bawkenstanes Manor to excessive jealousy." She felt uncomfortable under Susanna's steady stare. This was not a subject she had wanted to discuss, but she had come to the conclusion that it might be relevant. "Louise took women, as well as men, as her lovers."

Jennet gasped. "Then she *was* embracing another woman!"

"What woman?" Susanna demanded.

The whole story tumbled out then, all Margery Cottelling had said. "She did not see her face," Jennet said, "and I thought she must be mistaken. Women do not…women…do they?"

"I suppose one must be widely read or else acquainted with a certain sort of person to know about such things," Annabel allowed.

"It is hardly surprising they are not spoken of, not when neither the Roman Catholic church nor the New Religion, both of which are controlled by men, even acknowledge that such a sin exists," Susanna agreed, "although both faiths are quick to condemn men who prefer men."

"'Tis monstrous," Jennet whispered, an expression of extreme distaste distorting her features.

Now it was Susanna's turn to be uncomfortable, but she did not let embarrassment stop her from asking the obvious question. "Were you her lover, Annabel? Is that why you were so concerned for her? Or was that, mayhap, why you killed her?"

Annabel had not expected the last question. Of a sudden her knees felt wobbly, forcing her to brace one hand against a bedpost. "I was her friend, not her lover." Except that once, after which shame and confusion had very nearly driven her to abandon Louise's friendship altogether. Forcing the memory to the back of her mind, Annabel stiffened her spine and soldiered on. "As for the other, I have told you before that I did not kill her."

"You have told me a great many things, some of them outright lies."

"That is not one of them, and I think you know it. Indeed, it would appear we have both come to the same conclusion. A woman could be driven to kill her lover if that lover shared her favors."

"Who did Margery see?" Susanna asked. "Who was Louise's lover?"

"Lady Bridget," Annabel said without hesitation. "Louise would never have taken the risk of being caught with a servant."

Jennet offered no opinion. Grappling with a concept so foreign to her experience seemed to have left her bereft of speech. Annabel was grateful for small favors.

"Lady Bridget would not have been pleased to learn she shared Louise with Sir Richard," Annabel continued, "or that Louise had been with Wymond Tallboys, either, since she intended him for her daughter."

"I am not certain *she* did." Susanna repeated the fragment of conversation Nell Hawley had remembered, along with the rest of her exchange with the girl.

Distracted from the question of Louise's lovers and which of them might have killed her, Annabel asked, "Do you mean to support Nell against her parents?"

"If I can. I'd planned to go to Bawkenstanes Manor this morning while Lady Bridget was at the baths and replace her poppy syrup with this." She held up a phial of a dark, thick liquid. "It might be better if you make the exchange. No one will question your presence in her chamber."

"Only her tiring maid is permitted access to her private storage chests and boxes."

"It may not matter," Susanna said thoughtfully. "If either of Nell's parents killed Louise, the wedding will undoubtedly be called off."

"You are that confident you can determine the murderer's identity?" Skeptical, Annabel pushed herself away from the bed and crossed to Susanna's writing box. She plucked up the list of suspects. None had been crossed off.

"They all have secrets," Susanna remarked, taking it back from her. "So do you."

Annabel acknowledged that with a nod.

"You say you did not kill Louise, and I am inclined to believe you, but how, then, did you hear of her death?"

Annabel hesitated. There were things she could not yet reveal, not even to Susanna Appleton, but she could answer this one question honestly. "I lied to you before. I did not learn of her death until I returned to Bawkenstanes Manor. I had come back to Buxton in the guise of Louise's good-sister paying a visit, hoping to persuade her to abandon the scheme to rescue the queen of Scots."

And that, Annabel thought, would have to satisfy Susanna for the present. The whole truth would come out soon enough. There was no way now to avoid it.

37

Bawkenstanes Manor

WILL HAWLEY'S wary glance traveled from Rosamond to Diony and Lina and back again to Rosamond. No one else was in earshot as they confronted him in a remote corner of the stable.

"What do you want?" The panic in his eyes belied his belligerent tone. "I did nothing to your precious kittens, Ros. I know they disappeared, but they must have run off on their own."

"Before you could capture and torture them? How disappointed you must have been." Rosamond reveled in the knowledge that she'd been right to take Dowsabella and Ailse to Mama. "What did you have in mind? Twigs tied to their tails? Trapping them in a wheel?"

"Is that any worse than Cook using a dog to turn the spit?"

"Cook rewards the mongrel for his efforts. You like to make small animals suffer." Her hands clenched into fists and she knew the expression on her face must be very fierce because Will backed away until he came up hard against the stable wall.

"What do you want from me?" This time both Will's voice and his demeanor conveyed less bluster and more wariness.

"The truth," Rosamond said. She must not allow herself to get distracted. She'd already rescued the kittens. Now she was trying to help Nell. A whole day had passed since Mama promised to find Lady Bridget's poppy syrup and she'd done nothing. With Will's cooperation, Rosamond intended to take care of the matter herself.

"Hurry, Rosamond. Someone may come."

Rosamond ignored Diony's warning. No one came into the stables at this time of day. The grooms were at their dinner. So were most of the servants at Bawkenstanes Manor.

"The truth," Rosamond repeated. "No evasions. No lies. If you cooperate, nothing you confess will be repeated to anyone else."

"Nothing?"

She hesitated, wondering if she had gone too far with that promise, but she was certain Will had not tried to kill her—he'd been running in the footrace—and any lesser crime could be overlooked. "Nothing."

"What do you want to know?"

A sudden sound had her glancing nervously over her shoulder, but it was only one of the horses moving in its stall. She took it for a timely reminder that they had no time to waste. The menials might be safely out of the way, but they could always be interrupted by an upper servant, or by Sir Richard or Lady Bridget.

"Did you tell your father we saw Nell come out of Poole's Cavern with the musician?"

"Is that what this is about?" He looked relieved.

"Did you?" She gave him a hard poke in the chest.

"Yes! You knew I meant to."

"Did he reward you for betraying your sister?"

Whether moved by her disgust or embarrassed by his failure to profit by his action, Will could no longer meet her eyes. Instead he stared at the stone floor and mumbled, "Father acted as he should."

"Your father forced Nell into a betrothal she did not want."

"He was afraid she would make a clandestine marriage with Giles Bannister. It is his duty as a parent to do what is best for his family." Will's old belligerence was returning. He even managed to sound self-righteous.

"It is the duty of Nell's *friends* to prove he used unfair means to do so." Rosamond was about explain to Will what he could do to help them when he suddenly squared his shoulders and stood up straight.

"You know nothing." Will adopted a haughty and superior tone. "A father is entitled to use any means necessary to protect his family's reputation."

Caught off guard, Rosamond just blinked at him for a moment. Then her heart began to beat a little faster. "Any means necessary?" she echoed, her thoughts leaping from Nell to Madame Poitier. "Even murder?"

"If the musician sullied Nell's honor, he'd have the right to beat the fellow."

"That's not what I meant." But Rosamond was reluctant to bring up Madame Poitier's name. She'd told neither Diony nor Lina that she suspected the Frenchwoman had been murdered.

"Father would challenge anyone who insulted his honor to a duel." Will sounded proud, which made no sense at all to Rosamond. "It is not murder to kill a man in a duel."

She rather thought it was, but this was not the time to debate that issue.

Before Rosamond could pose another question, Lina asked one. "What if he struck someone in anger?" Her voice quavered as she added, "If a man hits a woman or a child, sometimes they die."

"That's not murder either," Will insisted, "merely an unfortunate accident. Besides, all fathers beat their children. How else should they maintain discipline?"

Appalled, Rosamond stared at him. "Sir Richard beats you?" How could she have lived all this time at Bawkenstanes Manor and not known of it?

"When I deserve it." Will sounded defensive. "And he only hits Mother when she provokes him past reason. Never Nell, though, not even after I told him I'd seen her with a man."

Rosamond glanced at her two friends. Diony looked as sickened as Rosamond felt but Lina was nodding. Like Will, she seemed to think it natural that fathers should inflict pain on their children and husbands beat their wives.

"I do not believe you," Rosamond said. "Lady Bridget would not put up with such treatment. Nor will I when I am wed. If my husband tries to strike me, I will hit him back. And if he raises his hand to me again, I will poison him!"

"More like you'll do what Mother does," Will said with a sneer. "You'll dose yourself with poppy syrup for the pain and pretend all's well with the world."

❦38❦

Bawkenstanes Manor

ELEANOR felt decidedly unwell after her session in the First Chief Bath. Her legs pained her less than usual, but she was nauseated and light-headed. The sensations continued even after she returned to her own chamber at Bawkenstanes Manor and reclined on the bed.

"Faith," she muttered, "I have not felt so ill since…"

She paused, considering. Was it possible?

Before she could contemplate further changes in her body, one of Lady Bridget's servants arrived with a message delivered in her absence. "The rider said it was from your husband, madam," the young stableboy said. "Gave me a half groat to make sure you got it right away and another to say naught of it to anyone else."

Eleanor added a twopence piece of her own, bringing the lad's earnings to four pennies, a magnificent sum for so little work. She did not know how much stableboys were paid per annum but Melka's wages for an entire year were but six shillings and eightpence.

She settled back against several bladders full of hot water—another part of the Buxton "cure"—to peruse the letter. Walter had written in code, one he and Eleanor had devised together, and although it was doubtful anyone else could interpret the message, it made a very pretty love letter on the surface. The disadvantage to this system was that it did not allow for the inclusion of specific information. Still, what there was tantalized. Walter acknowledged receiving her letter, which meant he knew that Susanna was at Buxton and that a Frenchwoman had been murdered. The instructions he sent were cryptic but explicit—leave at once.

Where was he?

What else did he know?

With a sigh, Eleanor folded the missive and tucked it into the bosom of the fashionable doublet she wore instead of a bodice. "Help me into my chair, Melka," she ordered. "Then fetch Lady Appleton to me."

Susanna arrived within a short time, to Eleanor's satisfaction, but her reaction to what Walter had written was less pleasing.

Susanna studied the letter with ill-disguised amusement. "A poem to his lady's eyebrow? And to call your red lips rubious—that does seem a bit extreme!"

"Eyebrow is our word for intelligence gatherer and used in that context means there is one here." She did not bother translating word-for-word.

"Annabel?"

"If she is the one he refers to, then when he wrote this letter he did not know her identity, else he'd have found a way to name her." True, they did not have a code word for Annabel MacReynolds, as they did for Susanna and Rosamond, and even for Melka and for Walter's man, Jacob, but Walter was clever. He'd have found some way to indicate "Annabel" to Eleanor if he'd known she was here. When she'd written to him, Eleanor had deliberately held back that information. She did not know why. Certes, it had not been because she'd been convinced that Annabel's reasons for being at Buxton were as benign as the Scotswoman claimed.

"So, he does not give a name, only a vague sort of warning." Susanna looked pensive.

"He expects me to keep myself and Rosamond safe from harm. I rather imagine he wants us to accomplish that by accompanying you back to Leigh Abbey."

"In other words, he'd like all of us out of the way." Susanna tapped her lips with her fingertips and looked thoughtful. "No doubt he knows of some plan already in place to thwart any plot involving the queen of Scots, but how can he ask us to abandon our quest for justice in the matter of murder?"

Eleanor did not much care if Louise Poitier's killer was caught or not, so long as no further attempts were made on Rosamond. "He did not want me to come here in the first place," she informed Susanna. "He knows the reputation of Spaw and other places that offer medicinal waters."

"Then I am surprised he did not come with you."

"He could not. The queen commanded his presence elsewhere."

"France? The Continent? Mayhap Spaw?"

"You know he keeps such information to himself. I am astonished he deigned to reveal as much as he did in this letter."

"When did you write to him?"

"While you and Rosamond were away. I sent the letter to Jacob in London. Jacob will have forwarded it by diplomatic courier. Nothing else could produce such a prompt reply."

"Not Spaw, then. But France is a possibility. And Walter once knew Paris well."

Eleanor fiddled with the wheel on her chair, making it jiggle back and forth. Susanna was too calm. She gave no indication she meant to leave Buxton. She must know more than she was saying, more than she was willing to share. Annoyed, Eleanor snapped at her.

"What difference does it make where he is? We are here and he is not. We will decide what is best to do. Do you trust Annabel?"

"No." With an economy of words, Susanna told Eleanor what she'd learned of Annabel's movements between Louise's death and Annabel's return to Buxton. She summarized Annabel's vague explanations, including her revelations concerning Louise's preferences in lovers.

"I am not surprised," Eleanor said, referring to the latter, and described the scene between Lady Bridget and the beautiful young woman in the baths.

"You know Lady Bridget better than I do. Would she have killed Louise rather than let some man have her?"

"I do not think it likely. Could a quarrel that night at the baths have ended in an accidental drowning? *That*, I can well imagine. It is interesting," she mused, "that Lady Bridget refers to Louise as the French mistress."

"She calls most people by their position in her household—musician, husband, son, waiting gentlewoman."

"Yes, but in this case might the term not have a double meaning?"

They contemplated that thought in silence while Susanna helped herself to a piece of marchpane and Eleanor ate a sugared almond from the selection of comfits Melka had set out.

"I must speak to Rosamond before I return to New Hall. And Annabel, too. A matter concerning Nell Hawley's marriage." She explained their quest, ignoring Eleanor's raised eyebrows and disapproving look.

"All this fuss about a marriage. Why is Sir Richard so set upon it?"

"Why are you so set upon marrying Rosamond to Will?"

"He is the grandson of an earl. What more did he need to recommend him?" With a grimace, Eleanor acknowledged that she had changed her mind. "There will be other opportunities for Rosamond. If she survives her stay here. Mayhap Walter is right. We should leave and take Rosamond with us. Whether Annabel is a murderer or not, I am certain she is involved in espionage."

"What if Annabel is working for England? What if *she* is the agent Walter wrote of?"

"If Annabel is no longer working for France, there is even less reason to trust her. Someone who has changed allegiance once may more easily do so again."

❊39❊

May 17, 1575
Bawkenstanes Manor

"I HATE weaving garlands," Rosamond complained. "It is as dull a chore as darning stockings."

But the real cause of her discontent was her suspicion that Mama was keeping secrets from her again. Late yesterday afternoon, some time after Rosamond's confrontation with Will in the stable, Mama had taken her aside for an all-too-brief exchange of news. Rosamond had told Mama everything Will had said before they were interrupted by the unexpected arrival of a messenger and the return of one of the stableboys. Mama had told her nothing except that Annabel had successfully substituted a harmless potion for Lady Bridget's poppy syrup.

"I do not see what all the fuss is about weddings," Rosamond added.

"Why should you?" Lina muttered. "Your parents never bothered with one."

Startled by the hostility in her friend's voice, Rosamond stared at her. She'd never made any secret of the fact that she was a bastard, but she did not often talk about it. Until now neither Lina nor Diony had given any hint that they thought less of her for being base-born.

"I do not know why you worry so about being married off to Will Hawley," Lina continued. "Lady Bridget will never allow it, no matter how big your dowry is. She'd sooner see him married to Diony."

"You know nothing about it." She glanced at Diony, but the other girl's face was impassive.

"I know what Madame Poitier said."

Rosamond's eyes narrowed. "Why should she talk to you about such things?"

Tears pooled in Lina's eyes. "She liked me."

Holding on to her temper by a thread, Rosamond thought hard. Lina had been devoted to the Frenchwoman because she'd reminded Lina of her late mother—they'd had the same unusual eye color. Rosamond tried to imagine how she'd have felt if Mother had died when Rosamond was three, instead of abandoning her to go off to the Continent with her new husband. If she'd not been fostered with Mama, Rosamond supposed, she might have become attached to another woman simply because she resembled her real mother. Seen in that light, Lina's feelings were not so curious. But Madame Poitier had gone out of her way to befriend Lina, and Rosamond suddenly wondered why. "Did Madame Poitier know you before she came here?"

"No." But bright color crept into Lina's cheeks.

Rosamond seized the half-finished garland out of her hands and flung it across the room. "What are you hiding? She was murdered, Lina. How am I to discover who killed her if you keep secrets?"

The pink cheeks blanched. Eyes wide, Lina stared at Rosamond. "Murdered?"

"Did you not guess?" Diony asked. "Why else has Rosamond been asking so many questions? Why else did Lady Appleton come here?"

"I did not think.... I—" She glared at Rosamond, as if she were, somehow, to blame. "You did not seem pleased to see her, or your mother!"

Impatient, Rosamond glared at her. "I was not. I wrote to a friend for information on poisoned mushrooms. I never expected—what?"

"What have mushrooms to do with this?"

"Madame Poitier's mushroom box disappeared after her death. I thought she might have been poisoned, then left by the well to make it seem an accident, and—"

"But I have the box," Lina interrupted. "I...I wanted something to remember her by."

"More secrets!"

"You're a fine one to complain about keeping secrets," Diony snapped. "If you'd told us what you were thinking, you'd have known weeks ago that you were wrong ."

"*Was* I wrong?"

Stubborn pride had Rosamond stalking over to Lina's wardrobe chest. She flung open the lid and burrowed through the expensive garments until she found a small, oblong wooden box decorated with paintings of flowers. She unlatched and opened it but gave a start of surprise when she saw what it contained.

"What happened to the mushrooms?" she demanded, reaching for a folded square of parchment that was the only thing inside.

"I ate them."

Diony gave a shout of laughter. "If you'd only stopped and thought about it, Rosamond, you'd have realized that any sensible murderer who used poisoned mushrooms as a weapon would not have had to bother making Madame Poitier's death look like a drowning. Everyone would have assumed she'd picked the wrong mushroom by mistake. No one would have questioned the verdict of accidental death. I do not think it was murder at all. I think you just wanted to call attention to yourself."

Rosamond heard the criticism, but it washed over her. She was too dumbstruck by what she'd found in the mushroom box.

Eyes snapping with anger, Lina stormed across the chamber and reached for the paper. "Give me that."

Rosamond clung to the paper. "Is what this says true?"

Lina snatched it away. Her defiant stance and red cheeks were enough to give Rosamond her answer.

❊❀40❀❊

New Hall

SUSANNA sent for Eleanor, Rosamond, and Annabel as soon as word came from Chatsworth that Giles Bannister had left the countess of Shrewsbury's service abruptly and without notice. When they were assembled in her lodgings at New Hall she shared this intelligence with them.

"He's coming for Nell," Rosamond declared. "He means to carry her off and marry her."

"I do not think so, Rosamond. Your mother received a letter from Sir Walter in which he warns her there is an intelligence gatherer at Bawkenstanes Manor." She glanced at Annabel. "We thought it might be you, but now I wonder...What do we know of Giles Bannister?"

"I know no more than you do, for I arrived here only a few weeks before you did."

Susanna's gaze sharpened. Annabel looked troubled by the revelation. She also looked guilty. Did she know more about Bannister than she'd said? Or was she hiding something more sinister?

When she'd arranged herself on the window seat, Susanna turned to Eleanor, who was seated in her carrying chair. Her two sturdy chairmen waited below, ready to transport her back to Bawkenstanes Manor at a moment's notice. "A pity Sir Walter did not send you a name."

"Yes, and I do much regret that I did not send one to him." Eleanor glared at Annabel, making it clear she still considered the Scotswoman a threat.

Annabel leaned back against the window casement, sighed deeply, and closed her eyes. "He would have warned you if he knew I was here."

"A musician would make an excellent intelligence gatherer," Jennet mused. "Always in the background like a piece of furniture.

He might have come here to watch for conspirators. Did he suspect Madame Poitier, I wonder? Did he kill her to thwart her plot?"

Rosamond looked from Jennet to her mother and then at Susanna. "Do you mean to say he *is* a spy? That he is not in love with Nell at all?"

"If he is an intelligence gatherer, a woman would be a fool to believe his avowals of undying devotion." Bitterness leaked through Eleanor's voice. "And since he has disappeared without marrying her, no doubt he's gone for good."

"Poor Nell," Rosamond murmured.

Annabel's eyes flew open. "If he killed Louise, he's no fit husband for anyone!"

Susanna wondered if she would ever understand how Annabel's mind worked, but there was no time now to dwell on the Scotswoman's inconsistent attitude toward murder. She drew out the list she had made. The names had not changed. "Tallboys seems unlikely, and Nell could do worse than marry him, Rosamond. Giles Bannister is a possibility, but we know of no connection between him and Louise."

"There was none or she'd have told me of it." Annabel's curtness conveyed absolute certainty.

"She did not tell you everything, Mistress MacReynolds." Rosamond sounded so smug that Susanna exchanged a look of concern with Eleanor. "I was right to think the missing mushroom box was important."

"Not poison?" Eleanor's astonished voice echoed Susanna's disbelief.

"No. But the box had a false bottom and inside was a document that revealed Madame Poitier's real reason for coming to Bawkenstanes Manor."

"Do not keep us in suspense, Rosamond," Susanna chided her. "What was this document and what did it say?"

"And how did you find it?" Annabel asked.

Rosamond, to draw out the drama, answered the last ques-

tion first, explaining how she'd discovered that Lina had kept the
box as a memento. "She found the paper and kept it in the box
after she ate all the mushrooms."

"That child will eat anything," Jennet muttered.

"The page was a letter written by Madame Poitier's father on
his deathbed. A confession of sorts. He said he'd concealed facts
about her birth."

"Louise knew she was a bastard," Annabel said in irritation.
"She cared not a whit if she was, or what her father thought of her.
He kept her for a time, but tired of having her about and sent her
to a cousin who served a lady at court. Her own intelligence and
beauty led to her advancement there."

Plainly delighted to have information even Annabel lacked,
Rosamond smirked at her. "But she did not know until after her
father's death who her mother was. According to the letter,
Madame Poitier's—"

"Her name was not Poitier," Annabel interrupted. "She never
married. Her father's surname was Guay. She was Louise Guay."

"It is her *mother's* name that is important," Rosamond said. "It
was Leland. Joan Leland. She was an English gentlewoman whose
family lived in exile in France during the reign of Queen Mary
Tudor. Joan fell in love with a Frenchman, even though he was
married and a Catholic, and bore his child out of wedlock. Her
parents were so appalled that they gave the baby to the father to
raise and took Joan back to England, where she was later married
off to a wealthy merchant as his second wife. He already had children by his first wife, and Joan gave birth to her second daughter
before she died."

"Godlina Walkenden," Susanna murmured, remembering
what Rosamond had said about eyes. Lina's mother's had been the
same unusual shade of violet as Louise's.

"Lina was Madame—was Louise Guay's half sister," Rosamond affirmed, "and Lina's presence there was the real reason
Louise came to Bawkenstanes Manor."

"Do you claim Godlina Walkenden had naught to do with treason?" Annabel asked.

"We have only your word, Mistress MacReynolds," said Rosamond, "that there *was* treason afoot."

"And your stepfather's," Eleanor reminded her.

Rosamond's stricken expression spoke volumes. "Even if *Madame Poitier* was plotting against England, I am certain Lina is not involved in treason."

"She must know that the designs she's been embroidering have a connection to the queen of Scots." Jennet did not trouble to hide her skepticism.

Rosamond shook her head. "She copied them from some that Louise had done, as a tribute to her late sister."

For a moment no one said anything. Then Annabel cleared her throat. "A pity this discovery brings us no closer to the identity of Louise's killer."

Susanna sighed and added a notation to her list of suspects. If Louise had merely used the scheme to free Mary Stewart as an excuse to come to Buxton, then the other conspirators could have become suspicious that she had divided loyalties. If they'd feared she'd betray their plans to the authorities, they might have decided to rid themselves of a liability. One of *them* could have killed her.

41

JENNET went down to the kitchens at New Hall after Annabel, Eleanor, and Rosamond returned to Bawkenstanes Manor. Lady Appleton required nourishment. She'd forget to eat if someone did not look after her. After Jennet gave orders for a modest repast to be sent up, she stepped outside for a moment to clear her head. At times it seemed to her that half the populace of England led double lives as intelligence gatherers.

She set out at a brisk pace along the path that led to the bowling green. Much as she hated to admit it, Jennet had decided that Lady Appleton was right. She did feel better for a bit of exercise. She did not have to pause so often now to catch her breath, and her kirtle used less lace to fasten.

Jennet was almost at the end of the long, grassy alley, empty of players at this hour of the day, when she caught sight of movement in the hedges. She stopped dead and stared. Without thinking, she issued a challenge: "Who goes there?"

Giles Bannister stepped out of cover. "A word with you, goodwife."

She whirled and would have fled, but he was too swift for her. He caught her arm and hauled her back against him, clamping one hand firmly over her mouth.

"Stay, Jennet. I am not your enemy."

She struggled futilely in his grip.

"You must take me to your mistress. Now. I bring word from Sir Walter."

At the mention of that name, Jennet went still. He released her at once.

"What do you know of Sir Walter?"

"I know he was once one of the queen's most trusted intelligence gatherers."

"*He* was trusted. Are *you*?"

"He sent word to his wife that there was an intelligence gatherer here. He meant me. I was sent here to observe and report, but I failed to realize the importance of what I overheard between the woman who calls herself Jacquinetta Devereux and your mistress on the day you first came to Bawkenstanes Manor."

When Jennet finally got her dropped jaw back in place, she took Giles Bannister to Lady Appleton.

"So you made the thump we heard in the next room," Lady

Appleton murmured when he'd repeated what he'd told Jennet. "But why did you say nothing ere now?"

"I was obliged to consult with my superiors before I acted. It is as well I did so. Mistress MacReynolds was known to them and came to Derbyshire under their auspices."

"To kill Louise?"

"To eliminate the conspirators. There were reports of Papist agents at Chatsworth, South Wingfield, and Buxton—all houses in which Mary of Scotland has been lodged and might be allowed to visit again. The plan, it appears, was to spirit the queen of Scots away to the convent of Saint Pierre in Rheims, where Renée de Guise resides. She is Queen Mary's aunt. In this matter of Mary Stewart, the Scots are allied with England. They do not want to risk a return to Catholic rule any more than we do. The Scots regent sent Mistress MacReynolds to deal with the problem."

"Do you mean to say that if Annabel did kill Louise, she'd not be prosecuted for the crime?"

Giles nodded.

"But if that is what happened, why did Annabel come back?" Lady Appleton asked. "If she fulfilled her mission, assassinated Louise and the other conspirators, she should have gone on to Scotland to reap her reward."

"I do not know the answer to that question, madam. Indeed, I did not know anything of her role in this until I left Chatsworth and reported to…to my superior."

Lady Appleton lifted a questioning brow, but no name was forthcoming. Someone who knew *her*, doubtless, and how she'd helped Sir Walter in the past.

"I do not think Annabel killed her friend," Lady Appleton said after a moment. "I think she returned here hoping to convince Louise to accompany her to Scotland, since she'd just dealt the conspiracy a fatal blow. When she learned of Louise's death, she stayed to discover who murdered her."

"Then who *did* kill Louise?" Jennet asked.

Lady Appleton glanced at the paper she'd been studying when Jennet and Giles Bannister had burst into her chamber. "Someone at Bawkenstanes Manor," she said, "and with your help, music master, I believe we can trick the murderer into confessing."

✺42✺

Bawkenstanes Manor

SUSANNA secreted Giles Bannister behind the arras in the same south-facing upstairs chamber at Bawkenstanes Manor where she'd first been reunited with Rosamond. Her plan was simple. She would gather all her suspects and witnesses together in this room—she'd sent Jennet to summon them—and present them with a carefully worded account of the facts she had uncovered about Louise Poitier's death. She hoped to provoke a reaction from the murderer, but failing that, she would produce Lady Bridget's music master and claim he'd seen the killer leave Bawkenstanes Manor on the night Louise died. At the threat of being identified, someone would react. Susanna felt certain of it.

A short time later, they were all there. Lady Bridget claimed the bench by one of the windows overlooking the gardens. Sir Richard and Wymond Tallboys stood in front of the other. Margery, Annabel, Nell, and Rosamond's two friends were once again seated on cushions with needlework in hand. Will Hawley leaned against one of the paneled walls, affecting disinterest by picking at a hangnail, while Eleanor wheeled her chair as close to Lady Bridget's bench as she could get. Jennet had made herself unobtrusive, blending into the arras behind her. Rosamond, determined not to miss the slightest betraying flash of expression, had chosen a spot by the door from which she could see everyone clearly. Susanna's vantage point farther along the same wall gave her a equally excellent view. She, too, remained standing.

"By your leave, Lady Bridget," Susanna began, "I have a tale to tell." And she began to sketch out, with slight alterations, the events of the night of Louise Poitier's death, starting with three girls creeping out of the manor house. "They meant to take a moonlit swim," she explained.

Identical looks of acute discomfort appeared on Diony's and Lina's faces, but Rosamond's expression was defiant. Her bravado earned her an admiring grin from Will.

"Louise Poitier realized they were gone and guessed where they might be. She followed them but while the girls entered through a broken spot in the wall around the pool, she knew where a key to New Hall was hidden. She let herself in and made her way to the First Chief Bath where she confronted the girls and ordered them back to their beds. She did not accompany them. Mayhap she wished to show her faith that they would obey her. Or mayhap she delayed to assure herself that no candle had been left untended."

That was Susanna's own theory—the girls had left a candle behind and Louise, after her meeting with Annabel, had detoured into the First Chief Bath to fetch it. She did not intend to mention that the key had been provided by Henry Flower or that Annabel had been at New Hall that night. Annabel had not killed Louise.

"Whatever her reason, staying behind was a fatal mistake. Someone else was there that night, someone who had followed Louise from Bawkenstanes Manor without realizing the girls were already at the bath. That person may have remained outside New Hall when Louise went in or crept in after her, but since the girls left the way they'd come, they were not seen. They were, I think, heard. Louise's killer knew she was talking with someone and assumed that person was her lover."

"Killer?" Margery echoed. "Are you saying that Louise was murdered?"

"I am, Mistress Cottelling."

A chorus of shocked exclamations broke out from those who had not already been told that the death was suspicious. Susanna searched in vain for the flicker of emotion that would give one of them away, but there was no betraying expression on anyone's face. Of them all, only Rosamond had a countenance like an open book—she could not hide her avid interest as she, too, watched the others for the slightest hint of guilt.

In her mind, Susanna pictured the scene on that moonlit night in March. Had the murderer stood at the bottom of the staircase, straining to hear when two voices spoke softly in the chamber Annabel had appropriated? Their words had been treasonous, not amorous, but the killer had no way of knowing that. "It must have appeared that Louise had arranged an assignation," she said aloud. "She was killed in the belief she had betrayed one lover with another."

A heavy silence hung over the chamber. No one spoke. No one dared meet another suspect's eyes.

Susanna stifled a sigh. It was unreasonable to expect a confession this soon. "There was a violent confrontation in the First Chief Bath," she announced, hoping she was right and that her bold statement would convince the killer that she had proof of what she said. "By accident or design, Louise Poitier ended up in the pool and drowned. The killer might have left her there, had rage and a desire for revenge against the rival who had stolen Louise's affections not risen to the surface along with the body. Instead the murderer fished her out and took her to a place where she was sure to be discovered the next morning by a group of people on their way from Bawkenstanes Manor to the chapel, a group that included Louise's new lover. The body was placed beside the well and the gate was left unlocked. It only remained for the killer to make certain that fact was noticed and investigated."

Susanna looked directly at Lady Bridget, but her face betrayed fury, not guilt. She made a sound of pain and rage and whirled around to glare at the two men standing together near the window—Wymond Tallboys and Richard Hawley.

"You!" she shrieked. "You killed her!" And she flung herself straight at her husband. The nails on her right hand raked across his face. Her left fist struck his chest.

Giles Bannister, hidden behind the arras, rushed out and attempted to restrain Lady Bridget. He'd been waiting for Susanna's signal to make his presence known. The plan had been to have him claim he'd seen someone leave the manor on the night of Louise's death. Someone he was now prepared to identify.

At the sight of him, Nell gasped, but her mother paid Giles no mind other than to kick and claw him in an attempt to break free and do further damage to her husband. All her venom was directed at him.

"Beast! Villain!" she screamed at Sir Richard. "You came to me fresh from killing her."

"Calm yourself, madam," Susanna said. "Tell us what you know and he will be punished."

Lady Bridget's hair had come loose and her eyes were wild, but she regained enough of her composure to focus on Susanna and obey. "You want to know what happened that night, Lady Appleton? Well, I will tell you. This fiend burst into my chamber well after midnight and forced himself upon me. His skin was ice-cold. And his hair was wet. And he hurt me," she finished with a wail of outrage.

Drawing himself up to his full height and holding himself stiffly, Sir Richard sneered at his wife. "I did no more that night than claim my rights as your husband."

The attempt at arrogance suffered from his continual dabbing at the blood dripping from his cheek.

"Murderer!" Lady Bridget screamed.

"Lying trull! Be silent, or by God's nightcap I will silence you!" Sir Richard would have struck her if Tallboys had not held his free arm. The other man's face was chalk white but grimly determined.

"Unhand me," Sir Richard snapped. "I am master here."

Red in the face and bosom heaving, Lady Bridget threw up her hands as if she meant to claw him again. Then a laugh burst from her. "You will pay, Richard. They will hang you." Still laughing, she turned to Susanna. "I owe you a debt, Lady Appleton. I knew I'd married a cruel man, but I'd never have suspected he was a murderer."

"Are you certain he is?" Susanna asked mildly, still a trifle bemused by the sudden turn of events. She had expected to discover Lady Bridget was the guilty party.

"Oh, yes. It was my beloved husband who made sure I noticed the missing padlock. If my son had not rushed in first, my husband would have positioned himself in the perfect location from which to observe my reaction to finding Louise. As it was, he reveled in my anguish, though he never accused me of being with her in New Hall. He only said I would regret it if I ever betrayed him again."

Lady Bridget's bitter tone still had an undercurrent of hysteria. "He wanted me to suffer. Fool! I was not his rival. She intended to marry Wymond Tallboys, for all that she could scarce tolerate his lovemaking. I suppose he was the one she met at New Hall."

Susanna did not correct the assumption.

Tallboys, shaken by the sordid revelations about a woman he had wanted to wed, let his grip on Sir Richard slacken. Louise's murderer took advantage of the moment to twist free and bolt for the door, but Rosamond was in his path.

A cold chill ran down Susanna's spine. "Get out of his way!" she shouted, terrified that Sir Richard would seize the girl and use her as a hostage. He had already tried to kill her once, after he'd overheard her talking about the night of Louise's murder with her friends. He'd doubtless have killed all three of them if Rosamond's silence afterward had not convinced him they'd seen nothing after all.

Susanna, Tallboys, Bannister, even Lady Bridget rushed toward Sir Richard, but Annabel got to him first. She pushed Rosamond aside, raised the blade she'd held concealed in her long skirts, and calmly stabbed Louise Poitier's murderer through the heart.

꧁꧂

NO ONE stopped Annabel from leaving for Scotland. Even Will Hawley accepted that she'd acted to save Rosamond's life. Wymond Tallboys, on his authority as a justice of the peace, declined to make an arrest.

Giles Bannister departed soon after Annabel, to report to his superiors in the English government, but he meant to return to Bawkenstanes Manor. Lady Bridget's confirmation that the posset Sir Richard had given Nell was drugged, together with Wymond Tallboys's newfound disinclination to wed into the Hawley family, assured that the betrothal would be nullified.

Tallboys himself was next to ride away. He took Diony with him. Godlina Walkenden, Lady Bridget declared, must return at once to her father in London.

That left only Rosamond's fate undecided.

"Well, Eleanor," Susanna said when Rosamond had gone off to help Lina pack, "what is to be done with your daughter? Will you take her back with you to Priory House?"

"I believe I am with child."

"I am pleased for you, if that is what you want, but it does not answer my question about Rosamond."

"Yes, it does. There is no point in sugar-coating the truth, Susanna. You are more a mother to her than I ever was. I should like to do better this time, and that will not be possible if Rosamond is under the same roof as a constant reminder of my failures. You take her."

The thought of having her foster daughter with her again filled Susanna with pleasure, but she was not sure that returning to Leigh Abbey was best for Rosamond. "She already feels she's been shunted from one place to another because no one wants her."

"Shall we stage a loud quarrel for her benefit? Both claim we cannot bear to be without her? I will let you win." Eleanor chuckled. "She'll rebel out of habit, no matter what we decide, but you are better able to deal with her tantrums than I am."

"I left Rosamond with you and Walter at Priory House four years ago because I believed you two would be better able to discipline her. I spoil her."

Eleanor turned in her chair until she could see Jennet, who had been standing unobtrusively by the arras that had hidden Giles earlier. Melka was beside her, equally a part of the furniture. They'd both heard every word and Jennet's pained expression warned Susanna how she felt about the suggestion that Rosamond return to Leigh Abbey.

"Let Jennet supervise Rosamond." Eleanor laughed again. "The matter is settled, Susanna. I do not want the girl back and she cannot stay here."

Susanna gave up the argument. She did long to have Rosamond with her again, to supervise her education, to instill in her the values that she held dear. She caught Jennet's eye. "Will you help me control Rosamond's worst excesses?"

"Can we lock her in her room until she marries?" Jennet asked. "Madam, Rob's school in Canterbury is but five miles away."

Susanna repressed a smile. "Much too far to travel often, and Rob's days are full. He has no time for anything but his studies." Jennet did not look convinced. "You underestimate Rob and the strength of his desire to go on to Cambridge, if you think he will let Rosamond lure him into trouble."

"No, madam. You underestimate Rosamond." And then, so softly that Susanna could pretend she had not heard, Jennet added, "But she underestimates me."

❦FINIS❦

A Note from the Author

Poole's Cavern, Buxton, and the other Derbyshire locations mentioned in this novel are real places. Bawkenstanes Manor, however, is entirely a figment of my imagination, as are the May Day celebrations at Buxton in 1575. The Chatsworth that stands today is not Bess of Hardwick's creation, but a later house that bears little resemblance to what was there in that year. New Hall at Buxton exists as a small part of what is now the Old Hall Hotel. Extensive rebuilding has taken place in the intervening centuries. South Wingfield Manor survives only as a ruin. All books referred to and quoted from in the text are also real, including those dealing with the proper way to utilize the healing waters at Buxton.

About the Author

KATHY LYNN EMERSON has been interested in the Elizabethan period all her life. In addition to books and stories in the *Face Down* series, she has used that setting in several romances, and has written nonfiction for writers and scholars about it. She has also begun another historical series set in nineteenth-century America.

Emerson lives in Maine with her husband and cats. She welcomes visitors and e-mail at www.KathyLynnEmerson.com.

MORE MYSTERIES
FROM PERSEVERANCE PRESS
🂡 *For the New Golden Age* 🂡

Available now—

The Last Full Measure, A Katy Green Mystery
by Hal Glatzer
ISBN 1-880284-84-7
In late November 1941, swing musician Katy Green joins two old friends in a dance band on the SS *Lurline*. En route to Hawaii, the ship—like the world at large—is riven by intrigues both political and personal, and by a murder that might be a foretaste of war.

Paradise Lost, A Novel of Suspense
by Taffy Cannon
ISBN 1-880284-80-4
Appearances deceive in the kidnapping of two young women from a posh Santa Barbara health spa, as relatives and the public at large try to meet environmental ransom demands, and the clock ticks toward the deadline.

Crimson Snow, A Hilda Johansson Mystery
by Jeanne M. Dams
ISBN 1-880284-79-0
The murder of a popular schoolteacher shocks South Bend, Indiana. Young Erik Johansson was in Miss Jacobs's class, but his sister Hilda, housemaid to the prominent Studebaker family and preoccupied with her pending marriage, refuses to investigate this time—until Erik forces her hand. Based on an unsolved case from 1904.

Face Down Below the Banqueting House, A Lady Appleton Mystery
by Kathy Lynn Emerson
ISBN 1-880284-71-5
Shortly before a royal visit to Leigh Abbey, the home of sixteenth-century sleuth Susanna Appleton, a man dies in a fall from a banqueting house. Is his death part of some treasonous plot against Elizabeth Tudor? Or is it merely murder?

Evil Intentions, A Feng Shui Mystery
by Denise Osborne
ISBN 1-880284-77-4
A shocking and questionable suicide linked to white slavery and to members of an elite Washington D.C. family embroils Feng Shui practitioner Salome Waterhouse in an investigation that threatens everyone involved.

Tropic of Murder, **A Nick Hoffman Mystery**
by Lev Raphael
ISBN 1-880284-68-5
Professor Nick Hoffman flees mounting chaos at the State University of Michigan for a Caribbean getaway, but his winter paradise turns into a nightmare of deceit, danger, and revenge.

Death Duties, **A Port Silva Mystery**
by Janet LaPierre
ISBN 1-880284-74-X
The mother-and-daughter private investigative team introduced in Shamus-nominated *Keepers*, Patience and Verity Mackellar, take on a challenging new case. A visitor to Port Silva hires them to clear her grandfather of anonymous charges that caused his suicide there thirty years earlier.

A Fugue in Hell's Kitchen, **A Katy Green Mystery**
by Hal Glatzer
ISBN 1-880284-70-7
In New York City in 1939, musician Katy Green's hunt for a stolen music manuscript turns into a fugue of mayhem, madness, and death. Prequel to *Too Dead To Swing*.

The Affair of the Incognito Tenant, **A Mystery With Sherlock Holmes**
by Lora Roberts
ISBN 1-880284-67-7
In 1903 in a Sussex village, a young, widowed housekeeper welcomes the mysterious Mr. Sigerson to the manor house in her charge—and unknowingly opens the door to theft, bloody terror, and murder.

Silence Is Golden, **A Connor Westphal Mystery**
by Penny Warner
ISBN 1-880284-66-9
When the folks of Flat Skunk rediscover gold in them thar hills, the modern-day stampede brings money-hungry miners to the Gold Country town, and headlines for deaf reporter Connor Westphal's newspaper—not to mention murder.

The Beastly Bloodline, **A Delilah Doolittle Pet Detective Mystery**
by Patricia Guiver
ISBN 1-880284-69-3
Wild horses ordinarily couldn't drag British expatriate Delilah to a dude ranch. But when a wealthy client asks her to solve the mysterious death of a valuable show horse, she runs into some rude dudes trying to cut her out of the herd—and finds herself on a trail ride to murder.

Death, Bones, and Stately Homes,
A Tori Miracle Pennsylvania Dutch Mystery
by Valerie S. Malmont
ISBN 1-880284-65-0
Finding a tuxedo-clad skeleton, Tori Miracle fears it could halt Lickin Creek's annual house tour. While dealing with disappearing and reappearing bodies, a stalker, and an escaped convict, Tori unravels the secrets of the Bride's House and Morgan Manor, which the townsfolk wish to hide.

Slippery Slopes and Other Deadly Things,
A Carrie Carlin Biofeedback Mystery
by Nancy Tesler
ISBN 1-880284-64-2
Biofeedback practitioner/single mom/amateur sleuth Carrie Carlin is up to her neck in snow, sex, and strangulation when her stress management convention is interrupted by murder on the slopes of a Vermont ski resort.

REFERENCE / MYSTERY WRITING
How To Write Killer Fiction:
The Funhouse of Mystery & the Roller Coaster of Suspense
by Carolyn Wheat
ISBN 1-880284-62-6
The highly regarded author of the Cass Jameson legal mysteries explains the difference between mysteries (the art of the whodunit) and novels of suspense (the hero's journey) and offers tips and inspiration for writing in either genre. Wheat shows how to make your book work, from the first word to the final revision.

Another Fine Mess, **A Bridget Montrose Mystery**
by Lora Roberts
ISBN 1-880284-54-5
Bridget Montrose wrote a surprise bestseller, but now her publisher wants another one. A writers' retreat seems the perfect opportunity to work in the rarefied company of other authors…except that one of them has a different ending in mind.

Flash Point, **A Susan Kim Delancey Mystery**
by Nancy Baker Jacobs
ISBN 1-880284-56-1
A serial arsonist is killing young mothers in the Bay Area. Now Susan Kim Delancey, California's newly appointed chief arson investigator, is in a race against time to catch the murderer and find the dead women's missing babies—before more lives end in flames.

Open Season on Lawyers, A Novel of Suspense
by Taffy Cannon
ISBN 1-880284-51-0

Too Dead To Swing, A Katy Green Mystery
by Hal Glatzer
ISBN 1-880284-53-7.

The Tumbleweed Murders, A Claire Sharples Botanical Mystery
by Rebecca Rothenberg, completed by Taffy Cannon
ISBN 1-880284-43-X

Keepers, A Port Silva Mystery
by Janet LaPierre
Shamus Award nominee, *Best Paperback Original 2001*
ISBN 1-880284-44-8

Blind Side, A Connor Westphal Mystery
by Penny Warner
ISBN 1-880284-42-1

The Kidnapping of Rosie Dawn, A Joe Barley Mystery
by Eric Wright
Barry Award, *Best Paperback Original 2000*. Edgar, Ellis, and Anthony Award
nominee
ISBN 1-880284-40-5

Guns and Roses, An Irish Eyes Travel Mystery
by Taffy Cannon
Agatha and Macavity Award nominee, *Best Novel 2000*
ISBN 1-880284-34-0

Royal Flush, A Jake Samson & Rosie Vicente Mystery
by Shelley Singer
ISBN 1-880284-33-2

Baby Mine, A Port Silva Mystery
by Janet LaPierre
ISBN 1-880284-32-4

**Available from your local bookstore or from
Perseverance Press/John Daniel & Co. at (800) 662-8351
or www.danielpublishing.com/perseverance.**